AN OTHER PLACE

ALSO BY DARREN DASH

THE EVIL AND THE PURE

"*The Evil And The Pure* is a deliciously dark delight; a gritty, realistic look at the depths of human depravity. The twists and turns have you reeling with shock. A glory to read. 5/5 stars." **Matthew R Bell's BookBlogBonanza.**

"A thoughtful and enthralling examination of a society that is seedy, corrupt and painfully uncompromising. Few writers can so easily and powerfully communicate the complexities of people dragged into a world of darkness and despair." **Safie Maken Finlay, author.**

"I found myself brilliantly horrified and captivated as I read and was taken along on a dark journey with a range of dangerous, sick and even innocent characters." **Chase That Horizon.**

"an amazing read… a book you won't want to end… It's got the cast complexity of a Maeve Binchy novel as if written by a violent madman, and I mean that as a compliment! 5/5 stars." **Kelly Smith Reviews.**

SUNBURN

"vivid and unrelenting… the novel offers captivating tension and brutal, gory fun." -- **Kirkus Reviews.**

"A well-written and disturbing piece of fiction. The plot reads like an international horror movie, enticing the reader with a series of detailed and comedic chapters before exploding into a vision of blood-chilling gore." **Books, Films & Random Lunacy.**

"This demonic masterpiece does not fail to disappoint even the biggest of horror fans." **Crossing Pixies.**

"The elements of classic horror are very much present here. *Sunburn* held me firmly in the moment, demanding my full attention right to the very last page." **Thoughts Of An Overactive Imagination.**

"Like the *Hostel* films, they have a lot of set up and then shizzle hits the fan… and then hits it again for good measure!" **Dark Readers.**

AN OTHER PLACE

DARREN DASH

HOME OF THE
DAMNED LTD

An Other Place

by Darren Dash

Copyright © 2016 by Home Of The Damned Ltd

Cover image by Stephen Toomey

Cover design by Liam Fitzgerald.
http://www.frequency.ie/

Edited by Zoe Markham
http://markhamcorrect.com/

First electronic edition published by Home Of The Damned Ltd December 1st 2016

First physical edition published by Home Of The Damned Ltd December 1st 2016

The right of Darren Dash to be identified as the Author of the Work has been asserted by him in accordance with the Copyright, Designs and Patents Act 1988.

All rights reserved. No part of this publication may be reproduced, stored in a retrieval system, or transmitted, in any form or by any means without the prior written permission of the publisher, nor be otherwise circulated in any form of binding or cover other than that in which it is published and without a similar condition being imposed on the subsequent purchaser.

All characters in this publication are fictitious and any resemblance to real persons, living or dead is purely coincidental.

www.darrendashbooks.com

www.homeofthedamned.com

6

ONE

I've come to Amsterdam for work, not leisure, and have no intention of savouring the seedy pleasures of its red light district until I find myself wandering by a row of garishly illuminated windows on my way back to my hotel during a late lunch break. I glance at the ladies on display out of curiosity, the way every visitor does, and a red-head in a nurse's uniform catches my eye. It isn't the saucy outfit – if I go down that route, bunny costumes are more my thing – but the colour of her hair. It strikes me that I've never had sex with a red before, and I pause to consider if that's genuinely the case. She smiles at me and crooks a finger in the middle of that pause, and like a peckish fish I'm hooked.

"What do you do?" the hooker asks me twenty minutes later, as she's squeezing back into her white, PVC dress. I'm lying on a mattress, still naked, staring at a large photo of Marilyn Monroe pinned to the ceiling.

"Hmm?" I grunt.

"What do you do? she asks again. She's from Scotland, this lady of the night (well, afternoon), hence the red hair. I'm sure there's an interesting story in what she's doing in Europe's most infamous city, but I'm not in the mood for stories.

"I'm the King Kong of troubleshooters," I tell her, smiling at Marilyn, feeling sated and happy after shooting my load.

The hooker casts me a startled look. "You're some kind of an assassin?"

I snort with laughter and consider playing up to her misconception – *Yeah, doll, I'm a killer of men, an annihilator of souls* – but I'm too tired. "A troubleshooter's someone who fixes things," I explain. "I work with computers and sort them out when they go wrong."

"Oh." She sounds disappointed. "Is it a good job?"

"It pays the bills but you probably make more than me," I laugh, figuring it's best not to reveal how well I do, or she might seduce me again and charge more the next time. I sit up and reach for my trousers.

"Will you be in Amsterdam long?" she wants to know.

"Maybe another day or two. I'm trying to string out the job that I'm on. Some of my friends are here and I want to hang with them."

"If you guys are looking for company..." she simpers.

"You'll do me a good deal?" I grin.

"For a fellow Londoner, always," she says.

"You're from London? I thought you were Scottish."

"I am," she says, "but I lived in London for seven years before I came here."

"Soho?" I smile.

"No," she sniffs. "I had a proper job, working in a bank."

Seems I'm going to get her life story whether I'm interested or not. "So what happened?" I ask.

She looks at me, considers it, then shakes her head. "Don't worry, I won't bore you with the details."

"I'll tip you another ten for that," I chuckle.

"If you really want to tip me, bring your friends round,"

she says.

"I will if they're keen, and they almost always are," I wink. "Do you do group rates?"

"Of course. I'm especially generous to the gentleman who brings extra punters along." She's fully dressed now. I pull on the rest of my clothes and slip into my shoes. "Anything else you'd like?" she asks as I'm tying my laces. She runs the back of her right index finger under her nose. "I can do you a good price."

"No thanks," I say. "Not my scene."

"Don't forget to introduce me to your friends," she says as I head for the door.

"I won't," I promise, but it's a lie. I won't be coming back here. I tend to steer clear of hookers who try to sell me drugs. I don't believe in mixing my vices.

I don't return to my hotel but head straight back to the offices. They're a small but successful firm. They trade in diamonds, or something along those lines. I rarely learn much about my clients. The company I work for sets up networks all over the world, for various businesses. As a troubleshooter, all I need to know about are the systems. Anything else is a distraction. I fly in, do my job, fly out. No time for fraternising with the locals, and to be honest, not much inclination either.

A virus has crippled the network here. Not one of the newer, nastier strains, but an old, familiar foe. Normally I'd aim to have it sorted by closing time today, so that I could catch a late flight home, but like I told the hooker, I'm in no rush on this one, not since I engaged with Hughie and Battles by chance earlier in the day.

The three of us go way back. We met in college in our late teens, when we were studying business, and all dropped out around the same time, for different reasons. We rented a flat together for a couple of years and had a whale of a time while we were deciding what to do with our futures. Our paths took us apart after that but we've stayed in touch, albeit sporadically.

Hughie works for a major international bank, helping wealthy clients hide their money in global boltholes unknown to the taxman, while Battles is a security expert, situated in the Middle East at the moment, helping equally wealthy clients keep themselves from being blown up.

We only found out that we were all in Amsterdam this morning, when Battles posted a picture of himself on Facebook, standing outside a sex shop, asking the question of his Followers, *Where am I?* Hughie was among the first to respond, with, *No way! Me too! Shall we meet for a small, sweet sherry after work?* I wasn't long in adding, *If you fancy making it a threesome, I'm in town too.*

It's been nearly two years since our last get-together. That was in Moscow, middle of winter, so cold you had to drink half a bottle of vodka a day to stop your piss from freezing inside you. Battles was wearing an experimental device, with electrodes strapped to his testicles. Went to urinate in a frozen fountain after a night on the hard stuff and nearly electrocuted himself.

Golden memories.

I get itchy thinking about my friends and those carefree, younger times. I can't focus on work, so I flick off the screen and stretch. "That's it for today," I tell the worried manager who's been hovering by my shoulder, waiting for a progress report. "A debugging program will run through the night. I'll check it in the morning and see where we're at. If all goes well, hopefully we'll be in the clear by the end of play tomorrow."

"What about the other computers?" he asks. "Should we turn them off?"

"No need," I tell him. "Work away as normal. The system will be sluggish but you can't do any more damage."

He smiles with relief. "Thank you, Mr Riplan. Have you any plans for tonight? If not, would you like to join my wife and I for dinner?"

"That's OK," I tell him. "I'm going to have a quiet one, do some work from my hotel. But don't expect me too early. I want to give the program time to finish. No point sitting here for hours on end, staring at a blank screen."

"Of course not," he agrees. "Take all the time you want. We'll expect you when we see you."

"Cheers," I smile. "I hope you enjoy your meal with your wife." Then I swing my jacket over a shoulder and text the two boys as I'm heading for the street — *Let the games commence!*

I wasn't lying when I told the hooker that drugs weren't my scene – I did that shit for a few years, and it was fun, but you've got to know when to get out – but partying in

Amsterdam and not getting high is like going to Ireland and not getting wet — just isn't going to happen.

Hughie and Battles come to Amsterdam regularly, so I leave everything in their hands. They arrange a party in Hughie's pad – a rented apartment that he uses whenever he visits the city – and ask their contacts to deliver weed, coke and girls, while I pick up a few slabs of beer en route, so that I don't feel like a complete leech. We smoke a few joints and down several cans, catching up while we're waiting for the ladies to arrive. They do lines with us when they get here, telling us how handsome we are, that they like English men the most. One girl does a striptease and soon everybody's naked and we're fucking on the carpets and the furniture, in the bath and on top of the TV, swapping ladies (a fresh condom each time — these working girls don't take chances) and betting on who's going to last the longest before we collapse from the coke and the sex.

It's a fast, fun night, a throwback to our hedonistic heyday when we thought we were immortal, and doesn't stop when we send the girls on their merry way. "I want a bagel," Battles says, and as soon as the words are out, Hughie and I want one too.

"God, yes, a bagel," I gasp. "Where are the bagels, Hughie?"

"Bagels are your department, Riplan," he says. "We supplied the drugs and the girls. All you brought were some cans. You owe us."

"Come on then," I say, heading for the door.

"Bagel quest," Battles sings, and we take up the chant as

we dance through the streets. "Bagel quest, bagel quest!" Soon five or six random strangers have joined us and we're cha-chaing along, legs flying every which way, "Bagel quest, bagel quest, where the fuck are the bay-gulls?"

Belly full of delicious bagels. I've three more in a bag for breakfast. We're back at Hughie's. We picked up a couple of replacement girls along the way but couldn't work up the energy to start banging, so they've scarpered. Just the three of us now, getting high, talking shit.

"Made a couple hundred k last week," Battles boasts. He has crazy, spiked, blond hair, looks like the bastard love child of Sonic the Hedgehog. "A guy I was supposed to bust for one of my clients, to keep him away from the client's daughter. A smuggler into everything you can think of — drugs, weapons, white slaves."

"Fuck off," I jeer. "That's newspaper bolloxology. White women don't get kidnapped and sold into slavery, not in the real world."

"Of course they do," Battles snaps. "Most operators focus on girls from piss-poor villages in Russia, since it's like picking apples in an orchard, but shrewder, braver guys like my one target pretty little Westerners and ship them off to some leery old Arab or African."

"I don't believe you," I laugh.

"It's true," he shouts. "On my mother's grave. He showed me photos."

"How much does a French or Italian lady cost?" Hughie asks, eyes hooded as he brushes a few fingers through his impeccably styled hair to check that every lock's in place. Always the banker, maybe he's wondering if he can afford to buy a white slave for his boss for Christmas.

"Dunno," Battles says. "He was tight-lipped about that. Said he only discusses prices with people who are serious about paying. Anyway, he was hot for my client's daughter, so I was hired to..."

Battles tells us how he put together a file on the smuggler but allowed himself to be bought off when the smuggler got wind of what he was up to and made him an offer. "Would have been easier to kill me," Battles says, "but I'd left copies of the file with different lawyers, so he knew I'd have screwed him from beyond the grave."

"What about your client?" I ask.

"Still paying me," Battles beams. "I convinced him that the creep was a gent of the highest order and had plans to put a ring on the daughter's finger. They're going out for dinner this weekend. Wouldn't surprise me if the old guy offers to make the smuggler his partner."

The dapper Hughie starts up with his success stories when Battles runs out of steam. The way he talks, half the currency of Europe passes through his hands in an average week, and he always takes a slice of the action. He's bought a small yacht, keeps several mistresses, is buying shares in promising startup companies.

To keep pace with the big boys, I tell them I'm planting dormant viruses on the quiet, every time I work on a system, and that over the next several years I'm going to activate them one by one and demand a king's ransom from the companies I'm currently in the act of helping. A load of horseshit, and they know it, but they pretend to be impressed.

In truth, while I'm not enjoying as much success as Hughie and Battles (at least judged by what they *say* they're earning), I'm not doing too badly. Twenty-eight years old and well on my way to my first million. Of course a million doesn't mean that much in this day and age but it'll still be nice to rack it up. Another two years, maybe three, and I'll be able to launch my own company. I could do it now but I'd be small fry. I want to wait, build up my profile, so I can start on a high. Everywhere I go, I see losers who went for broke too soon. I've no intention of ending up like them, bankrupt and out of ideas by the time I hit thirty.

NRE is what I'll call the company, Newman Riplan Enterprises. My parents named me Newman after some character on that old *Seinfeld* show. I've never watched it but it was their favourite programme back when they were young and in love and in the business of banging out babies.

"NRE," I murmur, but only shake my head when Hughie asks what that means, not wanting to reveal too much for fear one of the buggers would copyright the name to piss me off. I know I'd do it to them if given the chance — anything for a wind-up and a laugh.

Hughie rolls another joint and it makes the rounds. We're well stoned by this stage. I tried reading the time a few minutes ago but the numbers on the clock kept swirling and blurring.

"I've got to stop soon," I mumble. "I've a virus to shoot down in the morning."

"Fuck viruses," Hughie snorts, forcing a tumbler of tequila into my hands — he must have picked that up when we went out for the bagels.

"Rock 'n' roll!" Battles hisses, and I understand him well enough to know that he's challenging me to match them. Since I was never one to duck a challenge, I gulp, forward my regrets to my morning self in a mental email, and drink.

Later. Or sooner. I can't remember. Time's all screwed inside my head. I close my eyes. Next thing I know, I'm standing over the toilet. Have I pissed or was I about to? I look down but the dirty brown water tells me nothing. Fuck it. I tuck myself away. I can always return if my bladder starts stinging.

Battles is on the phone when I get back. "I love you, Mum," he's bellowing. "I've always loved you. You're my main squeeze. I'd marry you if I could, I swear it. I'd kill Dad and take you for myself, only…"

"How crazy is that bastard?" I laugh.

"Not as crazy as you think," Hughie cackles. "It's not *his* mum he's onto — it's *yours*. That's why he's using your phone and your accent."

It takes a few seconds for that to sink in. When it does, I leap across the couch and rip the phone from Battles. "Hello?" I groan.

"Newman?" my bewildered-sounding mother says. "Is that you? What on –"

I hit the red button, which is very small and hard to locate in my ragged state. "You fucker!" I roar at the giggling Battles and advance on him menacingly, but I begin to laugh before I reach him and soon I'm on my knees, weeping happily. "You son of a bitch. I'm going to... going to... Oh, fuck it."

"What are you doing?" Hughie asks as I hit redial on my phone.

"Ringing her back," I say. "Going to put things straight." She answers on the third ring. Hughie and Battles are laughing, so I hiss at them to shut the fuck up. "Mum?" I say seriously.

"Newman?" she asks.

"Yeah, it's me. I'm sorry... it wasn't... Battles took... Oh, hell." I pretend to gnaw on the end of the phone, then put it to the side of my face again and say in my most businesslike tone, "Mother, please describe to me – in very careful detail – exactly what undergarments you're wearing."

Behind me, Hughie and Battles explode.

Much later. I've drunk and smoked myself sober. Everything's clear again. I make a note on my phone to ring Mum – it's too late to bother her now – and apologise. I don't see my parents that often but I like to keep them sweet.

Hughie and Battles are beginning to sober up too. We stare at the mess of a room, the empty cans, tequila stains, joint stubs, white stains.

"Are you going to have to clean this up?" I ask.

"Am I fuck," Hughie replies. "The landlord can sweep it before the next tenants arrive. I pay enough not to have to worry about shit like that."

"This is horrible," Battles moans. "I can count my fingers. Look — ten of them. I don't want to be able to count my fingers. I want to rock 'n' fucking roll!"

"There are more cans in the fridge," Hughie tells him. "A bottle of vodka in the freezer too, I think."

"No good," Battles snarls. "I'm past that shit. What happened to the coke?"

"Up our noses," Hughie sighs.

"All of it?" Battles says in disbelief.

"We had company," Hughie reminds him. "The ladies accounted for their fair share."

"What about...?" Battles starts rooting in his pockets, before producing a bag of dreamy white. "My emergency stash."

"You kept that quiet," Hughie rumbles.

"I had a feeling it'd be a long night," Battles says, moving to the table to lay three lines.

"I don't know about this," I mutter.

"Got to keep the party going," Hughie winks.

"But it's come to its natural end," I complain. "I feel good now, exhausted but good. I've worked the earlier shit out of my system. If I go back to my hotel and grab some shuteye, I can catch up with the day and..."

"I don't have much," Battles says. "It won't go far. Just enough to set us up nicely for breakfast."

"We're in the middle of Amsterdam," I stall. "If that hits

the spot, we'll go out and buy more."

"Newman," Hughie says steadily, "you have to learn to trust yourself." He leans over, snorts a line through a rolled-up fifty, then passes it across. I should reject it but it's been two years since our last blow-out and who knows how long it will be until our paths cross again, so even though I know it's a bad idea, I roll my eyes, take the note and surrender to the fates.

I'm so wasted, I feel like I've crawled out of the pages of a Hunter S. Thompson book. Of course we didn't stop after Battles' emergency supply. We went straight out to track down more. Coming on top of everything we consumed earlier, it sets my head spinning so fast that I vomit with vertigo. I flop about the apartment, blubbering, giggling, hallucinating. Hughie and Battles are in better shape – they could always go at it harder than me – but only marginally.

An hour or two later, I'm not feeling *quite* so rough, and my mouth has started to work again. In fact my mouth beats my brain back to consciousness, and as I tune into the conversation, I find that I'm the one talking, letting off steam about how over-worked I am.

"Nine months since my last break," I growl. "And that was just a long weekend. I'm being exploited. When I get home, I'm going up to the... boss or his... PA, and I'll... I'll..."

"You'll do fuck all," Hughie laughs, "because by then you'll be sober and thinking straight."

"Will not," I pout. "I'll stay high and fly back on my own

fucking wings. We got any more snow?"

"All out again," Battles says mournfully. "The snow is no-go, Joe. Let's go get some more."

"Amen," I pant and stagger for the door.

"Hold up, hoss," Hughie says, yanking me back. "We promised ourselves not to let this get out of hand."

"Too late for that," I tell him.

"Never too late," Hughie says. "Besides, snow isn't the answer. What's needed now is..." His face lights up as he stumbles upon an idea. "That's it. A holiday you crave, so a holiday you shall have. Come on." He lurches to his feet and darts into his bedroom. Moments later he emerges, stuffing something into his jacket's inside pocket, before leading us out into the dawn.

"Where are we going?" I ask as we worm our way through the streets, the early morning air sobering me up the tiniest bit.

"Looking for a taxi," Hughie says.

"And after that?" I ask.

Hughie winks. "Wait and see, Cinderella, wait and see."

We eventually find a taxi and pile in. Hughie asks for the name of Battles's hotel and mine, then tells the driver to take us to both, before settling back to sigh the sigh of a man relishing a moment of true inspiration. Battles and I ask him what he's planning but he ignores us and stares out at the city as it slowly starts coming to life.

Battles and I grow quiet, then silent, and while we're en route to whichever of our hotels the driver is taking us to first, in the middle of trying to work out what Hughie might be up to, my eyelids flutter shut and sleep claims me for its own.

We're still in the taxi when I jolt back to life. "Where are we?" I ask, looking around blearily. "Did we get to the hotels yet?"

"Yes," Hughie says.

"He let himself into our rooms," Battles grumbles. "Wouldn't say what he was after."

"How'd you get into mine?" I ask.

"Your room key wasn't hard to find," Hughie laughs. "I packed your clothes and checked you out."

"You did what?" I gasp. "Why?"

"You won't be going back there," Hughie says.

"But the offices... the virus..." I sputter.

"You can call in later," he says. "Tell them you had to return home for a family emergency."

"Where are you taking me?" I wheeze, worried about where we're heading, thoughts of white slavers filling my head. I'm on the point of asking the driver to stop, so I can make a break for freedom, when I spot a sign for Schiphol. "The airport!" I shout.

Hughie claps slowly. "You've eagle eyes, Riplan. Should have known you'd rumble me sooner or later."

"What's at the airport?" I ask suspiciously.

"Planes, you fuckwit." Hughie looks back at me and decides it's time to share his big idea. "You need a holiday but we all know you won't take one. You'll go back to London after this gig, another virus will crop up, your boss will send you off somewhere else and you won't complain because if you give him shit he'll hand you your cards and bring in someone new. Right?"

"Right," I sigh.

"Well, worry no more," Hughie says. "You *are* going on holiday, and you're going today."

I blink dumbly and frown. "Come again?"

"We're going to pack you off somewhere foreign," Hughie chuckles. "I have your passport, and the bag with your clothes is in the boot. We'll get to the airport, book you a ticket on the first flight out, you hop aboard, fall asleep, and when you wake up you'll probably be full of regrets, but you'll be out of here and there'll be nothing you can do about it. You'll have skipped the job and missed your flight to London, so you'll have no choice but to sit back and enjoy yourself, since the shit's going to hit the fan no matter what."

I scratch an ear uncertainly. "I don't know about this," I mutter. "The holiday bit's fine but leaving a job halfway through... I could get sacked for that."

"Bollocks," Hughie snorts. "You'll claim you had a nervous breakdown, say you were working too hard, that you snapped and took off, and next thing you knew, two weeks had passed and you'd worked up a tan and were on a plane back home and can't remember a thing about it."

Hughie is glowing, falling more in love with his idea with every passing word.

"Your boss won't be able to say boo," he assures me. "Sane men don't take off and disappear for two weeks. It'd be different if you went missing for a day or two, but if you come back after a real holiday, not having rung him once while you were away, he'll have to accept your word that you lost the run of yourself. He won't be able to sack you, because if it went before a tribunal and they found out you broke down because you hadn't been granted a proper break in two years, he'd be hung out to dry."

"Sounds reasonable to me," Battles says, which should be the sign to bail – if he approves of it, you can bet the idea's a stinker – but in my dazed condition I let the warning slip by unnoticed.

"Yeah," I whisper, "it sounds sweet. Nobody will be able to say I planned it, because I didn't. Just, suddenly, out of the blue…" I slap my knee and grin.

"Yes?" Hughie asks, eyebrows raised.

"Yes," I echo.

"Yes!" he whoops and bangs the roof of the taxi with his fists, which sets the driver off with a rapid batch of threatening Dutch curses.

Hughie and Battles take charge of securing me a ticket. They sit me down in a dark corner, stick a pill between my lips to keep me quiet – I don't dare ask what it is – and get busy on their phones. I doze off and next thing I know I'm being shaken awake and dragged to my feet.

"C'mon," Hughie yells, "we've got to hurry or you'll miss your plane."

"Are you guys coming too?" I ask as they hustle me towards security and start fiddling with their belts ahead of having to remove them.

"We booked cheapo flights for ourselves," Hughie explains, "so we can come with you to your gate."

"We want the whole thing to be a shock," Battles says, fully on board with the idea now. "We don't want you to know where we're sending you until you get off the plane."

"We'll escort you to the gate," Hughie says, "keep the destination a secret if we can, then leave you there and head back to our hotels."

"Are you sure?" I mumble. "This must be costing you a fortune."

"Too late to gripe about that," Hughie laughs. "The tickets are non-refundable."

They scan our boarding passes from our phones, being careful not to let me see mine, then hurry me through fast-track and into the heart of the sprawling airport. I've no liquids in my bag – Hughie left them all at the hotel – so I want to stop and restock, but they tell me I can do that at the far side.

"That's given me a thought," Hughie mutters and darts into a shop by himself. He comes back with ear plugs and an eye mask.

"For the plane?" I scowl. "I'm obviously not flying first class then, or they'd have provided me with a set on board."

"We're rich," Battles sniffs, "but we're cheapskates. You're in economy."

"But we did get you a nice seat close to the front of the cabin and next to a window," Hughie laughs. "Either way, these aren't for the plane. We'll use them to deafen and blind you when we get to the gate, to keep the surprise intact."

"You aren't sending me somewhere horrible, are you?" I ask, slowing down. "Like the DRC or Afghanistan?"

"Would we do something like that?" Hughie smiles.

"Of course we fucking would," Battles bellows. "But we haven't."

"You'll like this," Hughie says. "We want you to enjoy yourself and come back refreshed, so that next time we don't have to listen to you bitch all night about how hard you're working."

I decide to trust them and start moving again. "The magical mystery tour," I giggle, trying to get into the spirit of things.

"That's it," Hughie hoots. "You're a lucky fucker. I wish I had mates as great as us. Nobody's ever bundled me off like this."

"I'll bundle you off if you want," Battles says earnestly.

Hughie arcs an eyebrow. "Yeah, and sell me to the fucking slave trade. I bet I'd fetch a top price."

"You're kidding," Battles says. "I wouldn't be able to give you away as a freebie with a herd of camels."

"Anyway," Hughie says to me, giving Battles the cold shoulder, "I had a lovely fortnight in the Caribbean a couple of months ago, so I'm good on the holiday front, but if we meet in similar circumstances and I'm in the same condition as you were this time…" He gives my cheek a pinch. "Think of me then, eh?"

They make me stick in the ear plugs and don the eye

mask before we get to the gate, then sit with me until the flight's called and almost everyone has boarded. When the last few stragglers are rocking up, they remove the plugs and mask and hand me my small travel bag.

"I don't have much in this," I note. "I only planned to be away for a night or two."

"You can get some new gear on hols," Hughie says. "There are plenty of shops where you're going."

"Not a desert island, then?" I smile.

Hughie winks and claps my back. Battles treats me to a great big man hug.

"You two really are the best friends," I say when I'm released. "Thanks for this. It's extravagant and crazy and I love you both for it."

"Easy there, Newman," Hughie tuts. "We don't want any waterworks."

With that they about-face, leave me at the check-in desk and mosey off into the sunset, to wend their way back through the airport and security and out to the city beyond. I almost call after them, to ask if it will be a long flight, but I guess I'll find out soon enough.

My phone and passport are scanned and handed back to me by a smiling flight attendant. "I hope you enjoy your flight with us today," she titters.

"It's not the flight I'm concerned about," I tell her, "but where I end up."

She looks at me oddly, so I force a smile and move on before she says anything to give the game away — having come this far, it would be a shame to spoil the surprise now.

I join the line down the gangway – not too long, since most of my fellow passengers have already boarded – and nervously jiggle from foot to foot as I prepare for my flight into the unknown.

TWO

I'm worried that I'm behaving erratically – breathing heavily, twitching my head, hands shaking – and will be ejected from the plane by the crew, but none of the stewards pays me any attention, so I mustn't be as out of it as I fear. I make my way to my seat, put my bag up overhead, smile apologetically at the woman and her daughter who have to get up to let me slide in by the window, then settle back and shut my eyes.

I only meant to rest my eyes for a minute but the next thing I know, I'm staring down on a sea of white clouds. I've missed take-off and – a quick check of my watch – the first hour of the flight, which is probably no bad thing. I stretch my legs, rub my neck and groan.

"You're awake," someone says and I glance over. It's the girl, no more than ten or eleven years old. Her mother is smiling at her as she addresses me. "You were snoring."

"Sorry," I yawn. "I had a long night."

"That's not uncommon in Amsterdam," the woman says. "I had a few long nights there myself before this one came along." She nudges her daughter, who laughs as if it's a great joke. Give her another couple of years and she'll be rolling her eyes at any sort of interaction like that.

"Have they served the drinks?" I ask.

"Yes," the mother says.

"I wanted to wake you," the daughter pipes up, "but Mummy said to let you sleep."

"Mummies know best," I grin, then press the button for the flight attendants.

A stewardess is with me less than a minute later, smiling and warm. "Can I help you, sir?"

"I know I missed it," I murmur, "but I was wondering if I could have a drink? My throat's really dry and –"

"Not a problem," she interrupts. "What would you like?"

"Black tea and a big glass of water?" I ask.

"Coming right up," she says and goes off to get the drinks. She has an American or Canadian accent, which makes me suspect I might be bound for the Americas, though I guess the flight could be headed in the opposite direction too.

The stewardess returns with the tea and a bottle of water. I gulp from the bottle first, then sip the tea, sighing with contentment.

"Tea's a great soother," the woman with the daughter says.

"Yeah," I grunt, hoping she'll stop there. I've been polite to her and the girl but my head's pounding and I don't want to engage in a lengthy conversation.

"You're from London, aren't you?" she asks.

"Yeah."

"I thought so," she says brightly. "The accent. I love London, so full of history. The architecture's amazing. And all the galleries. I used to..."

She babbles on about her visits to London, how she loves the Tower and Spitalfields Market and walking along Southbank and good old Buck Palace. And isn't Trafalgar

Square wonderful? And the magical book shops in Charing Cross Road, although there are so few of them left these days. And...

"Excuse me," I say abruptly, lurching to my feet. "Call of nature."

"No problem," she says and stands up in the aisle. "Here, Jennifer, let Mr..."

"Riplan," I inform her, since I don't seem to have a choice.

"Stand up and let Mr Riplan out of his seat," she says.

The daughter – Jennifer – doesn't move across but draws her legs up and says, "There's plenty of room to pass."

The mother – I still don't know her name and I've no wish to – tuts but smiles at me to show she thinks this is an adorable bit of childhood rebellion. If I was the brat's father, I'd haul her out into the aisle and warn her not to be rude, but I know better than to tell other parents how to chastise their children, so I shuffle past, nod gruffly to the mother, and make a beeline for the toilets.

I didn't really need to go but since I'm here, I force out a few drops, then run the tap, splash water over my face and take deep breaths, forehead pressed to the mirror. I feel hot and bothered, the drugs still in my system, in need of several hours more sleep.

I wonder about my destination. This has to be the craziest shit I've ever pulled, letting those two maniacs book me on a mystery holiday. I could be headed anywhere. I'm tempted to check my phone but decide against it. I've come this far in the dark — it'd be a shame to chicken out now.

I splash more water over my face, use a bunch of paper towels to dry myself, then head back to my seat, breathing deep, trying to stay cool.

There's still lots of tea left and it's nicely tepid by this stage, just the way I like it. I realise as I drink that my ears are buzzing. Must be the drugs — normally I never suffer when flying. I'm going to be in for the mother of all headaches later, when the drugs, drink and travel catch up with me. Just thinking about the grief is enough to bring on the first throbbing pains.

"Excuse me, Mr Riplan?" It's the mother again, smiling at me as if we're old chums.

"Yeah?" I reply sourly.

"I was wondering... It's not much fun for a child being stuck in the middle. I know it would be an imposition, but we'd be so grateful if..."

"You want me to swap seats with your daughter," I say flatly.

"If you don't mind." She grins sweetly.

I should let the kid have the window seat. It's a big thing when you're young, looking out, spotting other planes streaking past, studying the land below. Any other time, I'd be happy to offer up my place, but the mother's grin pisses me off. She's not really asking me to move — she expects me to vacate my seat. I can tell that she thinks her daughter has a right to sit wherever she wants, that I should oblige her any way I can, and it's that sense of entitlement that inflames me.

"She can't have it," I say softly.

The woman blinks, her smile slipping. "I... well, of course, if there's a reason why you need to be by the window..."

"See this?" I growl, bouncing up and down a few times. "This is my chair. See that?" I slap the armrest of Jennifer's seat. "That's your daughter's. Hers. Mine. Hers. Understand?"

The poor woman stares at me, stunned, then grows indignant. "If that's the way you feel," she huffs.

"It is," I say obstinately, knowing I'm behaving like a five-year-old but too far into this to back out now.

Jennifer's lower lip is quivering and her eyes are filling with tears.

"It's alright," the mother says, trying to calm the girl, "you can swap seats with me."

"But I don't want to sit there," Jennifer snivels. "I want to sit beside the window."

"I know," comes the answer, "but you can't. That's *Mr Riplan's* seat."

"Damn right, baby," I chortle, figuring I might as well play the full pantomime villain.

I get comfy as the mother convinces Jennifer to take her seat, telling her that the aisle is the best place to sit, that it gets cold by the window. I'm feeling lousy now that the heat of the moment has faded, and almost offer up the cherished throne, but the mother would probably refuse it and that would leave me looking sad and defeated. Better to maintain the front and act like a callous son of a bitch.

"Is everything OK?" the stewardess who brought my tea and water asks, hearing Jennifer's sniffles as she's passing.

"Yes, thank you," the mother says icily.

"I wanted –" Jennifer starts to explain but I cut her short, not wanting the nice stewardess to hear of my pettiness.

"Any chance I could bother you for a bag of nuts?" I ask.

"Of course," the stewardess says and returns with a couple of small bags of mixed nuts and another bottle of water.

"You're a star," I thank her and she smiles beautifully. "Want one?" I ask the mother as I open the first bag. She sniffs and buries her head in the in-flight magazine. I shrug, flick a nut past my lips and chew away happily as the world slips by tens of thousands of feet beneath.

The mother and Jennifer haven't said a word for twenty minutes. I'm still chewing nuts, watching a TV show on my seat-back screen, the blind down. I did think of leaving it up and making a show of gazing out the window and cooing – "Wow! Those are some wild cloud formations. I doubt I'll ever see any like those again." – but I'm not *that* infantile.

I've come to the last few nuts at the bottom of the second bag. I upend it and let them slide into my mouth and bounce along my tongue. I'm thinking of asking the stewardess for a third bag – the salt seems to be helping me fight off the headache – when one of the nuts lodges in my windpipe. I begin choking and coughing.

"Are you alright?" the mother asks, alarm getting the better of her indignation. "Can I help?"

I shake my head and double forward, gasping for breath. I feel her hands on my back but I shrug them off. I'm not in serious trouble. I've had nuts go down the wrong way before. I'll jolt out of this by myself.

I gulp a few times, hoping my Adam's apple will dislodge the pesky nut. I hear the mother calling the stewardess and sense heads turning to see what the commotion is. I sit up straight, bang on my chest with my hands, then double over again and try to retch. The buzzing in my ears strengthens and I become oblivious to all surrounding sights and sounds, even the roar of the engines. I'm focused on the nut and my diminishing supply of oxygen. I rock forwards and backwards, eyes squeezed shut, lungs straining, tongue lashing from one cheek to another like a trapped, dying eel, and finally, when I'm beginning to really worry, out shoots the nut like a bullet from a gun. It hits the back of my teeth and lands on my tongue. I spit it into the palm of my hand, wipe round my mouth, relax back into my seat and turn to assure the mother, the stewardess and the others that the crisis is over... only to discover that I appear to be the only living human left on the plane.

THREE

It must be the drugs. I'm tripping. I have to be. And yet... I've never experienced anything like this before. Never even *heard* about anything like this.

The mother has turned into a plastic mannequin. So has Jennifer. So, it seems from a cursory look round, has everybody else.

I study the figure beside me, far calmer than I should be, sure that this is a surreal trip, one that I'll float out of any minute now. It looks like the mother – same build, similar facial contours – but there are differences. This woman's naked for one thing, and devoid of hair, none on her head or pubic areas. Her breasts lack nipples and she has no fingernails. Her lips are shut tight and there's a white, mucousy film covering her nostrils, ears and eyes.

"Mrs?" I say stupidly, wishing I'd bothered to ask her name. "Jennifer?" They don't answer or move. They're sitting stiffly, facing ahead, expressionless, hairless, nippleless. I poke the woman with a finger, which sinks in alarmingly. The mannequin isn't made of hardened plastic, as I assumed, but some sort of wax. It's soft and malleable, like hot wax, except it's cool as a winter morning pane of glass.

I pull back my finger, sniff and lick.

It tastes of candles.

I leave my seat and stand in the aisle, gazing round, going with the flow of the hallucination. The men have testicles and penises but they're small and hairless.

Everyone's sitting in the same position, facing forward, still as corpses, hands neatly tucked in by their sides.

I'm fully clothed, hair on my head. I prod my stomach and face and they feel the same as ever. I hurry back to the toilet and check in the mirror — no visible changes, except I'm flushed and sweating. I smile at my reflection and paddle my lower lip with my index finger. "Going loony, old boy," I chuckle. "Father always said it would happen."

I sit on the toilet seat and take a few deep breaths, even deeper than those I took earlier. This is starting to get to me. I'm scared. The trouble is, I'm thinking too clearly. I should be bewildered and groggy but I'm not. My head's in good shape. Even my headache's vanished. I know what it's like to trip and how my mind works when the wiring in my brain gets tangled, and this isn't the way it should be. This is more than a bad reaction to coke. This is *wrong*.

I wander up and down the plane like a lost little lamb. I've been prowling the same patch for... how long? An hour? Two? Three? Impossible to say, since my watch and phone have gone missing. They either disappeared when the people turned to dummies or were swiped from me unawares just prior to that.

I continue telling myself that this is a bad trip and keep trying to snap myself out of it – pinching my arms, pulling my hair, slamming my head against things – but no luck so far. In truth, I don't believe it *is* a trip. From the first moment I had a feeling this was something more. I don't know what that *more* might be, but if I was a betting man,

I'd wager a fair sum on full-blown madness.

I've tried communicating with the mannequins but they react to nothing. I've hit them, screamed at them, jabbed pens into them, without response. I even cut the hand off one of them with a knife I found in the galley — there was just a whitish goo inside, no bones or blood.

The door to the cockpit is closed. I've attacked it with my feet and hands, the knife, with arms I ripped off chairs, all to no avail — they started making those things pretty impenetrable in the wake of 9/11. I considered building a fire and trying to burn my way through but I didn't think it would work, and what if the fire spread? I'd be all alone in the middle of a raging inferno, no help in sight. I bang on the door from time to time, in the hope there's somebody alive up front, but if there is, they aren't responding.

There are the emergency doors of course but I haven't been able to find any parachutes and jumping out of a plane while it's in flight remains the most final of options.

Although having said that, I'm not sure we're actually in the air. I have the sensation of flight but the engines are dead as far as I can tell. The plane's silent, except for my laboured breathing and the pounding of my heart and feet. And it's pitch black outside. Not dark, like it is when flying at night, but *black*. No stars, no moon, no flashing wing-lights. Perhaps we're gliding, closer to the ground than we should be, thick cloud cover overhead.

I try the door to the cockpit again. "Can you hear me?" I scream, then try a Pink Floyd line. "Is there anybody out there?" Nothing. "Hello? I need help back here." No answer. A wave of panic sweeps through me and I begin pressing the call buttons above the heads of the mannequins. I stagger back along the aisle, randomly pressing buttons, stamping on the floor, peering out the windows, shouting at the dummies in the vain hope that one of them will react.

All to no avail.

Back in my seat. The mannequins of Jennifer and her mother lie sprawled on the floor. I threw them down partly to see if it would provoke a reaction – it didn't – but also to make some space. It's creepy as hell being surrounded by these silent, expressionless things. I need room to breathe, move, think.

I check my pulse, worried that my thrumming heart is about to burst, but I'm too agitated to take an accurate reading. Instead I get an idea to test the dummies. They've no pulse but if I press an ear to their chests, I detect a faint heartbeat. I contemplate cutting one of them open but decide against it. Not because I'm squeamish, but because it's the sort of dumb thing a person would do in an episode of *The Twilight Zone* — slice open a mannequin, only for everyone to become human again, thus ending up on a murder rap. I'm doing nothing desperate until I've run clear out of options.

(Sure. Like cutting off a hand isn't desperate.)

Could Hughie and Battles have had anything to do with this? Maybe I'm not on a real plane. Maybe we never left the ground. Perhaps this is a weird fairground ride, and any minute a door's going to open and my friends will fall in, laughing themselves sick. "Got you, Riplan! Freaked the shit out of you, huh? Is that brown pants stew we smell?"

The phrase *clutching at straws* races through my mind.

I'm still in my seat, wondering what to do, when I sense the plane descending. I'm not sure what tips me off – it's as silent as ever – but I know we're coming down.

I rush to the door of the cockpit and bang on it again. "Open up," I scream. "Tell me what's happening. Hey! Can you hear me? Are you..."

I stop. What if the pilot and his crew have turned into mindless, directionless mannequins too? That would explain why the engines were dead. What if we've been gliding along, as I suspected, but with no hand on the steering wheel, only for gravity to finally exert its control? We could be plummeting to a shrieking, fiery end.

I pound at the door, then hurry to the rear of the plane and settle down. I think this is the best place to be if we crash. I curl into a ball and say my prayers – I don't believe in a god, but at times like this I'm open to renegotiation – and brace myself.

The crash never comes. Instead the plane lands silently and smoothly. I hear no wheels being lowered or the squealing of rubber on tarmac. One second we're in the air, descending, the next we're on the ground, at a standstill. I can't explain how I know that, but I do.

We're down.

I hesitate, then shuffle over to the window, hoping to

spot lights outside, but it's still unnaturally black out there. I look for something to break the glass with – dangerous if I'm wrong and we're in the air – when all of a sudden the door to the cockpit slams open. After so much silence, the sound is startling and I cringe, terrified.

I stare at the open door, expecting a monster to come barrelling through, but I can't see a thing up there. I'm a long way back but I'm pretty sure there's nobody about. I take a step towards the front. Another. I make it about halfway up the cabin when, in perfect unison, the previously lifeless wax mannequins rise to their feet and start stepping out into the aisle.

FOUR

I panic when I find myself surrounded and lash out with my fists. The dummies don't react, just stand there and stare blankly ahead. After a few mad seconds I come to my senses, calm down (relatively speaking) and push through those nearest me to the seats they've vacated. My heart's still thumping wildly but I'm over the worst of the shock.

I observe the mannequins carefully, wondering what they'll do next. If they don't start moving again shortly, I'll continue my trek to the cockpit to find out if there's –

"Alright, you lot," someone roars. "Let's move it out."

Startled, I half-stand and peer over the top of the seat in front of me. In the mouth of the cockpit I spot two men standing to either side of the door. I call out to them but my voice is lost when the mannequins kick into life and march forward, blocking my view of the men and creating a din which I'd have to scream to be heard above.

I cower back in my seat, awed by the sight of the dummies marching up the aisle. They move robotically, eerier and more menacing than a pack of shambling zombies in a horror film.

I mean to get up and follow as the last mannequins pass by but my legs won't work. I have a terrible image of the two men leaving with the dummies, shutting the door and locking me inside forever, but even that dark thought isn't enough to jolt me into action. For the moment I'm as immobile as the wax figures were during the final stages of the flight.

*

The mannequins have disappeared, into the cockpit and out, I assume, through a door. The plane's silent again and feels significantly cooler. After several long seconds, footsteps approach. I hear the two men talking.

"A good crop," one says. He has a deep, strangely accentless voice.

"Best load we've had in a while," the other man agrees. His voice is slightly higher than his companion's and also impossible to place.

"Everything looks clean," the deep-voiced one says. "Why don't we knock off early?"

"No way," the other replies with a laugh. "Your predecessor tried that, only for the Alchemist to pop up and..."

He spots me and stops. I smile at him nervously, then stand and clear my throat. "H-hi," I stutter, "I'm –"

"This is why we don't knock off early, Phil," the man says, shooting a warning look at his partner.

The deep-voiced man gawps at me. "Who is he, Bryan?" he asks, then follows it up with a bewildered, "*What* is he?"

"A human," Bryan replies, "just like us."

"How'd he get on the drone hold?" Phil asks. "I didn't see anybody come in."

"He's not from here," Bryan says.

"Not from the city?" Phil's eyes widen. "But then where...?"

Bryan shrugs. "Dunno. I asked the Alchemist once. He told me to mind my own business, so I did."

The two men are dressed in dark blue uniforms, boots up to their thighs, peaked caps, burly gloves. Phil is white-skinned, Bryan a light brown. They don't look sinister or alien. They resemble a pair of jaded delivery men more than anything else.

"Excuse me," I say falteringly, "but what the hell's going on? What happened to all those people? Who are you? Where am I?"

"He doesn't know where he is," Phil giggles.

"Don't mock him," Bryan snaps. "If you ever find a human like this in a drone hold, treat him with respect or risk the wrath of the Alchemist."

"Sorry," Phil says, blanching at the idea of getting on the wrong side of whoever this Alchemist guy is.

"Where am I?" I bleat, trying (but failing) not to sound hysterical.

"Where do you think you are?" Bryan responds politely.

"I don't fucking know," I shout. "If I knew, I wouldn't be asking. I'd..." I take a deep breath and count to five. "Sorry, but I'm freaked out big time. One second I'm choking on a nut, the next I'm on a plane full of... of... whatever the hell those dummies are. And now..." I shake my head miserably.

"No use crying over spilt sap," Bryan says. "What's done is done. Now, if you don't mind moving along, we've jobs to be getting on with."

I stare at him incredulously. "Move along?" I screech.

"Have to," he says. "You can't stay here. We'll be sealing it when we're done. No food, no drink, no way out. You wouldn't last long."

I stare at the door of the cockpit, then back at Bryan. "But where will I go?" I whimper.

Bryan shrugs. "I don't want to be cruel but it's not my concern," he says. "We're just off-loaders. We make sure all the drones get off safely – sometimes one gets stuck in its seat – then clean up any mess."

"Drones?" I press him. "You mean the wax people?"

"Right," he says.

"What are they?" I ask. "They look like the people who were on the plane with me, but –"

"I really am sorry," Bryan says, taking my elbow and gently but firmly leading me up the aisle, "but we can't stay and chat. Drone holds don't clean themselves, you know."

"Bits of the drones fall off from time to time," Phil chips in. "Ears, noses, fingers, even a few teeth, though we don't get many of those, worse luck."

"Where will I go?" I whine again, shaking free and standing my ground.

"Out the door," Bryan sighs, exchanging a look with Phil that very clearly says, *This guy's crazy.*

I study the two men, then half-turn towards the cockpit. "What's out there?" I ask quietly, fearfully.

"The drone port," Bryan answers. "Beyond that, the city."

"What city?" I ask.

"What city do you think it is?" comes the infuriating response.

"I'm... not dead, am I?"

It's a difficult, delicate question to phrase, but Phil and Bryan laugh rudely, displaying not even the slightest sliver of sympathy.

"He thinks he's dead," Phil exclaims.

"Lots of them in his position think that," Bryan chuckles. "I had one once who lay down and refused to get off. He said he wouldn't move till somebody got him a coffin, whatever the snuff that is. Had to drag him out by his ears."

Bryan starts guiding me towards the cockpit again. I argue with him and ask one more time what's happening and where I am and what lies beyond the cockpit but he says nothing except, "This way, sir, this way please." Phil follows, giggling at my questions, telling Bryan he's ready to step in if I act up.

We reach the cockpit door and Bryan lets go of my arm. "Here we are," he says. "Through there, then the door on your left and down the steps. That'll bring you to the port. Where you go from there is your business."

I stare into the dark cockpit. There's nobody at the controls. No sign of the pilot or his crew. "Please," I sob, beginning to crack. "Tell me where I am, what's going on. Is this a dream? Am I tripping? Do you –"

Phil cuffs the back of my head and shoves me into the cockpit. "Get off our snuffing drone hold," he snarls.

"Steady," Bryan says. "Remember what I told you about treating people like him with respect."

"I don't care," Phil says. "Who the snuff is this guy, to come on our drone hold and start questioning us?"

"He's just confused and scared," Bryan says calmly.

"Well, he'd better scram before I give him something to be properly scared about," Phil says and shakes a boot at me. "Clear out before I chop your head off and claim I thought you were a drone."

Bryan rolls his eyes but cocks his thumb and gestures sharply with it. "Go on," he says softly, "before this fool does something you'll both regret."

From his tone of voice I can tell we're done talking, and since I like my head where it is on my shoulders, I scrabble to my feet, glance one final time about the deserted cockpit, then rush to the door on my left and start down the steps.

I'm on a sprawling, bare stretch of tarmac. To the far left I spot a bus, into which the wax mannequins – *drones*, Phil and Bryan called them – are piling. A little to my right lie two small buildings. Behind them and running all round the tarmac is a towering wall. Looking up, I can see only the pitch black sky that I spotted when in flight.

It's an even choice as to where I go next — the bus or the buildings. Since almost all the drones have boarded the bus, I decide to head for that first, in case it pulls away before I have a chance to examine it.

I arrive just as the last drone is entering. The bus is a strange affair. It looks new but there's no glass in the windows and no lights of any kind. It's a dull red colour. The drones sit inside, as still as they'd been on the plane.

While I'm studying the bus, an old man with grey hair appears from round the far side. He jumps when he spots me, then relaxes. "Hello, stranger," he says in a friendly tone. "Who are you? I've been asking for an assistant for ages. You ain't him, I suppose?"

"No," I reply.

He sighs. "Didn't think you were. Still, we live in hope,

eh?" The old man offers me his hand. "Mannie's the name."

"Newman Riplan," I tell him as we shake.

"Two names?" He laughs kindly. "One not good enough for you? Let me guess — you're from off the drone hold?" I nod and he chuckles. "I can always tell. You ran into Phil and Bryan?"

"Yes."

"Bet they were none too obliging."

I smile thinly. "You could say that."

"A curt pair," Mannie says pleasantly, "but good workers, especially Bryan. He's been here nearly as long as me."

The bus starts and begins to roll away. I take an involuntary step after it but Mannie grabs my arm and shakes his head. "Not that way, young fella. The bus is for drones, not humans. You don't want to go with that lot."

"Why?" I ask. "What happens to them?"

"You'll find out," he promises, then claps briskly. "If those who've arrived in the drone holds before are anything to go by, I assume you're full of questions."

"Yes," I say eagerly. "Where am I? What is this place?"

Mannie clucks and says, "Where do you think you are?"

I pull a face. "That's what Bryan said."

Mannie nods understandingly. "You'll hear a lot more of it before your stay here is out," he assures me. "I wish I could tell you something different, but it's a question that doesn't mean anything to me, so I can't answer it. Come on," he says, starting back across the yard. "Maybe Jess will be able to tell you more, though I doubt it."

"Jess? Who's..." I stop. I've just spotted Phil and Bryan

entering one of the small buildings. The plane's nowhere to be seen. My gaze shoots high but there's no sign of it in the freaky black sky either. "Where'd the plane go?"

"Plane?" Mannie's eyebrows furrow, then lift. "Oh, you mean the drone hold." He shrugs. "They never stay long. Here one minute, gone the next, always when you least expect them. Come on," he says again. "I don't like hurrying you but I've got to go see if Phil and Bryan stole anything from the drone hold. They never do but it's my job to check."

Mannie leads me to the second building. Closer up, I notice that both buildings are set in the perimeter wall and there's not a single pane of glass to be spotted in the windows of either structure.

"Here you are," Mannie says, knocking on the door.

"Come in," a muffled voice responds.

Mannie pushes down the handle and the door swings open. "I'll leave you here," he says. "Jess doesn't like to be disturbed, so I keep out of her way as much as I can. But as fierce as she is, she's good at her job, so don't worry, you're in safe hands." He slaps my back and smiles encouragingly. "Chin up, young fella," he says, then strolls along to check on Bryan and Phil.

I gaze at the open door, then at the tarmac expanse behind me. No sign of the bus now either. I take a step back and study the wall. Impossibly tall and sheer. Looks like there's only one way to go, and that's forward, into the building. So in I march on shaking legs to see the apparently fierce but efficient Jess.

*

It's a plain room, the huge perimeter barrier serving as the rear wall. There's a long desk set beneath one of the glassless windows to my left, behind which sits a woman in her late thirties or early forties, plump, dressed in a uniform similar to those of the men in the yard, her face unadorned with make-up.

"Can I help you?" the woman asks, barely looking up. She scribbles something at the bottom of a sheet of paper and stacks it with a load of others.

"Are you Jess?" I ask hesitantly.

"Who else might I be?" she sniffs.

"Um... Mannie told me to come see you."

"Did he?" She scribbles on another sheet of paper, straightens the edge of the pile, then fixes her gaze on me. "A friend of his, are you? Looking for a job? As I told the last no-hoper he sent to me, this isn't —"

"I'm not his friend," I interrupt. "I'm not here about a job. I'm from the plane."

Her face is blank. "Plane?" she says, as if the word is bitter on her tongue.

"The drone hold," I elaborate.

Her eyes light up with understanding. "Oh. Yes. The Alchemist told me to be on the lookout for a newcomer but that was so long ago..." She tears through a stack of papers to her right, then another, and another. Finally she finds a form, licks the tip of her pen and gets down to business. "Name?"

"Newman Riplan," I answer automatically. "Um... The men on the drone hold, and Mannie. I asked them where I was but they —"

"Please," she snaps. "I can't record your details if you're distracting me with questions. Have you been here before?"

"Where?" I ask.

"Here," she says. "This port, this office, this city."

"I don't know," I cry. "Nobody's told me where I am. Is it London? Moscow? Sydney? How can I tell you if I've been here if I don't –"

"I'll take that as a no," she stops me, writing it down. She looks up and smiles tightly. "The answer to that question was obvious, I know, but I'm required to ask. Now..." She scans down to the next question. "What age are you?"

"Twenty-eight."

"Occupation?"

"I'm a troubleshooter. Computer systems."

She pauses. "Could you be more specific?"

"I fix viruses and things like that."

"You're some sort of medic?"

"No," I groan. "Computer viruses. I sort out operating systems that have gone haywire."

"I see," she says, but by the way she chews her lower lip, I can tell she doesn't. "These *com-pu-ters*... they're machines of some kind?"

Is she trying to be funny? By her puzzled frown, I don't think so. I spend a couple of minutes trying to explain what a computer is – something I've never had to do before, and it's more difficult than I would have imagined – and it ends with her inscribing on the sheet, *He fixes machines. A possible medical connection.*

"Do you know anything about drones?" she asks.

"Those wax dummies on the plane? No. Not a thing."

She ticks a box. "That's unfortunate. Still, you'll learn fast, I'm sure. It won't take long to adjust."

"Adjust to what?" I ask but she's already moved on to the next question.

"Have you any place to stay?"

"In the city?" She nods. "No."

"You don't know anybody here? No family or friends?"

"Hard to say when I don't know where this is," I note sarcastically but she ignores that.

"Have you any currency?"

"Some sterling, euros and my credit cards," I say, but when I search for my wallet, it isn't where it should be. I spend a few frantic seconds patting myself down but it's gone, the same as my watch and phone.

"No matter," Jess says when I express concern. "Your currency would have been worthless here anyway." She pulls out a drawer, reaches in and hands me a small bag tied at the top with yellow string. I open it and look inside. It's full of teeth.

"What the fuck?" I yell, dropping the bag.

"Those are what we use for business transactions," Jess says.

"*Teeth*?" I laugh sickly. "You're shitting me." She shakes her head. "Where did you get them?" I ask, picking up the bag again. "The tooth fairy?"

"From the drones," she says. "As soon as they arrive, they're taken to a factory, where their teeth are extracted and processed."

I shake loose a couple of the teeth and examine them. They have no roots and are perfectly white, no fillings or cavities. Tiny marks have been carved into the front and back of each. "Are there different denominations?" I ask wryly. "Is a long tooth worth more than a short one? An adult's more valuable than a kid's?"

"No," she says. "All teeth are the same. Now, the contents of that bag should be enough to tide you over for three or four days, but after that you're on your own. You'll have to find work and earn your living. This is the only hand-out you'll ever receive, so make the most of it."

"How much are teeth worth?" I ask, tucking the bag away, playing along with the madness. "What can you get with them?"

"One tooth buys a drone," Jess explains, "or basic clothing items or a torch. Two will ensure you a room in a low-class boarding house. And so on. It won't take you long to figure out the system. It isn't that complicated." She returns to the form and purses her lips. "There are other questions but most are only relevant in peculiar circumstances." She reads down to the bottom of the page, then flicks over. "Are you sexually active?"

"What business is that of yours?" I retort.

She shakes her pen at me. "Temper, Mr Riplan. I'm only trying to help."

"You want to help?" I snap. "Tell me the name of this shit hole. Where the hell am I?"

"Where do you think you are?" comes the immediate reply.

"Are you people programmed with that response?" I ask sourly.

"I'll need a sample of your blood," she says, producing a small pin.

"In your dreams," I snort.

"It won't hurt," she assures me.

"Damn right it won't," I agree, "because I refuse to submit to it. You aren't sticking me with anything, lady, so the sooner you rid yourself of that particular delusion, the better."

"I see," she purrs. "Subject refuses blood sample." She writes each word down as she says it. "I assume you'll also refuse saliva and sperm samples?"

I laugh out loud. "You assume right."

Jess sighs. "You're being most uncooperative, Mr Riplan, but then most of your kind usually are."

"Is that a racial slur?" I bristle.

"All I need to conclude is your signature," Jess says, ignoring my question. She turns the sheet of paper round and offers me the pen.

"No," I say. "I'm not giving up that easily. I don't know what's going on but I'm going to find out. We aren't finished until I say we are, and that won't be until you've answered my questions as obligingly as I've answered yours." I lean forward menacingly. "Why don't we start with –"

Jess's left hand slams a button on the desk. A pole with a rounded end jabs me hard in the stomach, driving me backwards. I fall out of my chair and land hard on the floor, wincing. "What the hell?" I yelp. "That hurt. I'm going to…"

I stop. I can see under the desk now. There are two wire nets, one either side of Jess's legs. Behind them squat a pair of grim-looking wolves. They're glaring at me, lips pulled back over their teeth. They don't growl but they don't have to — they're terrifying enough as they are.

"This second button," Jess says, tapping the top of the desk, "releases the wolves. They're fed regularly but never overfed, so they're always in the mood for a snack. It's been a long time since I was forced to unleash them but I've done it before and I'll do it again if the situation calls for it." She leans forward and holds out the paper and pen. "May I have your signature now, Mr Riplan?"

Cursing softly, I take the pen, lay the paper on the floor and jot down my name where indicated.

"Thank you," Jess says, smiling as she checks to make sure I've signed in the right place. "You've now completed registration and are free to proceed."

"Proceed where?" I ask, slowly – so as not to alarm her – getting to my feet.

"Why, into the city, of course," she says. "Unless you want to stay here and try to wrangle a job with the off-loaders."

I look about the sparse room and recall how barren the area outside was.

"How do I get out?" I ask. She points to a door in the wall, tucked away in the far left corner, which is why I didn't see it before. "Straight through?"

"Straight through," she confirms.

"What happens on the other side? Do I have to get a taxi into the centre of the city, is there a train, can I walk?"

"Mr Riplan," Jess says impatiently, "I'm not here to answer questions. I suggest you simply go your own way and take things as they come."

"Thanks," I say bitterly, "you've been a bundle of help."

"I do my best," she grins, then calls after me as I head for the door. "Have an enjoyable stay, Mr Riplan."

I pause with my hand on the knob. "What about leaving?" I ask. "Do I have to come back here to get out of this place?"

She shakes her head sombrely. "Nobody leaves, certainly not through here. This port is for incoming drones only, and an occasional surprise visitor like yourself. Our off-loaders have orders to deal brusquely with anyone trying to make trouble."

On that ominous note I take my leave of Jess, the off-loaders and their damn port. Turning the knob, I push open the door and find myself facing a long, dark corridor. Hesitating only the briefest of moments, I let the door close behind me and thrust ever deeper into the heart of the bewildering mystery.

FIVE

The tunnel's longer than I thought it would be. I've been walking a good ten minutes or more, no end in sight. It's lit by thick candles which hang from the ceiling, one every ten metres or so. Plain concrete walls. No markings. The echoes of my footsteps make it sound like the tunnel is full of people, but it isn't. I'm alone.

Still walking. How long's it been now? An hour? More? No way to tell. I stop and glance back but it's the same featureless tunnel whichever way I look. At least it's straight, with no junctions. All I have to do is walk. No choices to make. The state I'm in at the moment, I can do without distractions.

At last — a door. I stand with my hand on the knob for a few minutes, ear pressed to the wood, hearing nothing. I'm nervous. I know I have to leave but I don't want to. I've acclimatised to the dimly lit tunnel. There's no telling what lies beyond. Maybe I should turn and go for another stroll. Work up my courage. Wait until...

No. The longer I put it off, the harder it'll be. To hell with fear. I open the door and step through. I'm moving on.

As the door closes behind me, I find myself in a large, derelict building, maybe an abandoned factory or warehouse. I spot daylight ahead, through a gaping doorway, and inch towards it. My eyes adjust as I move nearer the light, so by the time I get there I can step out into it without hesitation.

I'm on a quiet city street. The question is, which city? I look round in hope of an immediate answer but there's no Eifel Tower, Burj Khalifa or Big Ben, just moderately tall brick buildings that could belong almost anywhere on the face of the earth.

A smartly dressed man is walking towards me. I step into his path and clear my throat. "Excuse me."

He stops and smiles helpfully. "Yes?"

I laugh uneasily. "This is going to sound like a weird question, but would you mind telling me where I am?"

"You're on a street," he says, not even a flicker of sarcasm in his tone.

"I know that," I sigh. "I mean, what city is this?"

"What city do you think it is?" he replies with mild curiosity.

I shake my head, disgusted, and step aside. Nodding at me amiably, he proceeds as before.

I take a good look at the outside of the building that houses the entrance to the tunnel — in case I have to retreat this way in the future — then turn my back on it and set off to explore.

This is one weird, messed-up excuse for a city. Superficially there's nothing strange about it — wide streets, not much garbage, people who look the same as people anywhere, cars carving up the peace and quiet — but it doesn't take long to confirm I've wandered far from Normalville.

The lack of glass is the most obvious anomaly. I haven't

spotted a single pane. The windows of buildings are mere holes in the walls. No windscreens on any of the cars. Nobody wearing glasses. The street-lamps – not lit yet – are just candles mounted on poles. No traffic lights.

I've stopped several people to ask where I am. All have answered the same — "Where do you think you are?" I've asked about the absence of glass but nobody knows what I mean. Most think I'm trying to say *grass* and point towards parks, of which there are many. I even flagged down a driver at one point, an elderly man with a warm smile, but he knew no more than the pedestrians. It was interesting to see inside the car though. No mirrors. I asked how he kept an eye on the traffic to his rear. "Why should that worry me?" he wanted to know. I noted that, without a mirror, he could be rammed from behind. "Why would anybody want to ram me?" was his honest, puzzled response.

There are no street signs either. I thought, if I couldn't prise the name of the city out of its inhabitants, at least they'd be able to tell me what street I was on, but no. Most folk stared at me oddly when I asked. "Names for streets?" one laughed. "Who'd bother naming a street? Might as well name clouds or drones."

The anonymous streets look pretty much the same. Whoever designed this city hadn't much of an imagination. Some buildings are bigger than others but none is painted or fancily decorated. No structure glitters with coloured lights or banners. Some have names – shops which go by simple titles such as Clothes, Nourishment, Candles – but most don't. I consider checking out one of the shops but I'm not ready yet. Later, when my brain's stopped making dull, grinding noises.

There are strange nooses hanging everywhere. Long thin bars jut out of holders on the walls, with wire loops dangling from the ends. I ask a passerby what they're for. "Protection," the lady says.

"Against what?" I ask.

"Whatever happens to attack you," she says with a shrug.

"Is it OK for me to examine one of them?"

"Sure," she says, so I ease a pole down from its holder. It's lighter than it looks. The wire runs down the side of the pole to a small spindle, making it possible to tighten or loosen the noose with a few turns of your hand. I think about taking it with me, but there are so many of them about, I figure it'd be needless, so I hang it back on the wall and return to my explorative meandering.

I find a phone box. I've passed several without realising what they were, because they're not like any phone boxes I've ever seen, just small wooden shacks attached to the sides of bigger buildings, no signs to explain what they're for. It's only now that I stop to examine one up close that I spot an old-fashioned, clunky phone inside and figure out their purpose.

I enter quickly, heart beating hopefully. I shut the sliding wooden door and study the phone by the light of a candle burning overhead. The phone is a thick, black model, the like of which I've only ever seen in movies or antique stores. No dial or buttons. No slots for coins or cards. Not even a number printed on it.

I pick up the receiver and hold it to my right ear. "Operator Lewgan," a bright voice chirrups over the line. "How may I help you?"

My mouth is too dry to form an answer.

"Hello," the operator says. "This is Operator Lewgan. How may I help you?"

I gulp and lick my lips. "I'm... my name is... Newman Riplan," I gasp. "I don't know where I am. I started to choke on a plane and the next thing I knew, everybody had turned to wax and –"

"I'm sorry, Mr Riplan," Operator Lewgan says, "but could you get to the point? Public contact boxes are provided for those who can't afford contact boxes of their own. They're not here for your amusement. If you wish to be put in contact with somebody, please say so and I'll do my best to connect you. If, however, you're merely taking advantage of our service to waste my time..."

"No!" I howl. "Don't hang up. I want to be connected."

"You wish to make a call?" she asks.

"Yes," I moan.

"Very well. With whom do you wish to be connected?"

"I'm not sure." I lick my lips again and brace myself for disappointment. "Can you tell me where I am?"

"Where do you think you are?" comes the answer I expected.

I grit my teeth and bang my head against the wall of the box but don't express my anger verbally. "I'm new here," I say as calmly as possible. "I'm not sure how things work.

Do I have to pay for this call or is it free?"

"It's free," Lewgan assures me. "A public service brought to the people of the city courtesy of the Alchemist."

"OK," I mutter. "Can you put me through to a number in London?"

"Where, sir?"

I close my eyes and count to five. "How about Amsterdam?"

"Sir?"

"Can I get any kind of outside line?"

"An outside line, sir?" She's bewildered.

"A line out of this city. I want to –"

"I'm sorry, sir," Lewgan interrupts, "but I don't know what you mean by *out of this city*."

I frown and slowly say, "I want an outside line."

"You mean you want to make your call from outside your contact box?"

"No," I snap. "I want to talk to someone in another city, London or Amsterdam, anywhere outside this godforsaken place, I don't care, just somewhere with glass and street names and –"

"An other city, sir?" Lewgan sounds confused. "There are no other cities."

"Don't be stupid," I growl.

"I assure you, sir, I'm not the one being stupid." She sounds snappish now.

"Look, just put me through to one of your superiors, someone who doesn't have shit for brains, and I'll discuss it with –"

The line goes dead. I curse and slam the receiver down,

then pick it up and listen. Silence on the other end. "Hello?" I mutter. "Anybody there?" No answer. Sighing, I lay it down more gently this time, then slide back the door and let myself out. So much for the age of unlimited global communication.

Back on the streets, I go looking for the honest and respectable upholders of the law. Even a city this offbeat has to be policed. It's just a matter of time before I spot an officer plodding his beat or chance upon a station. I'll get a few answers then, I'm sure. They won't be long putting me straight.

I've come a long way from the tunnel exit. I can't tell if I'm moving further into the city or out towards the suburbs, but I'm taking notice of more and more details as I go. Like the cars — they have no number plates. And buses don't have the name of their destination on the front. The scraps of writing that I see – on shop fronts mostly – are in English. No brand names on anybody's clothes. No planes overhead. I don't come across many children and those that I see are by themselves or with other youngsters.

I try asking some of the children where I am – kids are usually more responsive and less secretive than adults – but even the ones barely out of nappies simply stare at me curiously and reply, "Where do you think you are?"

No sign of the police yet, so I stop a man and woman and ask where I could find them.

"Police?" the man says, scratching the side of his jaw.

"What are those?" the woman asks.

"You know." I smile edgily. "Police. The coppers. Law enforcement officers."

The couple stare at me blankly.

"Who's in charge of this place?" I ask. "Who locks up the criminals?"

"Criminals?" the pair ask simultaneously.

"Robbers, rapists, muggers, joyriders. Who do you turn to for help if you're attacked?"

"We use the nooses," the man says.

"Choke the bastards to death," the woman agrees.

"That's OK?" I gasp. "You're allowed to murder people if you think they're in the wrong?"

"People?" The man frowns. "We don't use the nooses on people. People never attack us."

"So what do you use them on?" I ask, confused.

"Animals," he answers.

I stare at him oddly, then decide to try again. "But what if someone steals from you? What if someone grabs your girl and starts using her against her will? Who sorts things out then?"

The man shakes his head. "Nobody would do a thing like that."

"You mean there's no crime in this city?" I press.

"Not as you've described it," he says and the two take their leave.

So, no crime, no cops. Maybe there's an army or some kind of civil defence unit, or maybe this Alchemist I've heard a few people mention is responsible for law and order. But how to contact him? How to…

Contact. I spot another contact box at the corner of the street. I probably won't find help there but where else can I turn? Besides, the sun's starting to drop. If I don't root out some answers soon, I'll have to wait until morning to go looking again, and I don't like the idea of spending the night here in ignorance. So I head for the booth.

"Operator Lewgan. How may I help you?"

Damn. The same one. I grimace, then put on my sweetest voice. "Hi, my name's Newman Riplan, I was talking to you earlier. Sorry to bother you again but I –"

"Oh yes, I remember you, sir." She doesn't sound too happy to hear from me. "Have you rung to apologise or do you want to call me more names?"

I chuckle sickly. "Sorry about that, I don't know what came over me. It's been a crazy day and I let things get out of hand."

"Hmm," she grunts, considering my apology.

"I didn't mean to get shirty," I tell her. "I was bang out of order and I won't let it happen again."

"Very well," she thaws. "Apology accepted. What may I do for you Mr Riplan?"

I ask her if she knows what a policeman is. She doesn't. The army? Never heard of them. Civil defence? Clueless.

"But there must be *some* kind of law and order," I plead. "Who breaks up fights and arrests robbers? Who escorts little old ladies across the road to their Bingo halls?"

"I'm afraid I don't follow you, sir," Lewgan says. "Robbers? Bingo halls? What are they?"

"Never mind," I sigh. "What about the Alchemist? Where can I find him?"

"Nobody finds the Alchemist," she sniggers. "He comes and goes as he pleases, working from the shadows. I've only seen him a handful of times myself."

"But he's the main man?" I ask. "He runs things?"

She hesitates. "I wouldn't say that. The Alchemist is community-conscious. He sponsors public contact boxes, certain rest homes and nourishment establishments, but as for running things..." I sense her shaking her head.

"Where's the nearest airport with outbound flights?" I ask, changing tack.

"I'm sorry," she replies, "but I don't understand that question."

"I'm looking for airports, you know, where planes land and take-off."

"Planes?" she echoes.

"Drone holds," I correct myself, but even then she doesn't comprehend what I'm talking about. "What about train stations? Bus depots? I want out, lady, *out*." I have to struggle to stop myself from screaming.

"I'm sorry, sir," Lewgan says. "I can't help you. I know of no such things as stations and depots."

"But you know what trains and buses are, right?" I groan.

"I know what a bus is," she admits.

"Where can I find one?" I ask.

"On the streets," she answers. "They pass quite regularly."

"I know," I growl, "but where do they originate? Where's the bus terminal?"

"I'm sorry, sir, but I honestly don't —"

I hang up, exasperated, before I explode at her. I lean my head on the bulky phone for a couple of minutes, then pick up the receiver again.

"Operator Lewgan here. How may I help you?"

"I want the talking clock," I say dully.

"You again, Mr Riplan," she says with a small laugh. "I'm sorry, but I don't know what —"

Click.

It's getting darker by the minute and I'm relieved to see a moon and stars in the sky, not the distressingly pitch black maw that hung heavily over the airport.

Gangs of workers dressed in red robes are taking to the streets and lighting the candles which line every route. They use step-ladders and matches but in spite of their clumsy apparatus they work swiftly and soon the streets are aglow with flickering flames. As lost and dazed as I am, I have to admit the city looks picturesque in this light.

I ask the candle-lighters some questions but they know no more than anybody else. "Is this your full-time job?" I ask one.

"Sure," he says. "Not as easy as it looks, you know, especially when the wind is blowing. We have to replace the candles if they blow out. Sometimes we can be up the whole of the night."

"Why don't you use shutters?" I ask. "They'd block out the wind."

He laughs. "They'd also keep in most of the light."

"Not if they were made of glass," I note.

"What's glass?" He snorts when I explain. "A shutter you can see through? Get the snuff out of here. Do you think I have the brain of a drone?"

I ask another how long she's been working at this. She doesn't understand the question. "It's my job," she says. "It's what I do."

"Yes," I nod, "but how long have you been doing it?"

She shrugs and moves on, unable to answer.

That's something else I've noticed — there are no clocks or watches in this city. I'll investigate the matter further another time but not tonight. The streets are starting to empty and I'm beginning to feel uneasy, remembering what that person said about animals that attack. Hardly any cars are out now – with no lights, they rely on the glow of the candles, so most drivers wisely choose to get around on foot at night – and the place is disturbingly quiet. I've never known a city of this size to fall so silent.

I recall what Jess said about two drone teeth being good for a room in a low-grade boarding house. I've spotted a few of them in the course of my travels – they have no hotels or motels here, only boarding houses that are distinguishable by hand-written signs over the front doors – and decide it's time to book into one. I find a place that looks fairly shabby, pause by the door, pull out the bag of teeth, then enter.

The landlord is a thin man with dark hair that's severely parted down the middle, and a worried frown that never leaves his face, even when he smiles. He welcomes me as if I'm a long lost friend. "Hello! Good evening! Come in, come in. I'm Franz. Have you bags? Shall I take your coat? Do you want something to eat or drink? A sleeping partner, perhaps? All tastes catered for."

"No thanks," I say, thrown to be offered a hooker at such short acquaintance. "I'm just looking for a room."

"Oh," he sighs, disappointed. "Luxury or economy?"

"Economy."

He sighs again and his frown deepens. "With a window or without?"

I think about the glassless holes in the walls. It's a warm night but it could turn if a breeze kicks up. "Without," I tell him.

"That will be three teeth," he says and pockets the strange form of coin without interest. (I consider arguing the cost, since I was told it would be two teeth, but I'm too weary and ignorant of local protocol.)

"Do I have to sign anywhere?" I ask as he comes round the reception desk and leads the way to the stairs.

"Sign what?" he chuckles. "One of the walls?"

"What about the register?"

"What's that?" he says.

I shake my head. "Never mind. Lead on, McDuff."

"My name's Franz," he reminds me, then heads up.

The stairs are steep and I'm soon huffing behind the nimble-footed Franz. He notices my discomfort and slows. "I didn't get your name," he says as we continue at a more sedate pace.

"Newman Riplan," I tell him.

"Two names? So what would you like me to call you? Newman or Riplan?"

"Mr Riplan will be fine," I sniff, deciding I don't want to be on informal terms with a man who offers prostitutes to his guests as soon as they cross the threshold.

The halls are narrow and dark, lit by thin, sparse candles. It feels damp in here. I wouldn't like to be about when the weather turns cold. My room's on the third floor, second from the end. It's small and stingy, a single bed, rough covers, a sink set in one wall, a couple of candle holders.

"Where's the toilet?" I ask.

"What's that?" he replies.

"Don't tell me you don't have toilets in this place," I yell. "Where the hell do you go if you want to take a piss?"

"A piss?" Franz says.

"Yes, a..." I deflate and wave it away. Let the crazy people play their crazy games. I'll piss in the bed, see how he reacts to that. Do a dump in the middle of the floor. Heh.

"Do you want a wake-up call?" Franz asks, and at least that much is the same in this city of the obtuse.

"No thanks," I say, not having anything to rise early for.

"Have you no job?" he asks.

"Not at the moment," I tell him.

"Then how did you get the bag of teeth?" he asks. I tap my nose slyly. It feels good to be the one holding something back for a change. "Well, I hope you have a plentiful supply of them if you want to continue renting out the room, as I don't do discounts," Franz says with a dark look. "I'll see you in the morning, *Mr Riplan.*"

He leaves and I walk around, examining the walls, listening to the sounds of people in the neighbouring quarters. I'm starting to regret not asking for a room with a window. At least I'd have been able to stare out at the street. This dark, confined room feels like a prison cell. If I stay another night, maybe I'll switch. I wonder if it costs more or less for a room with a glassless window. Are holes in the wall considered a commodity or a liability in this place?

There's a small locker on the far side of the bed, for clothes and personal belongings. I check all the drawers, looking for signs of previous inhabitants, but find only dust. There isn't even a Gideon's Bible.

I slip off my shoes and sit on the bed. I don't feel sleepy. I've a feeling it's going to be a long, joyless night. I'm not brave enough to venture forth, not until I'm more familiar with the territory, so I'll just have to lie back and bear the solitude and uncertainty.

As I'm taking off my jacket to get comfortable I discover a small package I'd forgotten about. When I unwrap it I find the three bagels that I bought and set aside in good old Amsterdam. Cheered by this reaffirmation of a tangible, sensible world, I sit back against the headrest, squeeze out the first of the bagels, sniff to make sure it's still edible, and dourly devour my first meal in the city.

SIX

I don't recall falling asleep, but since I'm waking up, I must have. I lever myself off the bed and stare about the dark room, wondering where I am. It isn't long before the memories come flooding back. I groan and sit down. I'd been hoping it would turn out to be a dream, but apparently not. Whatever this place is – an afterworld, the result of bad coke or some alternate kind of universe – it looks like I'll be here a while longer.

Though I'm almost certain I fell asleep without undressing, I'm naked. My clothes are in the locker by the bed, neatly tucked away. I slip them on, then wash my hands in the sink. As I'm drying them on a dirty towel hanging by the sink, I wonder again about the absence of toilets. I normally go for a piss first thing in the morning. I consider urinating in the sink – I know I said I'd do it in the bed, to annoy the landlord, but when it comes to the crunch I can't – but my bladder feels oddly empty, so I leave it be and head downstairs after quenching the tiny candle stub that's left from the night before.

Franz is behind the desk, eager to convince me to part with more of my teeth. "Good morning, Mr Riplan. Did you enjoy your rest? Would you like a spot of breakfast? Shoes need shining? Clothes need cleaning?"

"No thanks," I say and the disapproving click of his tongue against the roof of his mouth is clearly audible.

"Do you wish to reserve your room for another night?" he asks coolly.

"Not at the moment," I say. "I didn't like being so closed-in. I might try a room with a window next time."

"Ah," he beams. (I guess from his reaction that rooms with windows cost more.) "An excellent idea. Nothing like a room with a view. Shall I reserve one for you?"

I jingle the bag of teeth thoughtfully, Franz's eyes fixed longingly on it. "I'll leave it for now," I decide. "I'm not sure if I'll be coming back tonight."

"Oh." Franz looks as if he's about to burst into tears. "Well, I'll hold a room for you anyway, just in case."

I thank him for being so considerate and start across the lobby. A thought slows me. "Excuse me," I say, turning, "but how do I find my way back?"

"Just mention my name to a public car driver," Franz replies.

"A public car," I repeat. "Is that a taxi?"

"Taxi?" Franz says.

"Never mind. All I have to do is mention you? I don't need to know the name of the street?"

"Name of the street?" Franz laughs. "Whoever heard of a street with a name?"

"Whoever indeed," I mutter to myself, smiling humourlessly.

It doesn't take long to spot a public car. They're plain, grey cars, with slightly rounded roofs. The words *Public Car* are scrawled across the doors on either side but there's no other form of identification, plate numbers or company names. I hail one and climb in. "Good morning," the driver says.

"Vin's the name. Where you headed?"

"Just drive about for a while, if that's OK," I tell him.

"Fine by me," Vin says and off we set.

Vin turns out to be as talkative as any normal cabbie but I learn no more from him than from anybody else in the city. When I ask where I am, he replies with the inevitable, "Where do you think you are?" He doesn't understand when I ask how long he's been a cabbie. He's never heard of glass.

"Don't you get cold when the weather's bad?" I ask.

"Sure," he laughs, "but I wrap up warm. The roof keeps out most of the rain and a bit of wind never hurt no one."

I ask about clocks and watches. "What are those?" he says.

"Devices for telling the time."

"Telling the time?" he frowns. "You mean they tell you if it's day or night? Big deal. Still, they might be handy for blind people. Where do you get them?"

I shake my head, bemused. "Clocks tell the exact time," I explain. "You have hours and minutes in this city, don't you?"

Vin shrugs. "Not that I've heard."

"No hours? No minutes? So how do you divide up time?"

"When it's light, it's day," he says, "and when it's dark, it's night."

"That's it?" I ask.

"That's it," Vin nods. "What more could there be?"

I press him for ages on the subject. I can't believe people here only measure time by day and night. I ask how long we've been driving. "A while," he says and can be no more precise than that. If he wants to meet somebody at a certain place at a certain time, how does he arrange it? He shrugs. "I just say, 'See you later' or 'Catch you around,' something like that." And if he has an appointment with a doctor or dentist? "I don't make appointments, just turn up and wait, no matter who it is I'm meeting." And on it goes.

I'm learning to ride with the tide. Arguing with these people is senseless. They see the world a certain way and can't understand anyone who sees it differently. The best way to deal with them is to accept their limitations and chip away at the madness in private. I'm going to have to figure the answers out myself. The citizens of this nameless city aren't advanced enough to provide any for me.

I have Vin drop me by a large fountain in a built-up square. I don't know which part of the city I'm in — I asked Vin where it started and ended and where the centre was, but he didn't know what I meant — but it looks like a nice area. The buildings are well maintained, the streets are spotless and the people lounging by the fountain are stylishly dressed.

"Any way of contacting you later?" I ask Vin, handing over the four teeth he requested. (That seems expensive compared with the price of renting a room for a night, but maybe boarding houses are cheap because there's a glut of rooms, or perhaps they're subsidised by that Alchemist fellow.) "Do you have a mobile phone?"

"A what?" Vin smiles, accustomed to my strange questions by now.

"A mobile contact box," I try.

"How could I have a contact box in the car?" he chuckles, shaking his head. "You've got some weird ideas, my friend, if you don't mind my saying so."

I grin. "I was just about to say the same about you." I tip him a tooth and he whistles appreciatively.

"Listen," he says, "I'm gonna circle for a while, see if I can pick up some customers. If I don't, do you want me to take you back later?"

"I'm not sure," I say.

"Well, I'll hang around on the off-chance," he says. "I don't get many customers as free with their teeth as you. Most folk would have bargained me down to two teeth for the ride, and that would have included the tip."

"So you conned me," I laugh.

"Snuff, no," he protests. "Four teeth's what I'm entitled to. It's just rare for someone to fork up the correct amount. In my line of work, you get used to living on less. It's refreshing to meet someone who plays things straight."

I bid farewell to Vin and stroll around the fountain. It's nothing special — a couple of poorly carved mermaids spout water from their open mouths — but looks glamorous compared to anything else that I've seen here. I find a dry spot and sit by the rim of the fountain, dangling my fingers in the cool water, keeping an eye on the people in the square, observing them as they go about their daily business.

They're a subdued bunch. They sit quietly, speaking in whispers if at all. There's a small boy perched on a nearby bench, as meditative as everybody else. On a day like this, if I was his age, I'd be racing around like a puppy, but he just sits there, lapping up the sun.

A woman passes, followed by one of the mannequins. It

carries a couple of boxes and trails after her like a slave. I've seen a few of the so-called drones engaged in similar tasks while driving around with Vin. Is this what they're used for? I'll have to make enquiries. In a way I feel closer to the drones than the people. The drones might be mindless automatons but at least they hail from the same world as me. They came in on the plane with me, so are proof that there must be an outside realm. Perhaps, if I find one that can talk, I'll be able to learn more about this place, why I'm here and where I am, and why I was the only one on the plane not to be transformed.

A scream diverts my attention. It's the first raised voice I've heard since arriving in this place. I leap to my feet and search for the source. It doesn't take long to spot the screamer. It's a woman, young, pretty, alone, pressed against the wall of a building on the opposite side of the fountain, trapped by two creatures that look like foxes. They're growling and advancing on her, snapping at her hands as she waves at the animals fearfully, uselessly.

"What's happening?" I ask a man to my right.

"An attack," he says. His gaze is glued to the scene – everybody's staring – but he makes no move to intercede.

"Are those foxes?" I ask and he nods. "What will they do to her?"

"Kill her," he says as if passing the time of day.

"Why?" I gasp.

He shrugs. "It's what animals do."

"We've got to stop this," I say with determination.

He turns and studies me. "Do you know her?"

"No."

"Are you a prostitutioner in search of fresh additions?"

"Of course not," I snap.

"Then why get involved?"

"Because... because..."

Fuck it. The foxes are closing in. If I stand here trying to explain humanity to this goon, it'll be too late to help. Grabbing one of the many nooses set around the fountain, I lurch towards the cornered woman. If I was back home I wouldn't interfere – I've seen people get mugged before and never stepped in to help – but in this alien city it feels good to at last be doing something proactive.

One of the foxes notices me. It turns, teeth bared, and leaps. I lash at it with the end of the pole and knock it sideways. It yelps, hits the ground, rolls and comes back at me. This time it dodges the pole but I manage to kick it in the head before its teeth can close around my leg. It squeals and bolts for good, leaving a trail of blood in its wake.

The second fox has remained focused on the woman. She's tired and her arms wave slowly and painfully now. I see it preparing to leap. I don't have long. I quickly widen the wire noose, then dart forward and slip it over the creature's head as it jumps. The noose digs into the fox's throat and hauls it back to the ground with a thud. Before the animal regains its senses, I twirl the spindle at the end of the pole. The noose tightens and slices into the flesh of the fox's neck. The predator thrashes wildly but I hold firm and within seconds it goes limp, then falls entirely still.

"Are you OK?" I ask the woman, stepping over the body of

the dead animal. She stares at me silently. She's trembling. Her arms and legs are covered with scratches. I move closer and she flattens against the wall. I raise my hands and take a couple of steps back. "It's alright, I won't harm you, I'm a friend, you don't need to be..."

Before I can finish, she ducks beneath my arms and flees. I make no attempt to catch her. I'm too astonished. "So that's how people here thank you for saving their lives," I mutter, glaring after the departing woman. "Go on, love," I jeer. "You don't want to hang about. No telling what you might catch. I..."

Oh, what's the use? She's terrified, not thinking clearly. I drop the noose, prod the dead fox with my foot, then turn my back on it and start towards the fountain, where people are returning to their previous pursuits, nobody in the least perturbed by the battle they've witnessed. Halfway there, I spot Vin in his car, turning a corner into the square. "Hey, Vin!" I yell and race after him. I've had enough of fountain-watching. Time to do what I should have done the minute I arrived in this godforsaken nightmare of a city — look for a pub and hit the hard stuff.

Just when I thought things couldn't get any worse, Vin doesn't know what beer is.

"Please tell me you're joking," I groan.

"I know a guy called Beera, if that's any use to you," Vin says helpfully.

"How about vodka? Whiskey? Tequila? Hell, I'd even take a Malibu."

Vin shakes his head. "Sorry."

"Then what do you drink to get drunk?" I ask desperately.

"What's drunk?" Vin replies.

"You know…" I roll my eyes and speak a few slurred sentences.

Vin stares at me oddly. "Why would you want to wind up in a state like that?"

"How about drugs?" I press. "Coke? Heroin? Acid?"

"Sorry," Vin says again.

"You mean to tell me you remain sober all the time?" I ask, aghast. "What do you drink when you go to a bar?"

"Bar?" Vin echoes.

"Christ," I moan, tugging my hair, "you don't know how depressed I'm getting back here. As if things weren't bad enough, now I find out I've wandered into Prohibition Central. I can't handle this place with all my senses intact. I need to get out of my head. There's got to be something I can ingest that'll set my brain spinning and make everything look rosy."

"I can take you to a nourishment house if you want something to drink," Vin says, "but I've never heard of one that serves mind-altering beverages."

I mull over his suggestion. It's been a long time since those bagels. I don't feel especially hungry, despite the fact I skipped breakfast, but a bit of grub certainly wouldn't go amiss.

"OK," I sigh. "Take me to the finest nourishment house this city has to offer."

"I know just the place," Vin assures me and off we set.

*

The nourishment house is run by a small man called Kipp. A dapper little fellow with a thin moustache that would have been all the rage in the early twentieth century. He welcomes the pair of us — I asked Vin if he wanted to eat with me and he happily accepted my offer — and leads us to a table in the centre of the room. It's a large, dark, sullen place, no paintings on the walls, no fancy lights, no plush carpets. No sign of a kitchen either. A load of drones stand by the rear wall. Not many customers, just five apart from ourselves, three of them eating alone.

"How's business, Vin?" Kipp asks. They're old friends. I guess that's why Vin brought me here, probably on a backhander for every new customer he brings in. I don't mind. We've all got livings to make.

"It's been good today," Vin says, "but lousy in general. I'm thinking of giving up the public car. No teeth in it. If not for the Alchemist's subsidy, I don't know how I'd make ends meet."

Kipp tuts sympathetically and says things are hard all over. "We need more drones," he growls, drawing up a chair, seemingly forgetting to take our order. He straightens the creases in his pants as he sits. "Last time I saw the Alchemist — and it's a while ago — I told him, I came straight out with it. There's barely enough to go round, and how many new ones trickling in? No more than a couple of hundred a day by my reckoning. 'We need more,' I told him flatly. 'We need more.'"

"What did the Alchemist say to that?" Vin asks.

Kipp shrugs. "What he always says — these things aren't

easily arranged, he'll look into it but can't make any promises."

"Where do you get the drones?" I ask, glancing at the pack by the wall.

"I pick them up at markets or off smugglers," Kipp says.

"And where do they get them?" I ask.

"No idea," Kipp says.

"Is the Alchemist responsible for importing the drones?"

"Importing?" Kipp looks confused but Vin laughs.

"Newman comes out with stuff like that all the time. I don't understand half the words he uses. But he's OK," Vin assures his friend, patting my arm. "He pays his way. He even tips."

I ask more questions about the drones but Kipp knows almost nothing about them. He's never heard of a drone hold or an off-loader. He's never wondered where the drones in the markets come from or where the drone smugglers – people who steal drones and sell them on at a marked-up price – get theirs. I mention Phil and Bryan, Mannie and Jess, but Kipp hasn't heard of them. Vin hasn't either, even though, as a public car driver, he claims to know everybody in the city.

"You know *everybody*?" I ask sceptically.

"Sure," he says. "It's my job."

"So how many people live here?" I ask.

"I dunno," he laughs. "I've never tried counting them."

"Reel off names for me and let's see how many you can get up to," I challenge him.

Vin shakes his head. "Doesn't work that way. The names

are in here –" He taps his head. "– but they only float to the top when somebody asks. I can't fish them out by myself."

Kipp sees the doubt in my eyes and jumps to his friend's defence. "It's true," he says. "You couldn't be a public car driver if you didn't know who people were and where they lived. Otherwise how would you find them?"

"What about a map?" I ask. By their blank expressions, I gather they don't have maps in this place. "So what happens if someone moves house or... No," I sigh, breaking off. "You know everybody in the city and where they live. Fine. I believe you. Why not? All I'm interested in now is food. What's on the menu, Kipp, my good man? Steak? Salmon? Venison?"

"There he goes again with the words," Vin laughs, slapping my back. "Just send over a couple of drinking drones for now," he tells Kipp.

The manager leaves. A short while later, two small drones – a boy and a girl – approach our table. They're naked, white films covering their facial orifices. They carry thick drinking straws, which they mechanically offer to us. Vin takes his and blows through it to make sure it's clean.

"What do we do with these?" I ask, regarding mine with trepidation.

"We use them to suck out the sap," Vin says. "Surely you've drank from a drone before?" I shake my head. "You mean it's been water all your life?" He whistles. "The more I get to know you, the weirder you seem. Not that that's a bad thing," he hastens to add. "Variety's the spice of life, or so people say."

Having finished blowing through his straw, Vin takes the sharp end – the straws are sharpened at one end, like spears – and holds it above the head of the boy. He grunts. "You're too tall. Down on your knees." The drone obeys. Then Vin, to my horror, drives the straw into the boy's head and twists until it's buried deep.

"What are you doing?" I bellow, jolting to my feet.

Vin looks up at me, astonished. "Drinking," he says and closes his lips around the flat end of the straw.

He starts to suck.

My stomach turns at the slurping noise and I feel my face blanch. Vin draws away from his straw and stares at me. "Are you alright?" he asks. Drops of a white, sticky liquid are smeared to his lips. It's the same substance I discovered when I cut off a drone's hand on the plane.

Kipp hurries over. "Is something wrong?"

My eyes are fixed on the drone's face. Its expression hasn't changed. No sign of pain or terror. I glance at the girl, standing by my side, waiting for me to stick my straw in. I picture myself jamming it into her head and sucking out her brain juice. Seconds later I'm bending over, dry-heaving.

"My goodness," Kipp gasps. "What's he doing? What's happening to him?"

"I don't know," Vin says, worried. "Maybe he's choking."

"I'm trying to throw up," I snarl, taking deep breaths, regaining control.

"Throw up what?" Kipp asks.

I ignore the question, get my insides back under control and straighten. "Do you do a lot of this?" I ask.

"Drinking from drones?" Vin says. "Of course. What else is there to drink apart from water?"

"Sap's good for you," Kipp chips in. "Puts hair on your ears."

"What about food?" I ask. "Do you eat the drones as well?"

"Certainly." Vin looks nervous now. "Are you telling me you've never dined on a drone before?"

"Never," I grunt.

"Then how have you survived?" Vin asks.

"I eat meat, fish, veg."

Vin's eyes widen and Kipp's jaw drops. "You eat *animals*?" the driver shouts.

"Sure. Why not?"

The two men exchange glances of horror. "That's sickening," Vin moans.

"I've never heard of such a thing," Kipp agrees.

"Have you no shame?" Vin asks me. "To openly admit your sins... If it was me, I'd have the good grace to keep my perverse tastes to myself."

"Whoa," I roar. "Hold on. You mean it's illegal to eat animals here?"

"Illegal?" Vin shrugs. "I don't know what that means. But nobody does it. The mere thought is enough to..." He shivers and clutches his stomach.

I slowly sit down. My guts are telling me to run but I'll have to eat eventually. Better to face the matter now, with locals to steer me, rather than later when I'm by myself.

"So how do you go about eating these things?" I ask.

"Do you just bite off the bits you want and swallow them raw?"

"If you like," Vin says, eyeing me uneasily. "Were you joking about eating animals?" he asks hopefully.

"Of course," I reply, forcing a laugh.

"Snuff it!" he exclaims, pounding the table. "And we fell for it." He nudges Kipp in the ribs. "We'll have to be sharper round this guy in future."

Kipp nods weakly. "You have a strange sense of humour," he admonishes me, "but that's a customer's privilege. Only, please, don't make jokes like that in front of my other customers. You might put them off their food and drive them away to eat somewhere else."

Kipp leaves and Vin explains about the devouring of the drones. The two by our table are only to drink from — the sap is sweeter in children. We'll pick an eating drone from those lined up at the rear, then choose which part of it we want to dine on. The drone will be led out of the nourishment house and taken to a processing plant nearby, where it will be carved apart and cooked to our specifications. The cuts will then be wheeled back and dished up.

"Why don't they carve and cook them here?" I ask.

"Too awkward," Vin says. "It's not an easy thing to cook a drone. If you apply a naked flame, they start to melt and it ruins the taste. They have to be wrapped in special kinds of paper and placed in strange cooking machines. I don't know much about it — cooks tend to keep their methods to themselves. Trade secrets."

"What happens to the bits we don't eat?" I ask.

"I guess they're sold on," Vin says. "Melted down for candle wax or mashed up to be —"

"Candle wax?" I interrupt.

"Sure," he says. "Where else would candles come from?"

I sit back and marvel at his acceptance of all this. Society here seems to be built around the mannequins. Their teeth serve as units of currency. They can be slaves, delicacies, a source of light and heat. I wonder what else they might be used for but don't ask — I'm half-afraid of the answers.

Vin sucks more juice from his drone. "If you don't want to drink," he says, "you don't have to. Makes no difference to me whether or not you like sap."

I study the expressionless girl, shudder at the thought of feasting upon her — remembering the girl from the plane, Jennifer, and wondering if someone is even now sticking a straw into *her* head — then steel my nerves and decide this is as good a time as any to immerse myself in the city's strange customs. I take the straw that the girl is holding out and position it above her skull. I hesitate, staring into her blank, white eyes.

"I can't just drive this into her brain," I groan. "It's barbaric."

"You don't have to drink from the head," Vin says. "There's sap all over. You can stick it in her arm, leg or stomach if that'll make you feel better."

"It will," I say and ask the drone to extend her left arm. I search for a vein but she hasn't any. "Do they feel pain?" I ask Vin.

He laughs. "How could a drone feel pain? They're not human, Newman. They're just drones, for snuff's sake. Go on, drink up, it'll do you good, maybe straighten out that twisted mess of a mind of yours."

I jab the sharp end of the straw into the girl's forearm and sap oozes up it. I stare down the bore, but the sight of the whitish liquid does my quivering stomach no good at all. Closing my eyes, I place my trembling lips round the top of the straw and suck. The sap rises swiftly and the first drops hit my tongue. It tastes peculiar, thick and creamy, slightly salty, a bit malty. Not unpleasant, but hardly a fitting substitute for a good pint of beer.

"Like it?" Vin asks as I release the straw and wipe my lips with the back of my right hand.

"Not bad," I say, "but not great either." I feel the sap sliding down the walls of my throat. It sits heavily in my stomach, like a strong shot of hot chocolate.

"Better than water," Vin laughs, drinking from his drone again.

"I guess," I sigh, though in future I'll stick to the lighter of the two options.

"Now," Vin says, "how about dinner? Let's go pick us a juicy-looking drone. You want an arm, leg, breast?"

"I'll let you choose," I say.

"OK," he smiles, "but I got to tell ya, I normally go for the arse cheek. Nothing like it in my opinion, though I know certain folk who don't think the same way. You can make your own choice if you'd rather a different cut."

I take a deep breath and manage a shaky smile. "Arse

cheek sounds great," I squeak, and tell myself – and my stomach – to pretend I'm in a Heston Blumenthal restaurant.

I ask Vin to drop me back to Franz's boarding house, figuring I might as well spend the night somewhere familiar, but get out of the car a few blocks away, to walk off some of the meal. The arse cheek wasn't all that bad. There was a waxy taste to it – I suppose that's inevitable – but it was more appetizing than the raw sap, nicely prepared and served, in appearance and texture a bit like dry fish. I was able to pretend it was an adventurous vegetarian dish. Mind you, there was one palate-juddering moment when I realised a waxy little bump that had been puzzling me must once have been a glistening buttock pimple.

Franz is delighted to see me. "I knew you'd be back," he grins. "I've reserved one of my best rooms for you. It's on the top floor, huge window, thick drapes to draw across it if you get cold, a candle in every corner."

"How much?" I ask.

"Five teeth," he twitters.

I check the contents of my bag. "I'll give you three."

His face drops. "Come now, Mr Riplan," he whines. "It's a top quality room. Five teeth is a bargain. I wouldn't rent it out to my closest friend for less."

"Tell you what..." I tip out the teeth and count them. "I'll pay you seventeen for five nights in advance." That'll leave me with a mere six teeth, but at least I won't have to worry about living arrangements for a while.

Franz nods grudgingly. "Deal. But no dinner, only breakfast, OK?"

"Fair enough," I say and let him lead me upstairs.

The room's a big improvement over my original one. No toilet, but the bed's more comfortable and it boasts two lockers and even a fair-sized wardrobe. It's hardly five-star accommodation but it'll suffice for the time being. I thank Franz for keeping it for me, then bid him good night and close the door.

I stroll to the window to take in the view but I'm not there more than a couple of minutes when there's a knock on the door. I open it, expecting Franz, but to my surprise it's a woman, and not just any woman, but the one I rescued from the foxes near the fountain.

"Hi," she says, smiling nervously as I gawp at her. "My name's Cheryl. I'm your new neighbour. Can I come in?"

SEVEN

Cheryl sits on the bed and fidgets with her hair, which hangs in two long braids down her back. She's my age or thereabouts, no beauty, but pretty. Dressed in a plain white frock. No make-up — the scratches on her face still look red and sore.

"I followed you to the nourishment house, then back here," she mumbles, not looking at me as she speaks. "Trailed you in a public car. I waited downstairs and asked the landlord which room you were staying in, then booked one three doors down, said I was a friend of yours and wanted to surprise you."

I chew my lower lip, considering her story. I'd find it hard to buy in London but nothing strikes me as implausible in this upside-down place. "Why?" I finally ask. "Why follow me and rent a room here?"

She shrugs. "It's getting late. I live in a boarding house like this one. Easier to stay here than walk home in the dark — I didn't have enough teeth left to pay for another public car."

"That doesn't explain why you followed me," I say softly.

She blushes. "I wanted to thank you. You saved my life."

"You could have thanked me back by the fountain," I note.

"I was scared," she whispers.

I kneel and lock gazes with her. "Why were you scared?"

She hesitates before answering. "I thought you were a prostitutioner."

"A pimp?"

"I don't know that word," she says.

"I'm sure it's the same thing," I mutter. "What made you think that?"

"You saved me," she says. "Only prostitutioners bother to save people when they're attacked. I belong to you now if you want me."

"*Belong?*" I shout and she cringes.

"Those who are saved from animals owe their lives to their saviours," she explains. "That's why prostitutioners sometimes rescue people — the saved person must work for them after that. I ran because I thought you wished to put me to work in a sex house. When you didn't give chase, I was confused. I followed you to offer my thanks if you weren't a prostitutioner."

"I'm not," I say stiffly.

"I guessed as much," she smiles. "That's why I'm here."

I stand and rub my chin. What a city. Do a good deed and you become a pimp. No wonder she ran. "What happens if somebody saves a person but doesn't want to own them?" I ask.

Cheryl shrugs. "I've never heard of that happening, so I don't know."

"You owe me nothing," I tell her. "As far as I'm concerned, you're free to walk away any time you like."

"Thank you," she sobs. "I hoped you'd say that but I couldn't be sure."

"Come on," I laugh, "don't cry."

"I can't help it," she sniffs. "I always cry when I'm happy..." She smiles up at me and wipes away a few tears.

"...which isn't very often."

The tears have dried and we've been chatting for ages. Cheryl is unable to answer any of my standard questions – "Where do you think you are?" "What's a plane?" "What does *outside* mean?" – but she fills me in on a lot of other details. This city's full of sex houses. Wild animals are a scourge and attacks on humans are a regular occurrence — she's surprised I haven't seen more of them.

"I'm new here," I say. "I come from a different place, another city."

"An *other* city?" she frowns. "I don't understand."

"Never mind," I sigh.

She doesn't know where the animals come from but the city's besieged by them.

"Why don't people fight?" I ask. "You could form protective groups and hunt them down."

"It's not that easy," she says.

"Why?"

She shrugs. "People have jobs to focus on. You have to work hard to earn drone teeth. It wouldn't pay to go round fighting animals all the time."

I ask how she came to this city but she doesn't understand the question. "I live here," she says.

"You've always lived here?"

"Yes."

"So you were born here?"

"Born?" She doesn't know what it means.

"You grew up here?" I try. "You've lived here since you

were a child?"

"I'm not a child," she smiles.

"But you were once," I chuckle.

She shakes her head. "How could I have been? Children are children, adults are adults."

"Sure," I say, "but children grow up to become adults."

"Are you playing a joke on me?" she laughs.

She has no recollection of her childhood. She truly believes she's been an adult her entire life. I ask how long that life has been but she can't answer — she has no concept of months or years.

"What about your parents?" I press. "Your mother and father?" She doesn't know what they are. "You've no family at all? You're an orphan?" No, it goes further than that. She *never* had parents. Nobody here has. Families don't exist. "So how were you born?" I ask again. "How do you reproduce?"

They're alien terms to her. Could it be she's mentally backwards, or could the people of this city truly be unaware of the laws of reproduction? My head says it must be the former, but in my gut I'm sure it's the latter.

"Do you know what sex is?" I ask.

"Of course," she giggles.

"Good," I smile. "Well, sometimes, after a couple have sex, something magical happens..." I explain the facts of life to her, impregnation and fertilisation, all that stuff. She stares at me as if I've two heads.

"You believe that crazy tale?" she asks.

"It's not a tale," I growl. "It's how living beings have

offspring, the way life replenishes itself."

"If you say so," she smirks.

"How else can people reproduce?" I challenge her. "Where do they come from?"

"We don't *come from* anywhere," she says. "We just are. We live here. We've always lived here."

"And always will live here?" I ask sceptically.

"No," she says. "We only live until we die."

So at least they know about death.

"Imagine a person growing in a woman's stomach," she giggles. "How would they fit?"

"They're babies when they're born," I explain.

"Right," she snorts. "And then they *grow*." She spreads her hands and jiggles her fingers. "Like magic. Baby one day, child the next, adult the next." She wags a finger at me. "You might fool some people with a story like that but not me."

"No?" I snap. "Well, wait until you get up the duff, see what you think then."

"Up the duff?" she enquires.

"Pregnant. When some guy shoots his load up you one dark night and –"

"No!" she gasps, covering my mouth with her hands. "Don't say such things, even in fun."

"What do you mean?" I grumble, swiping her hands away.

"This story of yours," she says. "If you truly believe it and aren't pulling my leg, then it's dangerous. You must forget it, Newman."

"What are you talking about?"

She takes my hands in hers and squeezes. "You must

never ejaculate inside a woman," she warns. "It's deadly, the worst thing a man could do to one of us. I hear stories, the way you do, about men who do it to women when they're asleep, but I'm sure they're only wild tales told to scare the listeners. Sometimes it happens by accident, and that's a tragedy, but a man who did it on purpose would be truly evil, and I don't want to believe that evil exists in that way."

"What do you mean?" I ask, alarmed by the depth of feeling in her voice. "What harm can a streak of sperm do?"

"I don't know," she tells me, "but I know this — if a man ejaculates inside a woman during sex, it means death. *Death*," she hisses, almost crushing my hands as she squeezes.

Cheryl hasn't eaten, so we traipse downstairs and order a meal from Franz. She has a full dinner, slices of drone stomach and breast, but I'm stuffed after my meal at Kipp's, so I just have a snack, a few crisp fingers. I'm thirsty, so I ask for a glass of water. Cheryl orders a mug of sap.

"You can get it in mugs?" I ask.

"Of course," she says. "Most people prefer to drink from the source but I've never liked having drones about while I'm eating. They give me the creeps."

Cheryl works in a drone processing factory. She's one of the people who melts them down and fashions them into candles. It's not a great job, she tells me, but the pay's good and it's easy work, no hard physical labour. She used to make cars. The pay was better but the hours were lousy and she got sick of having to scrape droil out from under her fingernails when she got home every night.

"Droil?" I ask.

"Drone oil," she says. "What do you think cars run on — fresh air?"

God bless those drones. Is there anything they can't be used for?

I tread carefully around sexual matters – you don't crack dirty jokes in the company of a woman who equates climax with death — but I'm fascinated by the concept of a city of people who engage in sex but know nothing about procreation. I get her talking about children, where they come from and how they survive. As she sees it, children are just small adults. They live in communes by themselves, in buildings called nurseries. They have little to do with big people and she doesn't know where they work or what rules they live by.

"The young and old don't live together?" I ask.

"No," she says. "Why would they?"

"Where I come from," I tell her, "people live in groups called families. Men and women marry and have kids. They make a home and –"

"What does *marry* mean?" she interrupts.

"It's when a man and woman agree to live together and share everything and have sex only with each other for the rest of their lives."

Her eyes go wide. "That's awful," she exclaims. "What a horrible idea. That's almost as bad as prostitution. Being tied to one person for the whole of your life!"

"It's pretty popular in my neck of the woods," I assure her.

She purses her lips. "If you say so, I'll believe you, but the thought of it leaves me cold."

"You have sex with a lot of men, then?" I ask rather artlessly.

"No, Mr Smutty," she pouts, "but I'm free to do so if I want. It's my choice. I'm not bound to anyone."

"What if you fall in love?" I ask. "You do have love here, don't you?"

"Naturally," she says. "I've been in love several times. I have sex with a man when I'm in love. Sometimes we share a room in a boarding house. We go for meals together and enjoy the company. Then, when we fall out of love, we say our farewells and go our own ways."

I blink. "Just like that? No complications?"

"What's complicated about it?" she says. "I fall in love, I fall out of love. It happens all the time, to everybody. But I've never heard of a person letting love turn their head to such a degree that they'll to commit to a lifelong relationship."

Cheryl sniggers at the thought of marriage. Franz, who's passing our table, stops and smiles. "Having a good time?" he asks.

"An enlightening time," Cheryl giggles, then tells Franz about my views on love and marriage.

He studies me owlishly and grimaces. "What a loathsome proposal. The last woman I fell in love with was a wretch of a being. She made my life a living hell. I put up with her because I was in love, and a man is beyond the reach of reason when he's in love, but the moment I snapped out of it –" He clicks his fingers. "– she was gone. I gave her a boot up the arse – pardon my language, Miss – and that was the end of her. I don't know how I would have coped if I'd been shackled to her in the manner you suggest." He frowns and goes about his rounds.

"What's the longest you've been in love?" I ask Cheryl.

"How do you mean?" she replies.

"What's the longest amount of time you've lived with a man? A week, a month, a year?" I'm hoping to catch her out – I still can't believe these people have no concept of time – but she's as blank-faced as ever.

"I've lived with men while I've been in love," she says, "and split from them when the love ends."

"But how many days have you lived with them?"

She shrugs. "I don't know. Who counts such things?"

"How far into the past can you remember?" I ask.

She cocks her head. "Another bizarre question."

"Come on," I urge her, "tell me if you can. Do you remember what you did yesterday?"

"Of course," she snorts.

"The day before?"

"Yes."

"How many days back can you go? You worked for a car-manufacturing firm. How long ago was that? Ten days? Twenty? A hundred?"

"I don't know," she says.

"You never keep track of time?"

"Should I?" she responds with a fragile smile. "I used to make cars, now I make candles. Does it matter how many days there have been between the two?"

"It does to me," I say.

"Ah, but you're an oddball," she laughs, scraping the end of my nose with one of her fingernails, and we leave the conversation there.

I walk Cheryl back to her room. She stands shyly in the doorway and smiles at me. "I'm glad I followed you but I can't figure you out," she says. "You're like no one I've ever met."

"All the girls say that," I wink.

"I mean it," she insists. "I think I might be falling in love with you but I'm not sure. Usually it only takes a couple of minutes to know I'm in love. With you..." She shakes her head.

"In love?" I mutter, thrown by her swiftness and bluntness.

"I think so," she nods.

"Where I come from, people generally don't fall in love that quickly," I tell her. "And they certainly don't announce it, even if they do."

"Whyever not?" she asks, puzzled.

I laugh – I've no answer to that – and decide, as I have with so many other things in this city, to go with the norm. If love's on the cards, fine, I'll let it play out as it will, and just bear in mind that the cards are unique to this place.

"Do you think it's a good or a bad thing to be unsure of your feelings?" I ask.

"I don't know," she sighs. "It's scary. How am I supposed

to act? Should I kiss you or shake your hand? Invite you to spend the night or slam the door in your face?"

I chuckle at her expression of consternation. "How about settling for a peck on the cheek?" I suggest. "Then you can sleep on it. Maybe things will be clearer in the morning."

"That sounds like a good plan," she smiles and brushes my cheek with her lips.

"Do you have a sleeping pill?" she asks as she pulls away. "Mine are in my old boarding house."

"I don't use pills," I tell her.

"Then how do you get to sleep?" she asks.

"I just nod off."

"How?" she persists.

I shrug. "I just close my eyes when I'm tired and drift off."

"That's it?" she asks incredulously. "You get weirder every time you open your mouth. Hold on, I might have a couple in my bag." She roots through the handbag that she's been carrying all evening and comes up with two small brown pills. "Ah, here we are. It always pays to have a couple set aside for emergencies." She hands me one of the pills. "You can have it. I'll fetch the rest of my supply tomorrow."

"What does it do?" I ask.

"Sends you to sleep," she says. "Everybody uses them. We'd be awake all night if we didn't."

"Are there side effects?" I ask but she doesn't know what that means. "OK," I say, kissing her cheek in return, "I'll give it a go. Will I see you in the morning?"

"I'm not sure," she says. "I go to work pretty early. You

might not be up."

"Well, if I'm not awake, give me a shout before you leave," I tell her.

"Alright," she says, and following one final puzzled glance at me, closes the door and retires for the night.

I stroll back to my room, studying the pill in my hand, smirking like a hyena. It doesn't take the smooth-talking Newman Riplan long to adjust to things. Less than two days in this hell hole, where everything's upside-down and round-about, and despite it all I've already picked up a girlfriend. That's pulling power!

Opening the door to my room, I pop the pill in my mouth. I don't know how long it will take to work but I'll surely have time to shit in the sink – I've been holding one back for a while now – and wash my teeth. Although now that I think about it, I don't have a toothbrush. I'll have to look for one tomorrow, or will that turn out to be something else they don't have here?

I'm heading for the sink, unbuttoning my shirt and figuring it would make more sense to brush my teeth with a finger before defecating, when my legs buckle. I lurch forward with a choked cry, fingers splaying, and everything goes black.

EIGHT

I'm back on the plane when my eyes open and the nice stewardess is leaning over me, concern in her expression. "Are you alright, Mr Riplan?" she says, touching my arm and smiling worriedly.

"What the fuck's happening?" I yell, bolting upright, eyes bulging. Most of the nearby passengers are turned in my direction, checking me out, and they're human, every one of them. No drones. "What's happening?" I ask again, quietly this time.

"You had an accident," the stewardess informs me. "You choked on a nut. You coughed it up before it could do any serious damage but then you went into a coma."

"We've been worried sick," the woman next to me – Jennifer's mother – says. "You didn't seem to be breathing. I had to send Jennifer to sit in another seat, she was so scared."

"How much time has passed?" I ask, touching the glass of the window pane, touching myself, the seat, the stewardess, making sure we're all real.

"Five or six minutes," the stewardess says. She wipes sweat from my forehead with a napkin. "You gave us quite a scare. We thought we were going to lose you."

"That's nothing like what *I* thought," I chuckle weakly. "If I told you what's been going through my mind while I was..."

I fall into silent contemplation. Was that all it was? A dream? Of course. It had to be. I knew that, deep down. I accepted it at face value while I was there, since it was the easiest thing to do, but I never really believed it was an actual city. It couldn't have been. No place on Earth could function the way that dream city did.

"I've got a monster of a headache," I say, caressing my throbbing temples.

"Don't worry," the stewardess says. "I'll get you some aspirin. I'd advise you to lie back and rest until we touch down. We don't have much further to go. There'll be a doctor waiting to examine you. Everything's going to be alright."

"Yes," I smile. "Things will be fine. Oh," I add as she starts to leave, "don't bother with the aspirin."

"What about your headache?" she asks.

I wave her concern away. "I don't mind, proves I'm back home again." She pulls an uncomprehending face, then carries on up the aisle. I lie back, beaming, and relish the discomfort of real world pain.

Casablanca! Those mad, glorious jokers have packed me off to Casablanca. It's a place I would never have thought of visiting. Like everybody else in the world, I've seen countless clips of the old Bogie movie over the years, but it wasn't even shot here – they filmed everything on a set back in those days – so why would I be interested in swinging by? But that randomness is what makes this such a perfect destination. If they'd sent me to New York or Dubai, I'd quickly be able to put a vacation plan together, but I've no idea what to expect when I leave the airport, which makes it the perfect mystery destination.

I wave away the questions of the doctor who was brought

to the lounge to give me the once-over. "I'm fine," I tell him. "I blacked out, that's all. Everything's back to normal, honest."

He's reluctant to let me go without a thorough examination but he can't force me to submit to a probe, so eventually he sighs, gives me his number and tells me to get in touch if I develop any worrying symptoms.

I find a note from Hughie and Battles in my passport as I'm lining up to go through Immigration. *Aren't we the most cunning of foxes!* it exclaims. *Hope you like the waters. Give the ghost of Ingrid Bergman one from us. Ring when you get back and tell us all about it.*

I also find a wad of Moroccan notes stuffed into a jacket pocket.

"Those beautiful sons of bitches," I mutter and head for the exit once my passport has been stamped.

A taxi – a proper one, with glass windows – transports me into the heart of the famous but unknown city. After a quick online search during the drive in, I book into a luxury hotel and take one of the best rooms in the house. It's going to cost a small fortune but we only live once, right? After what I've been through these past few days – mere minutes in real time, but try convincing my brain of that – I deserve some pampering.

I lock myself into my room, almost forgetting to tip the bellboy, and hasten to the mini bar. "Come to Poppa," I chortle, downing the first tiny bottle I can get my hands on. The taste is enough to elevate me to the ranks of the angels. No more *sap* for this troubleshooter. I'm back on terra firma, and from this day forth I'll take nothing for granted. I'm going to wring the most out of life. No more killing myself with work. At least two holidays a year, a minimum of two weeks each. No more cheap sex with hookers — I'll find a good woman and settle down into what I used to mockingly call the humdrum life. We'll have kids, a gaggle of them. And I'm going to wear two watches wherever I go and remind myself daily to be grateful for time and glass and street names and...

"Baths," I whisper, grinning as I trot to the oversized tub that comes with the high-end room. I never got round to asking if they had baths back in that nameless sham of a city, but even if they did, I bet they weren't as grand as this one. I fill the tub with hot, steaming water – it takes ages – then yelp when I step in and have to drain off some of the hot and replace it with cold. On the second attempt it's just right. I sink beneath the water, gurgling the lyrics to *Yellow Submarine*, and it's like a cocoon when I'm totally immersed, free of the pull of work, hangovers, near-death experiences and nightmarish cities, and if it wasn't for the lack of oxygen I'd happily lie submerged here forever.

Lying naked on a four-poster bed, sipping champagne. This is the life. I ring Hughie and Battles, tell them I've arrived, what the room's like, that I'm having a great time. Then I tell them about the nameless city, the drones, Cheryl and the rest. There's silence for a few seconds when I finish, then...

"Holy fuck," Hughie hoots. "That sounds wicked. Wish I could trip like that."

"Must have been the bagels that did it," Battles sniggers.

"I bet it freaked you out," Hughie says. "Were you a drooling mess while you were tripping?"

"Not really," I sniff. "I coped with it well, rode out the storm, accepted the city on its own terms, kept my head, tried to fit in with the locals."

We discuss it some more. Hughie fancies himself an amateur psychologist, so he tries analysing the nightmare. "Those drones must be how you see people," he says. "They were your subconscious telling you you're an aloof fucker, that the way you see it, people are here just to serve you and do your bidding."

"Fuck off," I laugh. "You're the one with the God complex, remember?"

When he was younger, Hughie used to think he was a divine incarnation.

"That was years ago," he snorts. "I've worked through my delusions. But you haven't. This was your inner self telling you to grow up and smell the roses."

"What about the city?" Battles asks in the background. "Why didn't the place have a name?"

"Because the inner mind doesn't have a name for itself," Hughie pontificates. "We call it the subconscious, but that's just a label we've stuck on."

"And glass?" I ask, intrigued despite my scepticism. "Why wasn't there any?"

"Because glass is a barrier," Hughie says, sounding as if he genuinely knows what he's talking about. "Your mind wants you to reach out to your fellow human beings, not cut yourself off from the world."

"You're stretching," I growl.

"Not at all," Hughie says smugly. "The woman – Cheryl – didn't want you coming inside her because you're afraid of commitment. You think you can screw around freely forever, but she was your brain telling you that you'll get your card stamped if you continue to play the field – you're bound to get a girl pregnant eventually – which will mean the death of your current, carefree life."

I want to snort with derision but I'm fascinated. I'm sure Hughie's making this up on the spur of the moment, but it seems logical to me and goes a long way towards explaining the dream to my satisfaction. I'd been keen to dismiss it as a bad trip, to forget about it as swiftly as I could, but this is encouraging me to give it more thought, in case I can work out other things about what my subconscious is trying to tell me.

"I could go on in this vein for ages," Hughie says without a trace of modesty, "but we have to get going. Planes of our own to catch."

"When will I see you again?" I ask.

"Weeks, months, years, what does it matter?" Hughie chuckles. "You won't be able to keep track of time when you're locked up in a nuthouse."

"Well," I say with a wry smile, "if I escape and catch up with you, the beers and gear are on me next time, and so are the flights to the city of the drones."

"See you, Newman," Hughie laughs.

"Have a good holiday," Battles says.

And then, together, they bellow, "Don't catch the clap!"

I watch TV for a couple of hours, replaying my conversation with Hughie, marvelling at my brain's hidden capabilities. I always thought I had a rather dull mind – those of us who make a living from computers usually do – but this has radically altered my view of myself. Seems I've got an imagination after all, and a beast of a one at that. Maybe I'll junk the computers and become a writer. Can't be that hard. Sit at a desk all day and type. Easy-peasy. Big money in it too, or so I'd imagine.

Heh. I picture myself on one of those slick American chat shows. "So, Newman, where do your ideas come from?"

"Well, I stuff myself full of beer and vodka, a bit of marijuana, some coke, shag a few brasses, then I climb aboard a plane – no clue where it's going, of course – choke on a nut and the ideas come flooding in."

There's a knock at the door. "Room service," a maid calls. That'll be the club sandwich. No matter where I stay in the world, if I'm ordering room service, I always start with the club sandwich.

"Hold on," I shout. I pull on a robe, then open the door and let her in. She carries the meal in on a tray and looks to me for directions.

"Just leave it by the TV," I tell her, digging in my pockets for loose change.

"Is it OK here, Newman?" the maid asks.

"Sure, that's..." I stop. "You called me Newman."

"So?" she smiles. "That's your name, isn't it?"

"Yes, but how do you know that? I've never been called by my first name when ordering room service before. Who the hell are…"

Her face changes, whitens and narrows. Her hair, which was short and dark, becomes long and fair, forming into two braids which hang down her back.

"Cheryl?" I gasp.

The maid/Cheryl smiles. "Time to wake up, Newman," she says.

"What are you talking about?" I moan.

"You told me to wake you." She reaches out, and though there's three or four metres of floor separating us, her hands brush the sides of my face, then tweak my ears. "Wake up, Newman," the maid/Cheryl says. "Wake up, wake up, wake…"

"…up."

My eyes open. They weren't closed in the real world but they open all the same. I stare at Cheryl's face wordlessly. She winks and squeezes my nose. "You're a deep sleeper," she says. "I was about to leave. I would have, only I was afraid you mightn't be here when I got back. Are you alright? You look confused."

I shake my head and sit up. "Wh-wh-where am I?" I stutter.

"Where do you think…" She stops and grimaces. "Let's not start that again. I know you don't like it. I'll be back before it gets dark. We'll go for a walk, get something to eat, see where the night leads us." She smiles. "What are you going to do today?"

"I don't know," I say weakly, feeling tears building. I hope she leaves before I start sobbing. Nothing I hate worse than crying in front of a woman.

"Well, take care," she says, kisses my forehead, then leaves, closing the door – the door of my room in Franz's boarding house, not the door of my hotel room in Casablanca – behind her.

I look round the room, to be entirely certain that I'm back in the city and not in Morocco, then let my head sink into the pillow and wail.

<u>NINE</u>

I stare at the sink for what must be hours on end, sinking deeper and deeper into depression, remembering the bed in Casablanca, the champagne, the bath, the TV. What do I have here? Not even a toilet to piss in.

How could I have slipped through the wormhole again? If this place was the product of a bad trip, why am I back? I returned to the real world. I spoke with Hughie and Battles. The drugs had worn off. I still had a headache but I wasn't stoned. So why aren't I in Casablanca, tucking into my club sandwich? It doesn't make any kind of sense. Unless...

Unless this is real.

The thought sends an Arctic chill through my bones. What if this city is the real world and that other one was just a construct of my warped mind? After all, I'm the only person here who believes in an outside, other cities and families, glass and beer. Can I be the only sane man in a city of lunatics, or is it the other way round? What proof have I that the world I believed I knew exists? Maybe it never did. Perhaps the plane, Amsterdam and everything before was an illusion. The pill might have set my mind twirling again, hence my detour to the imaginary Casablanca. Perhaps this nameless city has always been home and the other place was a mirage.

"No!" I scream and lurch to my feet. I refuse to accept that. I know what's real and what's false, and this city's fake to the core. My world *does* exist. I'm Newman Riplan, twenty-eight years old, the King Kong of troubleshooters, on my way to my first million. That's the truth. Those are the facts. I mustn't lose track of them, no matter how weird things get. Whatever this city is, it isn't mine. This isn't home. Never has been and never must be. A real world – my world – exists and I have to stay focused on that. I've returned once, so I'm sure I can do it again. And next time I won't lounge about in a hotel. Next time I'll seek help and find a way to stay and...

Next time. What the fuck am I saying, *next time*, as though I might have to wait years for another chance. I've got the means right here, right now. The sleeping pills. I don't have any on me but I'm sure they aren't hard to find. I can ask Franz. I don't have many teeth left but I'll bullshit him if I haven't enough. I won't show him the colour of my teeth until he's handed over a pill and then, if needs be, I'll do a runner, hole up some place dark and quiet, pop one and float on out, leave this dump behind once and for all.

The pills are the answer. Drugs got me into this mess and got me out of it for a few blissful hours last night. They'll get me out of it again. And if I keep snapping back, I'll just go on popping pills, every time I wake and return. This city won't beat me. I'm Newman Riplan. I don't know the meaning of defeat.

Pausing only to throw on some clothes – how come I'm naked? I didn't undress last night – I hurry out the door and race down the stairs, yelling for Franz.

He has pills and they're cheap, ten for one drone tooth. They're as common as muck, he tells me. I rush back upstairs once the exchange is complete and lock myself in. I sit on the bed and tip out one of the pills. I go to toss it back. Pause and lower my hand. What do I know about these? Maybe it's dangerous to take more than one a day. Perhaps I should wait.

No. Fuck waiting. Another day in this place, when I know the real world is a mere pill-pop away, would drive me loco. I'll take my chances. I lie back on the bed and make myself comfortable. Stare at the ceiling, then glance at the sink, the candles, the wardrobe. "Adios, amigos," I mutter and fire down the pill.

I black out like before, then the real world fades in, sunny and familiar. I'm lying on a bed in this world too – a beautiful four-poster in a five-star hotel room in Casablanca – staring serenely up at the billowing material of the canopy. I spread my lips into a victorious smile and bring my fists up. "Yes!"

Except something's wrong. My lips won't move and my arms won't raise. I try lifting my head, to see what's wrong, but my neck's stiff. Even my eyes are stuck, fixed on the one spot. What's going on? I try to speak but my vocal cords don't work. My mouth – slightly open – won't form words. In fact, now that I focus, I can't feel my lungs working. I listen carefully but don't hear my heart beating.

The door to the room opens and footsteps rush towards me. Faces appear above mine. One's the maid who was serving me when I flashed back to the dream city. The other's probably the manager. The maid is frightened, the manager worried.

"He just fell," the maid says. "I was bringing in his meal. He told me to put it over there. Then he muttered something I didn't catch and when I turned he was falling. I called one of the other maids to help me lift him onto the bed, then came to fetch you. I wasn't sure if we should move the body but I didn't want to leave him on the floor."

"You did the right thing," the manager says. He checks one eye, then the other, then puts an ear to my lips for a while. Sighs and shakes his head. "Dead."

Dead? Is he saying I'm *dead*? It's ludicrous. I can't be. How could I see or hear them if I was dead? It's obvious I'm not my natural self — I wouldn't be immobile if I was — but I'm sure as hell not a stiff. I've suffered a stroke or brain aneurysm, something that's floored me, but I'm still alive, capable of thought and feeling.

The maid and manager leave, closing the door behind them. I hope they've gone to fetch a doctor. A medic won't be long clearing things up. I smile — inside only — as I imagine him leaning over, stethoscope pressed to my chest. His eyes widen. "This man's alive!" he shouts and the room bursts into action at his words. I'll be rushed to hospital, hooked up to machines. They'll bring me round. When I can speak, I'll tell them about the other city and they'll give me something to make the dreams go away and everything will be fine, everything will return to normal and I'll be able to recover and continue with my life. That's how it's going to be. That's how it's going to be. That's how...

*

The doctor's a middle-aged woman. She examines me briskly, then engages in a conversation with the manager in a language I don't understand. She's probably asking lots of pertinent questions, what I had to eat and drink, how I'd been acting. She looks like a sensible lady. I bet she'll get in contact with the crew of the plane and learn of my earlier attack. She'll hear I was in a coma for several minutes. This won't be the first case of its type that she's experienced. She'll know how to handle it.

The doctor examines me again, prods me, lifts my arms, opens my mouth, looks down my throat, then checks my genitals – naughty! – and listens for sounds of a heartbeat. She shines a torch in my eyes and mutters something to the manager, who leaves the room. The doctor flicks off the torch and checks her watch. Come on, doc, speak in English. Give me the good news. Buck me up. Don't you know that coma victims can hear people speaking? Reassure me. Tell me it's…

With the second and fourth fingers of her right hand, the doctor slides down the lids of both my eyes. Then she places my hands on my stomach and neatly crosses them. Then she leaves.

Oh no. Oh no, oh no, oh no. No. No! *No*!

I scream as I'm eased onto a stretcher. I scream as I'm wheeled out of the room, along a corridor, down a lift and out of the hotel. I scream as I'm loaded into an ambulance. I scream as we drive slowly through the streets of Casablanca, no sirens blaring, no hurry to deliver my body. I scream as I'm lifted out and taken somewhere cool, dark, beyond the realms of hope. I scream as I've never screamed before, as I'll never scream again, but nobody hears. Nobody ever hears the screams of the dead.

Time slows to a horribly thin trickle. People pass occasionally. I keep hoping one will notice me breathing, that somebody will take an interest and discover I'm still conscious, but they don't. How could they? Even *I* can't detect any signs of life in this washed out waste of a body. My mind's alert as ever but the rest of me…

How is this happening? How can I be dead and alive at the same time? Is this common? I never believed in heaven, not even as a kid. I've always thought the mind is a computer — shut off the power and that's it, nothingness, oblivion, the end. Was I wrong? Is the mind a soul, capable of surviving the body's end? If so, then surely I can free myself from the corpse, branch out and roam at will. If the mind and body thrive independently of one another, it should be possible to physically separate them.

I try leaving my flesh-clad shell, to no avail. This body has me in its clutches and it's not letting go. I imagine it laughing at my predicament, sneering, "If it's curtains for me, it's curtains for you, old buddy." No, that's crazy. A dead body can't sneer. I mustn't give in to hysteria. I have to concentrate on forcing a way out. It must be possible. Forget about my body. Put it behind me. Divorce it.

Easier said than done. My trouble is, I've always been a creature of the flesh. I never went in for meditation or mental escape. Maybe a more spiritually educated person could make headway, but I'm too used to the fusion of body and mind to extract one from the other.

Ghosts. I never thought they were real. I used to watch horror movies and read spooky stories, but it was all for fun, ludicrous escapism. If spirits did survive the body's end, the world would be full of them. With the billions of people who've died down through the millennia, you wouldn't be able to take more than a couple of steps without running into a sheet of ectoplasm. But what if only a lucky few are capable of evacuating their earthly shells? What if the minds – souls – live on, but confined to their bodies? The strong manage to break free, while the rest stay imprisoned, doomed to monotonous, motionless consciousness for all eternity.

I wish I could stop thinking like this but I can't. How can you stop thinking when thinking's all you've got? With a body it was easy to tune out my thoughts. I could exercise and focus on my physical being, or tank myself up with drugs and drift off into a blank, mental void. I could sleep. Can the dead sleep? Is there any rest for inactive ghosts? Any diversions? If not, I might as well be in hell itself, because I can think of no worse form of suffering than this.

For hours I stare at the backs of my eyelids, listening to the sounds of the room, anticipating the future with dread. Will there be an autopsy? Will I feel the pain as they slice into me? And afterwards. Will I be buried? What if they cremate me? I've always been terrified of dying in a fire. I imagine myself lying in an oven, flames roaring into life, the flesh burning off of me. A friend of a friend works in a crematorium. I got talking to him once at a party. He told me no fire is hot enough to reduce human bones to ash. When the body has been incinerated, they comb through the ashes and pick out the remaining bones, then stick them in a machine that crushes them into tiny pieces. Will I feel all that? Will I hear the shriek of the machine as it chews on my bones? Will...

My eyes! They're beginning to open!

Hardly daring to hope, I try moving my fingers. If I aim small, I figure I won't be too disappointed if I fail. Nothing happens at first – my eyelids are no longer moving either – but then the digits twitch and so do my lids. Opening my mouth, I breathe in the sweetest gasp of air in history, then jolt upright and ready myself to scream abuse at the idiots who had written me off as one of the dead.

The outraged scream dies on my lips. I'm not in a morgue or a hospital. Not even in Casablanca. I'm back in the city, in Franz's boarding house. The sun is low in the sky. I've slept through the majority of the day. It'll be night soon.

I walk around the room, enjoying the use of my limbs, taking deep breaths, giving my thoughts time to adapt. I don't know how I should feel. I've slipped from the real world again, so I should be miserable, desolate, aghast. But at least I'm alive here. In this city I don't have to lie on a slab, face-to-face with death.

Knuckles rap on my door and I stop. "Who's there?" I ask. It feels good to be speaking again, though my first words are shaky.

"It's Cheryl. Can I come in?"

I consider the request silently.

"Newman?" she calls, puzzled. "Are you alright?"

"I'm... fine," I croak, crossing to the door but not opening it. "Do you mind leaving me alone a while? I have a lot on my mind."

"But I thought we were going out," she says.

"I'm sorry but I don't want to go out with you tonight. Some other time."

"Newman, what's wrong?" She's moved closer to the door.

"Nothing," I lie. "I just need some time to myself. I'll call in on you later."

"Oh, you will, will you?" she huffs. "Well, maybe I won't be in. Maybe I'll be gone. I'm not –"

"Please," I groan. "I can't cope with this right now. Just go away and leave me be. If you're in when I call, fine. If not, that's fine too. At this precise moment I don't give a damn one way or the other."

"Alright," she says stiffly. "If that's how you want it. Goodbye."

Seconds later, a door slams. Silence descends. I use the solitude to think.

Hours later, I'm still thinking. It's dark in here. Franz came up earlier to light the candles but I wouldn't let him in. I've drawn the drapes across the window. I lie on the bed, a sleeping pill in hand, wondering whether or not I should take it. I've no desire to return to that slab and the horrors of a possible cremation, but what are the alternatives? Stay here? While life in the city is preferable to what I experienced when last in the real world, it's only marginally more attractive. And maybe I'll be alive this time if I go back. Maybe I took the second pill too soon after the first, resulting in the death-like state of my body. More time has passed. If I wait a few more hours and try again, maybe I'll...

The door handle twists and somebody tries forcing their way in. I glance across, disinterested, figuring it's Franz or Cheryl. Whoever's out there lets go of the handle when they discover the door's locked, but then there's the sound of keys jingling. The lock clicks and the door opens. I sit up and stare into the gloom, heart starting to thump.

"No lights," somebody says and I gather there's more than one intruder.

"Hang on, I've got a candle," a second voice mutters. A match strikes and a candle's lit. Two medium-sized men enter the room and close the door. They're carrying some weird kind of apparatus, I can't tell what it is.

"Who the fuck are you?" I bark as I struggle to my knees on the bed.

The men jump with alarm, dropping whatever it is that they were holding. When they see me glaring at them, they relax.

"Snuff, man," one of them chuckles, "you nearly stopped my heart. You shouldn't do that to people. We thought you were asleep."

"He's supposed to be asleep," the second man says, squinting at me. "Franz said he was a day worker."

"Maybe we got the wrong room," the first man says.

"Nah," the second man says, stepping closer. "I remember this one from the last couple of nights. He's the guy who's always dressed."

"Oh yeah," the first man says, joining his partner at the foot of the bed. "I took his clothes off last night, didn't I? Thought he'd be more comfortable that way. All heart, I am."

"Who are you?" I ask again, less harshly this time. They're not burglars, that much I'm sure of.

"I'm Andy," the first man says. "This is Isaac."

"How do," Isaac smiles.

"And you're..." Andy thinks for a moment. "Newman, right? Newman Riplan, the guy with two names?"

"Yes," I say, staring at them suspiciously.

"See that?" Andy beams, nudging Isaac in the ribs. "Am I great when it comes to names or what?"

"A wonder," Isaac says drily, then points at me. "Come on then, off with your clothes. We haven't got all night. Twelve more boarding houses after this one. Or is it thirteen?"

"It's fourteen," Andy pipes up. "A new place opened for business today."

"Is that on our route?" Isaac asks.

"Sure is," Andy says.

"Snuff!" Isaac curses.

"Excuse me," I mutter, "but who the hell are you?"

"Andy and Isaac," Andy says again.

"I've gathered that much," I sigh. "I mean, why are you in my room? What's your business here?"

"Oh," Isaac chuckles, "he wants to know what our job is."

"Oh," Andy smiles. "Why didn't he say? You have to speak plainly round us. We're not the brightest of men, are we, Isaac?"

"Wouldn't be enemaists if we were," Isaac grins.

"En-eh-mah-ists?" I echo uncertainly. It's not a word I'm familiar with.

"We're clean-up artists," Isaac giggles, patting the thing on the floor that they were carrying when they came in.

"Clean-*out* artists, you mean," Andy says, and the two howl with laughter.

"Look," I say impatiently, "I don't know what you jokers think you're up to, but if I don't get some answers pretty quickly, I'll call Franz and have him throw the pair of you out."

"We're enemaists," Andy says, as if that explains everything. "You know what an enemaist is, don't you?"

"No," I reply.

The men exchange a wry glance. "We've got a raw one," Isaac murmurs.

"Franz said he was odd," Andy nods. "I see now what he meant." He clears his throat. "Do you know what an enema is?"

"Of course," I snap, "but what does that have to do with…"

I stop. Enema. Enemaists. Uh-oh.

I lean forward and ogle the large container on the floor between the men. A long pipe sticks out of it and my nose detects a heavily disguised but unmistakably unpleasant scent. I recall looking in vain for toilets. Last night, when I took my first sleeping pill, I needed to shit. I didn't – I conked out before I could – but when I woke in the morning, the urge had passed. Now I know why.

"You give people enemas," I gasp.

"The boy's a genius," Isaac dead-pans.

My sphincter tightens at the thought of what the men have been up to in my room the past two nights. "What about urine?" I ask. "Do you drain that too?"

"Of course," Andy says. "Wouldn't do to leave it inside."

"Do you do this all over the city?" I ask light-headedly.

"Just our section," Isaac says, "and only boarding houses. Different teams handle private homes."

"You get paid more for privates," Andy sighs. "We used to be on privates but we got demoted. Complaints that we were taking liberties with some of our female customers."

"All fabricated of course," Isaac adds quickly.

"This is sick," I moan. "What's wrong with you people? Haven't you heard of toilets?"

"What are those?" Isaac asks.

I try explaining the principles of lavatories but I might as well be talking to a pair of chimps.

"A bowl," Isaac grins.

"With water in it," Andy adds.

"And pipes going through floors and out walls, under streets and…" Isaac can't continue, he's laughing so hard.

"We'll have to tell the rest of the gang about this," Andy cackles. "I don't suppose you could draw us one of these toilet thingies, could you?"

"Go fuck yourself," I snap.

"OK," Isaac says when he's calmed down, "no more

jokes. Drop your pants."

"What?" I back away from him nervously.

"We've got to clean you out," Isaac says. Can't leave that messy stuff inside. Think of the damage it would do." He lifts the tube leading into the dumper and points it at me. "Get the suds ready, Andy."

"Stop right there," I bellow. "The first man to set foot on this bed loses an eye. I'll claw it out with my fingers."

The pair of enemaists stare at me. "You don't want to be sluiced?" Andy asks.

"Are you insane?" Isaac growls.

"Maybe," I laugh hysterically. "But if you think I'm going to lie here and let you stick that thing up me, you're out of your minds."

"It doesn't hurt," Isaac assures me.

"Quite a pleasant sensation in fact," Andy says. "Lots of wealthy folk have their enemas while they're awake. Costs more but they think it's worth it."

"But we won't charge you extra," Isaac promises.

"You're not putting that thing up me," I roar again. "I won't have it. I've put up with a lot of shit lately, and I suppose it's only fair that I give some of it back, but I'll be damned if I do it like this."

"So what are you going to do?" Andy challenges me. "Just leave the piss and shit inside to accumulate? Does that sound reasonable?"

"I've no intention of letting it accumulate," I tell them. "I'll piss in the sink and shit in the parks. That'll see me right."

Their jaws drop. "Piss in the... the..." Andy can't bring himself to say it.

"He's an animal," Isaac gawps. "Nothing more than a filthy, mindless animal."

"The thought of it," Andy whimpers, face whitening.

"OK, sicko," Isaac says, "I'll give you one final opportunity. If you drop your pants now and apologise, we'll say no more about this. If you don't..."

"Yeah?" I jeer, secure in the knowledge that they don't have police here.

"If you don't, we'll spread the word," Isaac grunts. "Franz will kick you out. You'll be refused work wherever you go. Public car drivers won't let you in their cars. Nourishment houses won't accept you. You'll be treated like an animal and you'll end up with them, roaming the streets, foraging for food."

"You're bluffing," I snort.

"You reckon?" Isaac smiles thinly. "Come on then, Andy," he says, picking up the dumper. "We'll have a word with Franz, then go finish our rounds. I'd pack my bags now if I were you, *Mr Riplan*. I don't think Franz will wait for morning. No landlord is going to let a stranger piss in his sink. And though you'll probably be able to find a bed in another boarding house tonight, rest assured, this will be your final night indoors. By this time tomorrow, everyone will know about Newman Riplan and his disgusting predilections. The game, as they say, is up."

The two of them head for the door. I consider letting them go but their threat's a dire one. "Wait," I yap.

They stop and turn. "Yes, sir?" Andy asks, mockingly polite.

"If you ever get reincarnated," I say bitterly, "I hope you come back as an intestinal worm." Then, shaking my head grimly, I lie flat on my stomach and begin undoing the button on my trousers.

"Now you're being sensible," Isaac says, making his way back.

"Choke on it," I snarl, then shut my eyes and think of England.

Matters of the bowels attended to, Andy and Isaac depart, plunging me once again into darkness. Ignoring the empty feeling inside, I return to my original dilemma — the sleeping pill. The enemaists have pretty much decided things for me – I don't want to stay in a city where my privacy is invaded every night by a pair of grubby state employees who've been reprimanded for molesting sleeping women – but I hesitate a few final minutes, remembering what it felt like to be dead yet conscious, alert but motionless. I'm dreading the thought of return, of discovering I'm still dead, of maybe suffering in flames. But I have to try. One last go. Monte Carlo or bust.

I down the pill.

This time there's nothing. A veil of black that makes my room in the nameless city seem as bright as Las Vegas. No sense of body. No sounds or scents. It's a void, inhabited only by my consciousness.

Is this true death? Was my last experience merely an intermediate phase? If so, this place is far worse than the city. At least there's life there, odd as it is. This is an area of extinction. Even time can't penetrate this placeless place. I hang in the void for what seems an eternity, screaming silently. Days pass. Weeks. Months. Longer. Or maybe it's just been seconds. I can't say. This is like nothing I've ever experienced. Timelessness, pure and terrifying.

Eventually, long after I've thought all is lost, a faint light materialises far ahead. It drifts towards me slowly, growing steadily. I'd cry for joy if I could. I try moving to meet it but I'm pinned to an inescapable, non-material spot. Finally, after many more days, weeks or years, the light washes over me. I can feel the warmth even though I've no body. Then I shudder. I become aware of a physical form. Limbs twitch. A heart beats. Eyes open.

And I'm back. In the city.

I roll off the bed, check to make sure I'm real, that this room is real, that I'm not imagining it. Then I sink to the floor and weep. The sun rises outside the window – I can chart its course through the chink in the drapes – and when it gets to about midday I stop crying, pull back the curtains, wash my face in the sink and head down to explore the streets.

I'm here for good. I know that now. Time to swallow my pride and accept it. No more pills. No going back. I couldn't face that void a second time. Anything's better than nothingness, even if it's only a purgatorial dreamworld. My old life is part of an irretrievable past. This city is my home from this point onwards. I must make it my reality. As little as it is, it's all that I have.

TEN

Six days have passed. Or is it seven? I'm beginning to lose track of time, which is a good thing, seeing as how I'm the only person in the city who took any notice of it in the first place. The sooner I junk my preconceptions, the sooner I'll fit in.

It's not so bad a place once you get used to it. Simpler than the real world — I mean, the world I once knew. *This* is the real world now. I must keep reminding myself of that. People accept life as it is. No philosophers tearing their hair out by the roots, wrestling with the secrets of life. No bitter divorce battles. No lawyers, no family feuds, no war, no pollution. Hell, you don't even have to worry about bowel movements, as they're taken care of for you. (I sleep soundly now, though the first few nights – when, try as I might, I couldn't slip off – were pretty hairy.)

The only flies in the ointment are the animals. I've seen loads by this stage, wolves, bears, lions, snakes, along with mutated monstrosities I can't put names to. They roam the city at will and can attack any time, and the chances of someone coming to your rescue are slim. I don't play the hero any more. I've watched three people die and not stepped in to help. Cheryl warned me that prostitutioners don't take kindly to competition and would come after me if they got wind of my good deeds, assuming I was doing it to build up my own stable of sex slaves. Nobody knows where the animals come from or why there are so many of them. They just are, and in this city, that's explanation enough.

Cheryl and I are an item. I found her that night after my third and final sleeping pill. Made my apologies. Said I'd been on a down but had recovered from my slump and was ready to get on with life again. It didn't take her long to forgive me — one of the bonuses of short-term memories — and within hours we were out on the town together, wining and dining (well, sapping and lapping) and having a ball. Two nights later she arrived home from work and said she'd thought long and hard about it and had made up her mind — she was in love with me. As soon as she'd said it, she started to strip.

"What are you doing?" I asked.

"We have to bond," she said, "to make it official."

"Who am I to argue with the rules?" I grinned, loosening my belt.

Sex with Cheryl is fine. She's not the most passionate of lovers but she's game for most things. The only time she draws the line is when it comes to ejaculation inside her. She won't stand for it. In my hand, on the sheets, even over her stomach or breasts is fine, but never inside her vagina or mouth.

When I do ejaculate, I have to douse the sperm with a salt-like substance that's issued by the Alchemist (of whom I still know virtually nothing, aside from the fact that he has his fingers in pies all over the place) and can be found in small bottles in every room. I've asked Cheryl why it has to be done. She doesn't know but says it's vital. Her instincts tell her that the sperm can't be left as it is or bad things will happen.

They don't have condoms here, so it's sex as nature intended. I'm usually wary about unprotected sex, but since they don't seem to have any kind of venereal disease – Cheryl doesn't know what that is – I figure it's OK.

I wonder what Hughie would make of all this if I could return to the other world and tell him about it. Would he say it was a symptom of my fear of commitment, that since I don't want to be saddled with a paternity suit, I invent a city where women reject sperm, thus making impregnation impossible? For all I know, maybe that's what it is. If I'm dead in my world, perhaps this city is a construct thrown up by my dying brain to spare me the agonies of conscious nothingness. Maybe this happens to everyone when they die, and each of us creates an afterlife of our own design. That explanation makes as much sense as anything else I can think of.

But whether or not I'm onto something, thoughts of that nature are meaningless. This place is home now, so it's best not to question its validity. If I ask too many questions, I might undermine its structure and end up back in the void. Safer to buy into the dream and accept things as they are.

I've a job. I landed it yesterday. Cheryl earns enough to support us – she's moved into my room and Franz doesn't charge extra for two people sharing, so we've plenty of drone teeth – but I don't want to be a dependant. I never have been – even as a teenager I earned my own money, by charging friends to show them how to complete video games – and I don't intend to start now.

"What can you do?" Cheryl asked when I informed her of my wish to seek gainful employment. I told her about my years in the computer trade – she's learnt to hear out my stories of the other world without comment, even though she rarely understands what I'm talking about – and when I finished she paused, nodded and said again, "But what can you *do*?"

It was a problem. Computers aside, I'm not really good at anything. Never did much about the house. Couldn't even change a plug. Physical work wasn't for me.

"How about your place?" I asked. "Melting drones down can't be too difficult. What sort of qualifications would I need?"

"None," she said. "I'll put your name down for a position if you like. You'll get in eventually but you'll have to wait. There's a long line of candidates ahead of you. A couple of hundred people queue up by the admissions desk every day. Their places in the line are reserved."

We spent most of the night discussing it before Cheryl hit on a solution. "I know!" she cried. "We'll use that crazy imagination of yours and get you a job as a yarn spinner."

I'd seen those in nourishment houses when I went on dates with Cheryl. Since there are no televisions or radios, no music or major organised games, people rely on storytellers for entertainment when the sun goes down. The nourishment houses are full of them, men and women spinning tall tales, mostly about giant drones which come to life and eat people — the drones are vital even to fictional flights of fancy in this place.

"A yarn spinner? Me?" I laughed. "Don't be silly. I've never made up a story in my life. I was always useless at that kind of stuff, even in school."

"Nonsense," Cheryl gushed. "You make up the most wonderful stories I've ever heard. Things like glass, electrocity…"

"Electricity," I corrected her.

"…computers, planes and all the rest," she continued. "They're amazing tales. People will pay lots of teeth for stories like those."

I remained unconvinced but went with her to see Kipp the following evening. People were already eating when we arrived but it wasn't too busy, so Kipp was happy to chat. The nourishment house manager listened to Cheryl singing my praises, adjusting his cufflinks while he thought about whether or not to give me a chance.

"He does have a unique slant on life," Kipp agreed, "but can he translate it into captivating stories in front of an audience? A window filled with a panel of see-through, melted sand is an interesting idea, but something has to be *happening* in a story – somebody must be thrown through the window, or a killer drone has to be glimpsed through it – to grip people's attention and draw them in."

"He's right," I told Cheryl. "I couldn't do stuff like that. I'd come off sounding like a dull tourist guide. It'd be boring. People would tune out."

To be honest, I was terrified by Cheryl's proposal. I'd never dreamt of being a performer. I've always thought there was something freakish about people who put themselves on public display, forsaking the safety of obscurity for the bright lights of fickle fame. But Cheryl wouldn't listen. She was convinced of my talent.

"Give him a trial run," she pleaded with Kipp. "Put him on now –"

"*Now*?" I squeaked.

"– and he'll do a show for free. If things work out, we'll discuss terms later. If he flops, just drag him off and we'll pay for a meal, no hard feelings."

"OK," Kipp said reluctantly, "but if I sense he's losing the audience, I'll cut him short immediately."

"Thanks," Cheryl said. "You won't regret this."

"I can't go on now," I whined. "I'll have to prepare and compose my thoughts."

"Good luck, Newman," Cheryl said and gave me a quick peck on the cheek before ignoring my protests and pushing me into the spotlight. Well, not an actual spotlight — it was a raised, circular dais in the middle of the room, surrounded by thick candles. There was a light smattering of applause, then the house went silent. Deathly still.

"Hi," I mumbled, smiling stiffly. "My name's Newman Riplan. Um. Have you heard the one about the Irishwoman, the Scotswoman, the Welshwoman and the German Shepherd?"

Blank faces. I decided to scrap the joke and started talking about my job. I told them I was a troubleshooter who worked with computers, and began to describe what computers were and how they operated. I could sense people losing interest and saw Kipp edging closer to the stage. I was relieved at the thought of getting out of it so easily and pressed on with the technical jargon. Then a man in the audience raised his hand. Kipp had been about to haul me off but paused, not wanting to get in the way of a customer's question.

"Um, yes?" I smiled, confused.

"Excuse me," the man said, "but do these computers have something to do with drones? The way you talk about them, they sound alike — alive but not intelligent, able to be used but incapable of working by themselves, and you said they bite."

"No," I grinned, "I said *bytes*. That's..."

I stopped. Ears had perked up and suddenly I saw a way to hold the audience. Taking a deep breath, I set my eyes on the man – I found it was easier if I was speaking to a single person – and said, "Yes. Computers are machines that drones use."

Excited murmurs rippled round the nourishment house and Kipp took a few steps back.

"What are they for?" another man asked.

I sought him out, smiled when I spotted him, then adopted my solemnest voice. "Computers are machines which drones have built. Not ordinary drones, but clever ones. A gang of genius drones –" Genius drones were regular villains in many of the tales I'd heard. "– have built these machines called computers, designed to stimulate brain activity in the other drones, so that they can rise as a massive group and take over the city."

The audience members gasped and muttered loudly to one another, then leant forward raptly. I glanced around –

Kipp had withdrawn to take orders, while Cheryl was sitting in a corner, proudly smiling at me — then raised my voice and spun a yarn which was a rip-off of *War of the Worlds* and *Invasion of the Body Snatchers*.

And the crowd loved it.

Cue my new career.

I'm not on much of a salary — five drone teeth a night — but that will improve if I continue pulling in the crowds. My first two gigs have gone down a treat, but Kipp wants to be sure I can keep it up. Successful yarn spinners have to be able to deliver more than one basic type of story, as people get bored of the same old tale, even in this city of fractured memory. I don't think that'll be a problem. When I run out of computer stories, I can recycle some standard Earth ones and claim they're my own. Nobody here has heard of the Brothers Grimm, Shakespeare or Stephen King. Nobody's seen a movie or a TV show. I can take the plots and characters from the shows and movies I've watched, the books and comics that I've read, twist them round so people in this city can understand them, *et voilà!* an endless supply of material, meaning drone teeth galore.

"Plagiarism?" you say. Sorry, in this city without a name, I don't know what that means.

Speaking of names... I asked Kipp last night why everybody has only one name. I thought it might be significant. He just shrugged and said, "Who needs two?"

Vin — the public car driver — was with him. "I know a

few people with two names," Vin said. "Most took the second one so they could stand out. Snobs."

"But nobody's born with two?" I asked, then shook my head when they looked blank. "Sorry, I forgot, nobody gets born here, right?"

I asked what happened if two people had the same name but neither Vin nor Kipp had ever heard of that happening. The very idea puzzled them.

"Two people with the same name?" Vin asked. "How could that be? I wouldn't know which was which if somebody got in my car and asked for one of them."

"Society couldn't function under such conditions," Kipp agreed, "but it's a great idea for a horror story. Are you going to use it tonight, Newman? You could say computers were making people forget their proper names, giving them other people's, creating chaos so that the drones could revolt."

"Yeah," I said, "maybe."

"Two people with the same name," Vin said again and shivered. "Creepy."

I slip into a suit that I bought earlier today. The selection isn't great in the city stores, and the material is rougher than what I'm used to – it's made from recycled drone flesh, though I try not to think about that – but I look pretty good in the new gear. Better than I've been looking anyway — my old suit was fit for little more than the bin.

Cheryl is naked and washing her armpits. (No deodorant, which was a big turn-off at first, but my nose has adjusted.)

We recently got done making love. I feel like sneaking up behind her, wrapping my arms around her and squeezing tight, but I might get the suit wet and I don't want to risk damp patches this close to the show. Cheryl turns off the tap, dries her arms and catches me watching. "What are you looking at?" she asks, treating me to a full-frontal view.

"Nothing," I say bashfully.

She gazes down at her breasts. "If you think these are nothing, there's something wrong with you," she chuckles and gets into her dress. "What's the story going to be about tonight?" she asks as we go around extinguishing candles.

"It's a good one," I tell her. "I call it *Dracula*. It's about this drone with sharp teeth who sucks the blood out of humans." I pause by the last lit candle. One final glimpse round the room, then I wink at her – "I think you're going to like it. It packs a lot of *bite*." – and blow out the candle.

ELEVEN

I've been gigging – God, I sound like a roadie – for the better part of twenty nights now, straight through, no breaks. They don't have weekends in this city — hell, they don't even have week*days*. It's not tiring work, standing before an appreciative audience for a couple of hours every night, reliving old TV shows and movies and vaguely remembered comics and books, but I feel I'm due a rest. After all, that's what I flew out of Amsterdam for, a vacation, a chance to unwind.

I ask Cheryl how you go about booking time off.

"Ask for it," is her simple answer.

"That's all?"

"Sure," she says. "Nobody's expected to work constantly. Take tonight off if you're tired. Pop into Kipp's and tell him, so he has time to find a stand-in."

"You don't think he'll mind?"

"Of course not. He won't pay you for tonight, obviously, but he won't begrudge you the break. Employers are people just like us. He wants you fresh and in the mood, not drained and unenthusiastic."

According to Cheryl, that's how holidays function here. You take time off when you feel like it, as much as you want. It sounds like a crazy system but it works because people don't abuse it. Workers only take time off when there's a valid reason. Employers trust them and they repay that trust. The world I hailed from could have learnt a thing or two from these people.

*

Kipp's disappointed I won't be appearing – I've become his biggest draw and his nourishment house is packed every night when it's my turn to take the stage – but he doesn't complain. "Will you be back tomorrow?" he asks.

"Sure," I promise. "I only want a night off to recharge my batteries."

"Ah," he smiles, "*batteries*. Those are the weapons drones use to drain the energy out of humans, yes?"

"Got it in one," I grin.

Cheryl comes home early. She's taken the afternoon off and won't be going in tomorrow either, so we can stay up late and party through until the early hours of the morning.

We start with a pleasant bout of lovemaking, then wash ourselves using water in the sink – no baths or showers here, which I'm still struggling to accept – and get dressed. Cheryl takes my arm and we waltz downstairs like a couple of toffs on our way to the Proms. Franz spots us as we pass through the lobby and smiles. "Going out," he notes.

"Your powers of insight never fail to amaze," I smirk.

"Anywhere special?" he asks.

"Not really," Cheryl says. "We'll see where the night takes us." That's one of my phrases which she's adopted.

"Go with the flow," I say.

"Ride with the tide," Cheryl smiles. "Ruck with the ducks. Face the flood in the mud. Let loose in the juice."

Franz laughs and shakes his head. "You get crazier every day," he compliments us. "Enjoy yourselves."

"We'll be late back," I tell him. "If the enemaists miss us, ask them to send a day crew round in the morning."

"Will do," Franz says and out we glide.

It's a lovely evening, warm but not sticky, a gentle breeze, a full moon rising in the distance, a nice complement of stars twinkling in the darkening sky. If I knew anything about astrology I might be able to work out if the sky has any similarities to the one that hangs above the earth, but I'm clueless about such matters. I could never even find the North Star. Besides, what good would it do if I knew? This city's timeless and spaceless. To thrive here, I must be too.

We hail a public car, drive blindly for half an hour, and have the driver drop us off somewhere beyond our regular stomping ground. We stroll idly for a time, whispering to each other, watching the moon and stars come into their own. The streets empty as people lock themselves in for the night. Night owls will ooze out of their dens later, to while away the dark hours in nocturnal nourishment houses, but for the time being we're pretty much the only beaters of these deserted paths, apart from the candle lighters, enemaists and garbage collectors.

We visit a couple of nourishment houses, where we drink sap and nibble on a selection of crisp fingers and toes. I don't feel as easy devouring the mannequins as Cheryl and everyone else does but I'm getting used to it. I sucked direct from a drone's head a few nights ago, and although I felt queasy, I managed to keep my dinner down.

After another stroll we find a busy nourishment house

and tuck into a lavish meal. A comedian prattles away behind us while we eat. Most of his jokes are feeble, drone-related puns – "Why did the drone cross the road when it was busy and get killed? Because I told it to." "How many drones can you fit in a car? Fifty if you melt them down." "How do you confuse a drone? Shake a bag of teeth at it and ask if any look familiar." – but the people in the audience lap them up and howl with laughter. I pretend to chuckle but I've heard better in schoolyards.

We pay for the meal, stay seated until the comedian finishes his act, then re-emerge into the night.

"You didn't like the funny man, did you?" Cheryl asks as we trail along beneath the serene white moon.

"He was OK," I lie.

"Be honest," she says.

"Alright," I confess, "I didn't like him."

"Everybody else did," she comments. "Why didn't you?"

I snort. "Because he wasn't funny. He told dumb jokes that made fun of drones. Any fool could do that. Like, why did the drone cross the road? Because it was tied to the ostrich."

"What's an ostrich?" Cheryl asks.

"A big bird with a long neck."

"Bird?" she queries, which makes me realise I haven't seen any birds during my time here, so maybe they don't have them in the city.

"It's a creature that can fly," I explain. "I mean, birds in general can fly, but ostriches can't, because they're too big."

She nods thoughtfully, considers my impromptu joke, then bursts out laughing. "Because it was tied to the ostrich!" she howls, doubling over. "That's brilliant. Can I tell that one to Kipp and Franz and pretend it's mine?"

"Sure," I say, bemused.

"Do you know any more?" she asks.

I think back to my childhood and the silly jokes my friends and I would swap. "What do you call a thin drone with a finger up its nose? Slim Pickens." And then, of course, I have to try and explain who Slim Pickens is, which is difficult, since I've only the vaguest notion myself. But Cheryl laughs dutifully, even though she doesn't get it. Like everybody else, she's tickled pink by any joke that points the cruel finger of satire at the poor old harmless drones.

There's no river running through the city but there are plenty of canals. We find one with carefully tended flowerbeds on either bank, stretch out on a bench and stare at the stars. "Have you had a good night?" I ask.

"Beautiful," Cheryl says, cuddling up closer. "You're one of the sweetest lovers I've yet to enjoy."

The compliment makes me smile and frown at the same time. In the end I choose not to pass comment and instead say, "This is a nice area, isn't it?"

"Lovely," she says. "I've never seen a canal by night. Normally I don't venture far from home in the dark." She sits up and leans forward for a clearer view. Touches her face wonderingly. "I can't recall the last time I saw my reflection."

"Where I come from," I tell her, "we have mirrors – glass with a dark backing – which allow you to see yourself any time of the day or night."

"Amazing," Cheryl sighs, though I doubt she believes such things are real.

I wrap one of her braids around the fingers of my left hand, tug slightly, then seek her lips and kiss her. "Fancy a spot of moonlit skinny-dipping later?" I ask.

"What's that?" she replies.

"It's when you go for a swim with nothing on," I explain.

"Oh," she giggles, "I couldn't do a thing like that, not with people watching. Besides, I never learnt to swim."

"I could teach you," I offer.

"No thanks," she says.

"Don't you trust me?" I pout.

"Not really," she smiles.

I tickle her for teasing me, then kiss her again. "We'll do this more often," I promise, "pop out every six or seven nights for a walk and a meal." I nuzzle her neck. "Maybe even a swim. I was never much of a walker before, but now I…"

She's not listening.

"Cheryl?" I tug her hair again, smiling, but she doesn't look at me. She's staring at the water in the canal, her face starting to contort with terror. I lean forward to see what's troubling her and blink with confusion. The water's stained a deep red colour. "Is there a building on fire?" I ask, looking around, but I spot no flames. Besides, to discolour the water in this fashion, the fire would have to be directly upon us and I'd feel the heat.

Cheryl gets to her feet. Her hair unravels from my fingers. She raises her eyes and stares at the sky. I follow her example and gasp out loud.

It's the moon.

The moon has turned crimson.

For long seconds we gaze with awe at the fiery lunar surface. It's like nothing I've ever seen, as if the moon is actually burning, casting a rosy veil over the entire city. It's not just the canal that's red. So are Cheryl, the nearby buildings and the handful of people standing in sight, rooted to the spot as we are.

A howl shatters the eerie silence and Cheryl explodes into life. "Come on!" she cries. "We have to find a sandman."

"What are you talking about?" I mumble. "What's a –"

She grabs my hands, kisses them, then starts to run, dragging me along behind. "No time to explain," she pants as I race to keep up. "If we don't find a sandman, we're dead." Another howl pierces the red-limned night. I don't know what the hell is happening but I trust Cheryl. If she says we have to run, I'll run like the devil himself is after us.

We sprint along by the canal, Cheryl's gaze darting left and right, searching for this sandman of hers. She ducks up a side street and we emerge onto a main road. What I see stops me dead in my tracks and for a short while nothing can move me, not even Cheryl, who pounds at my chest and begs me to flee.

A woman is writhing in the middle of the road. She's torn off most of her clothes and ripped out much of her hair. Around her, people pour out of buildings like ants and scatter, screaming. The woman in the road is changing. Her face bulges beyond the bounds of human expression. Her nails lengthen. Her hands twist into claws. Her legs shorten and strengthen. Hair sprouts along the line of her backbone and across her shoulders. Her mouth widens and her teeth sharpen. Her face stretches, grows lupine. But if it's a werewolf she's becoming, it's like none I've seen before. The creature she's turning into is something unclassifiable. Her breasts wither. Her stomach bulges as if there's something inside struggling to get out. The colour of her skin darkens. Her eyes light up, two yellow sparks in a sea of red. She throws back her head and howls at the blood red moon.

Then she attacks.

She pounces on an old woman, slower than the rest. The victim shrieks and tries warding off the beast with her hands, to no avail. The animal plunges its claws into the woman's stomach and rips out her entrails, buries its snout in the cavity and chows down. The woman's body thrashes wildly for a few seconds, then goes limp. The creature guzzles a while longer, then shoves the body out of its way and looks for another target.

It spots *me*.

Even as it races towards me on all fours, blood dripping from its lips, eyes fixed on my stomach, teeth gnashing together like blades, howling like a banshee, I can't move. I've never experienced anything like this. I'm not conditioned to react. If I was a caveman, a primitive being, a creature of instinct, I might know how to defend myself, but I'm an educated man, civilized, cultured. Easy prey.

I see my death in front of me as the beast draws within range but still I can't do anything to save myself. Then, as I'm struggling to recall the prayers I learnt when I was a child, a wire noose drops over the savage's head and tightens round its throat. The beast's eyes bulge. It twists towards the person manipulating the noose, only for the wire to tighten another few notches. The animal shudders, wheezes, then drops to the ground, dead.

Cheryl — who else would bother to save a fool such as I? — releases the noose's handle, steps forward and slaps me hard across the face. "We can't stay here," she hisses. "You must come with me *now*. If you don't follow, I'll leave you. I love you, Newman, but I won't die for you."

I stare at her uncomprehendingly, then the words sink in. If I don't follow, she'll leave me alone, at the mercy of things like... My eyes flick to the dead animal, widen one final time with fear, then harden.

"Alright," I say evenly. "It took me by surprise but I won't be caught short again." I pluck a noose from a nearby wall — I know now why there are so many spread about the city — and test it while Cheryl finds a replacement for hers.

"Ready?" she asks.

"Ready," I grunt.

We advance.

We stick close to one another and hurry through the streets, Cheryl leading the way. I've seen fifteen or more of the animals running wild, howling and gorging on human blood and guts. We've avoided their attention so far — plenty of other targets at large – but it can only be a matter of time before another sets its sights on one or both of us. I want to duck into a building and hole up but Cheryl presses on, determined to find the being she refers to as the sandman.

"Why don't we hide?" I ask as she pauses for breath.

She shakes her head. "They could sniff us out. Only a sandman can guarantee our safety."

"What do the sandmen look like?" I ask.

"They're... watch out!" she screams. I spin on my heels. There's a man lying by a street lamp. He's been injured, his left arm a bloody mess, torn to shreds. As I watch, his body pulses, then starts to change. He's turning into one of the beasts.

Stepping forward, I emotionlessly slip the noose over his head and put an end to his suffering. This is the first human life I've ever taken but I don't pause to consider the enormity of my actions. There'll be time for that later if I get out of this alive.

"Bites transmit the disease?" I ask Cheryl as I grab another noose, and she nods. "But how does it start? Where did the creatures come from?"

"I don't know," she says. "The ones who turn first are always women, but as for how or why..." She shakes her head, picks a direction and runs. Cursing beneath my breath, I lumber after her, promising myself that if one of the beasts sinks its teeth into me, I'll slip the noose over my head and spare somebody else the dirty job. I'd rather kill myself than turn into one of these hellish things.

*

My lungs and legs are starting to give up on me when Cheryl rounds a corner and shouts with glee. Catching up, I spot a figure in a long brown cloak, surrounded by four men with thick machetes. Cheryl hurries towards them and I follow warily, keeping a close eye on the men with the blades, trusting nobody.

The figure in the cloak is a woman. She smiles as we draw close. "Nice night," she says as conversationally as you please.

My jaw drops but Cheryl manages to force a polite reply. "Yes, it's lovely."

The woman in the cloak holds up a small brown bag and shakes it teasingly. "I bet I know what you want. Sand, right?"

Cheryl smiles shakily and wheezes, "Right."

The woman hoots merrily. "I knew it. But can you pay, little one, can you pay?"

Cheryl rifles through her purse. "I have... seventeen teeth," she counts, then hands them over. "Newman?"

I plough through my pockets, saving the questions. "Eighteen... twenty-two... twenty-eight." I pass them to the woman in the cloak.

"Forty-five," the woman purrs, sliding the teeth from one hand to the other. A beast rounds the corner and leaps towards us, howling thirstily. One of the armed men steps forward and hacks off its head with a well-timed slice. "Forty-five," the woman says again.

"Is it enough?" Cheryl asks nervously.

"You're a couple short," the woman replies solemnly, but when Cheryl's face drops, she chuckles and tosses me the bag. "Just my little joke. Forty-five will be sufficient. This time."

"Thank you," Cheryl sobs, snatching the bag from me and bursting into tears of uncontainable joy.

"My pleasure," the woman says, patting Cheryl on the head. "Come," she snaps at the men with the machetes. "I have four more bags to dispense. Let's move on. Our work here is done."

The four men pack in tightly about her and they drift away slowly, fearlessly.

"Who the hell was that?" I croak.

"The sandman," Cheryl says, laughing hysterically.

"Don't you mean sandwoman?"

She snorts and thrusts the bag under my nose. "Look!"

"What is it?" I ask, opening the top of the bag and peering inside. "Sand?" I dip my fingers in and poke around. "Sand," I snarl. "Is that all? Just sand?"

"'Just sand,' he says!" Cheryl laughs and snatches back the bag. "You wouldn't survive long on your own, would you, Newman Riplan? Come." She looks for a clear space in the middle of the road and leads me towards it. "Stand by my side."

"But we're in plain sight here," I protest. "We'll be —"

"Stand by my side!" she screams with such force that I wince. Grumbling, I step up beside her and wait for an animal to chance upon us and gobble us up. "Close your eyes," Cheryl says, holding the bag of sand above our heads.

"Why?" I ask suspiciously, then shut them swiftly when her lips tighten angrily.

"Here goes," I hear her say, then I feel sand pouring over my head, down my face and the back of my neck. Some trickles into my mouth and I spit it out. "Keep your eyes closed," Cheryl shouts, and even though she's next to me, she sounds far away. "Don't open them. Don't... there. Do you hear it?" A strange whistling sound fills the air. "Do you hear it?" Cheryl roars.

"Yes," I roar back. "What is it?"

"The magic of the sandmen. Don't open your eyes — you'll be blinded for life if you do." The noise increases and pierces my head like the mating calls of a thousand randy cats. Strong breezes rip up and down my body, inside and outside my clothes. The grains of sand lash my skin. It's like I'm being stung with nettles, but when I try moving a hand to brush the sand away, I'm immobile.

"I can't move!" I scream.

"It's alright," Cheryl replies. "Neither can I. This is natural. There's no need to worry. It'll be over soon. When the wind dies down..."

All of a sudden it stops, the wind and the whistling.

"Ah," Cheryl sighs, no longer having to shout. "There we go." She steps away from me and I sense her stretching her arms. "You can look now."

I open my eyelids a crack, then wider. I stare at my surroundings, stunned beyond words, unable to think, let alone speak.

I'm naked, stripped to the bone, no sign of my clothes, not even a shred. The sand has disappeared too, transformed into a domed cage which stands about seven metres in diameter and three high. A cage made up of interlocking, vertical bars, no more than fifteen centimetres of a gap between each. The bars curve up over our heads and block us off from the harsh, deadly, outside world. And the bars look like they're made of...

I walk across and touch a couple, to be certain. Yes. The bars are made of *glass*. It's impossible. It's crazy. It doesn't make sense.

But then, in this city, what does?

Slumping to my haunches, I flick one of the bars with a fingernail, listen to the comforting *ting*, then sink to the floor and weep. Cheryl joins me and for a long time we remain in that huddled position, crying wordlessly, holding onto one another for support, listening to the howls and screams of the savage city beyond.

The sun's blue when it rises in the morning. A glittering, vibrant, mountain lake blue. As bright as ever, as warming, the same size. But blue.

Outside the glass bars of the domed cage the road is littered with the bodies of the dead. Lykans – that's what Cheryl calls the beasts – feed on them, carving them open and burrowing for scraps. One spots us and hurls itself at the cage. The bars shake and vibrate but hold firm. The lykan thrusts an arm through but gives up when it realises it can't reach us. It returns to the corpses, pops a skull open, scrapes out a chunk of brain and tucks in.

When the lykans first attacked the cage, I was sure they'd break it, but they didn't. According to Cheryl, they can't.

The magic of the sandmen is too strong. She's taking this in her stride. Can't understand why I'm so distressed.

"They're just lykans, Newman," she laughs.

"This has happened before?" I ask.

"Of course," she says. "Many times."

"Why didn't you tell me about it?" I snarl.

She shrugs. "It's not something I think about, except when the moon turns."

I ask how frequently the moon changes colour but she can't answer that. "When it's white, it's white," she says. "When it's red, it's red."

"How long will it stay this way?"

"It varies. Sometimes a day or two, sometimes three or four."

Three or four days... I stare through the bars. Most of the lykans have moved on to fresher pastures, but there are still enough of them lurking nearby to make leaving the cage a definite no-no.

"What are we going to eat?" I ask. "What will we drink?"

"Drones," Cheryl says. "They'll come out in their droves soon. We'll call some over and feast at will."

"And when the sun and moon revert to normal?" I ask. "What happens then? Do the lykans change back?"

Cheryl shakes her head. "No," she says sadly. "You're lost once you turn."

"So what do we do about them?" I ask.

"They'll be taken care of," she promises but refuses to elaborate.

*

As Cheryl predicted, drones soon start passing by, oblivious to the marauding lykans, who pay them as little attention in return. Cheryl summons one to the cage. It sticks an arm through the bars and she chews the waxy flesh. Glances over her shoulder at me. "You want some of this or not?" she asks between mouthfuls.

I take a couple of steps forward and stare at the sappy interior which she's exposed. I study the drone's expressionless face. Sigh. Drop to my knees and grab the other arm.

The blue sun descends and the red moon rises. The screams of the lykans and their victims have been dying away all day and now silence falls over the city, broken only occasionally by the startled shriek of a rumbled hider and the gleeful howl of a ravaging lykan.

A boy no more than eight or nine races down the middle of our road, leaping over corpses and abandoned cars. It looks like he's making a beeline for us, to ask for help, but he swerves at the last second and continues past, barely sparing us a glance. About fifteen metres further on, a lykan leaps up from behind a mound of bodies, where it had been lying in wait.

"Look out!" I yell but it's too late. The child goes down to one brisk, clawing strike and doesn't even have time to scream.

I turn away from the miserable sight and stare bitterly at Cheryl.

"What's wrong?" she asks, shifting uncomfortably as I glare at her.

"*What's wrong?*" I explode. "We've just seen a child being torn to pieces by a once-human monstrosity, and you want to know *what's wrong?*"

She shrugs. "The kid wasn't fast enough to make it to safety. I didn't know him. Why should it be any concern of mine?"

"Don't you feel anything for your fellow human beings?" I snap.

"No," she answers plainly. "I care about you because I'm in love with you. And I hope Franz and Kipp pull through because I like them. And there are a couple of people at work I'll miss if they turn or are killed. But as for everyone else..." Again, the shrug. "What are they to me?"

"Jesus," I snort. "I thought *I* was a cold fish but you people... you're..." I shake my head with weary disgust. "Oh, just forget I spoke."

I stare moodily at the scenes of carnage, then up at the red-rinsed moon. No point blaming Cheryl. This is just how the locals are. There's no communal spirit. People are polite, obey the unwritten laws, pull together when they have to, but they don't care about one another. Maybe it's because they don't have families. Perhaps emotions can't fully develop in a society which prioritises the individual at the expense of...

Hell, hark at Mr Sociologist. That's what happens when sobriety sets in. A good booze up is what I need. A few pints, followed by some shots, and I'd be merrily chatting about work, holidays and strippers, not the *prioritising of individuals*.

Another lykan slams against the bars of the cage. This time I don't even blink. It drops to all fours and growls at me. I stare back at it and smile. "Don't suppose you know the way to the nearest off-licence, do you, guv?" In answer, it lifts a leg and pisses by the base of the dome. "Nope," I say cheerily, "thought not."

It's early afternoon the next day when the sun's blue mask fades to reveal its old, familiar face. The change is so gradual that it takes me several minutes to realise what's happening. Cheryl's asleep, having popped one of her pills a few hours ago. When it dawns on me that the madness has come to an end, I shake her roughly and jolt her out of her drug-induced slumber. "Cheryl. It's over. Wake up."

"What's happening?" she yawns, groggily rubbing her eyes. "Why are you waking me? It's too soon. I haven't slept long enough."

"It's over," I hoot, picking her up and twirling her round. "The sun's back to normal."

She looks up and scowls. "So it's back. I told you it would be."

"Aren't you excited?" I laugh. "We can leave now and —"

"No we can't," she says, still yawning. "We have to wait for the clearing."

"What are you talking about?" I frown.

She points towards a couple of lykans lurking nearby. "You want to go out while those are still on the loose? No," she chuckles as my face drops, "didn't think you would. Lie down, Newman. Take a pill. You'll know when it's properly over, trust me."

With that, she makes herself comfortable and drops off again, leaving me in the company of the lykans, to wonder what will happen during the *clearing*.

For a long time nothing changes. The sun drops. The moon – back to its normal colour – rises. Stars twinkle. Lykans brush by our cage or give the bars a shake to test them. Drones patrol the streets, to be fed on by the hungry. I haven't seen any humans since the boy ran by. Haven't heard any screams either.

I'm watching a lykan scratch behind its ears with a foot when all of a sudden it stops and sniffs the air. Two more a short way off are doing the same. After a few seconds, one turns and flees, but the others stand their ground, growling softly.

For several minutes there's a tense stalemate. The lykans hold tight, growling, looking worried. Then another lykan comes pounding round a corner and dashes past. Shortly after that, a pack of lykans tears into sight and floods by our cage. Two of them stop, hesitate, then retrace their steps and join the pair who didn't move as the rest fled. The four lykans look oddly courageous, like stubborn warriors guarding their turf as all hell breaks loose around them. I could almost admire them if they weren't so God damned bestial.

Footsteps approach, the sound of a group of people marching military-style. The lykans crowd closer together and crouch. A man rounds the corner, followed by nine others dressed in blue and red striped uniforms, carrying crossbows, swords strapped to their sides. The leader spots the lykans, stops and barks an order. Six of the soldiers — I'm assuming that's what they are — step forward, while he joins the three at the rear. Four of the six kneel, while the other two stay on their feet. All six aim their crossbows and prepare to fire.

The lykans are snarling now, howling threateningly, shaking their claws at the humans, warning them to stay away. One makes a darting feint but returns quickly to its comrades when nobody breaks ranks to meet its challenge. The four take a few nervous, backward paces, growl unintelligibly to one another, then get ready to attack. It's a noble but futile gesture and for the briefest second — before I remember what they are and what they've done — I will them on against the odds.

As one, the lykans roar viciously and lunge forward at incredible speed, fangs opening and shutting like steel traps, claws extended. The soldiers fire in unison. Six arrows find their targets and the four lykans shriek, jerk to a halt and plummet to the ground, jets of hot red blood already soaking the hair of their malformed chests and faces.

The four soldiers to the rear of the archers advance, swords drawn, and thrust the tips through the hearts of the lykans, taking no chances. The six with the crossbows reload, then join the others. The one who was leading the way when they turned the corner sheathes his sword, checks his crossbow and once more takes the frontal position while the other nine line up behind him. They resume their determined march.

As they pass the dome the leader smiles at me. "Good evening," he says, half-saluting with his sword.

"Evening," I reply automatically.

"Everything fine?" he asks.

"Dandy," I say weakly.

"We're almost done with the clearing," he says. "You should be out by dawn. Be careful though. A few always escape the net. I'd carry a noose for the next couple of days if I were you."

"Thanks for the advice," I mutter and watch wide-eyed as they file out of sight further down the road.

I describe the soldiers to Cheryl when she wakes but the news comes as no surprise. "They're the wolfers," she informs me matter-of-factly. "They work for the Alchemist. They turn up when the sun and moon sort themselves out, hunt the lykans, kill or drive them away."

"And that's the clearing?" I ask.

"The first stage, yes. The sandmen come next to dismantle the cages – they're the only ones who can break them down – then the baggers who remove the bodies and cart them away for burning or burial or whatever they do with them."

"Do you know what this cage is made of?" I ask as we wait for the sandman.

"Glass," Cheryl says.

"Are cages always made of glass?" She nods. "So how come you pretended not to know what glass was when I asked you about it before?"

"Did I?" She looks blank.

"I've been trying to describe glass to people ever since I arrived in this place and not one of you claimed to know anything about it."

She shrugs. "There are things I only know when I need them. When the moon or sun changes colour, I know I have to find a sandman and build a cage. The rest of the time, that information isn't needed, so my brain doesn't bother me with it."

"Of course it's needed," I argue heatedly. "If you knew the moon was going to do something crazy, you could have prepared for it. We could have bought bags of magic sand and carried them with us, so we wouldn't have had to risk life and limb while searching for a sandman."

She frowns. "I never thought of that."

"Maybe you should start thinking," I snort. Sometimes these people show no more sense than their drones. I'm surprised so many of them have lasted this long.

The sandman – a man this time – arrives with a minimum of pomp and four visibly less tense guards. "Stand in the centre, please," he says. Cheryl obeys immediately and I join her. "Close your eyes."

As I comply with his request, there's a shattering noise. My eyelids fly open and I discover myself standing in the middle of a circle of sand. I thought my clothes might have returned but they haven't. I cover my privates with my hands but the sandman shows no interest in my genitals, nor Cheryl's.

"Have a good day," the sandman says, turning away.

"Hold on," I shout, stepping towards him, only to find my path blocked by four bristling guards. I edge backwards and raise my hands to show I mean no harm.

"Let him be," the sandman says, then raises an eyebrow at me. "You wish to ask something?"

"I want to know what happened," I mutter. "Why did the moon change? How often does this happen? When can we expect it to change again?"

The sandman shrugs. "Who can predict the workings of the sun and moon? They change of their own will, not man's. Even the Alchemist can't say for certain when the transformations are due."

"Alright," I growl, "but why aren't your bags of magic sand readily available? They should be hanging up like nooses. Why leave their distribution until the last minute? And why are so few handed out?"

The sandman smiles benignly. "Maybe there's not enough sand to go around."

"You don't know?" I ask.

"No."

"Does the Alchemist?" I press.

"Possibly," the sandman says. "He supplies us with the bags."

"You've never asked him about it?"

The sandman laughs. "One doesn't question the ways of the Alchemist, not if one enjoys one's job."

"How can I meet the Alchemist? Where does he hang out?"

The sandman's nose crinkles. "The Alchemist doesn't make himself available to the general public. His responsibilities are many. He doesn't have time to waste on personal meetings. Having said that, I'll pass on any message you care to give me for him, if that's acceptable." The sandman smiles graciously.

"It's not," I grunt.

The sandman's smile freezes. "In that case, there's no more I can say. Good day to you, sir." He turns and walks away.

"Wait," I shout and start after him. The guards intervene again and this time the sandman doesn't stop them, so I play it safe, back off and let him leave.

"Come on," a nervous Cheryl says, taking hold of my arm and attempting to kiss away my frown. "Let's go find some clothes. There are shops where they'll be giving them away for free. It's part of the clearing."

"We should pick up the sand," I murmur. "It might come in useful next time."

"No," she says. "The magic only works once."

"How do you know?" I ask.

She shrugs. "I just do. Are you coming or not?"

I stare at the sand, then at the bodies of the lykans and slaughtered humans. The first few baggers appear, stocky men and women with large black bags, into which they pile the remains of the dead, lykan and human bundled in together. The baggers look bored, as if this was part of a mundane garbage collection.

"Yeah," I sigh, "I'm coming." Then I take Cheryl's hand and turn my back on the sand, the bloodshed and all the unanswered questions, and off we meander to find replacement clothing, Sunday shopping, city-style.

TWELVE

And so life returns to normal. The clearing takes another three days, by which time all the bodies have been disposed of and the blood washed away. Walking the streets, you'd never know there'd been massacres galore mere days before.

The population has slumped dramatically and suddenly the lines outside popular factories and nourishment houses are a thing of the past. Employers are desperate for workers, while shops and boarding houses are crying out for customers. I could get a day job if I wanted, top pay, to supplement my income from Kipp's, but I can't be bothered. I'm earning enough as things stand. Right now, time is more important to me than teeth.

Vin didn't survive the lykan assaults, one of the untold thousands of fatalities. Sorely missed by all who knew him. People might not boast many friends in this emotional iceberg of a city but Vin was popular. Lots of drone sap is devoured in his honour.

Franz and Kipp pulled through, Kipp in a cage like ours, Franz in the basement of his boarding house. It's the second time he's taken shelter there, he tells me one night as I'm pumping him for information about lykans and wolfers. He's been fortunate but doesn't fancy his chances a third time. "From now on I run and search for a sandman," he says. "There's nothing worse than being holed up in a makeshift cage, not a bar of glass in sight."

Everybody knows what glass is now. They still don't know the name of the city – "Where do you think you are?"

remains the common refrain if I ask — or what electricity is, but glass? Glass is what the sandmen's cages are made of. Every old fool knows that.

Except, a couple of days later, every old fool *doesn't*. They begin to forget as we move further away from the slaughter. The red moon and blue sun are forgotten and people stare at me oddly if I mention them. The lykans become creatures of myth again, popular in stories — in which they're normally man-eating drones — but not something grown people believe in. Glass — what's that? Even the popular Vin is cast adrift somewhere in the collective memory banks, lost to the confines of the past. You wouldn't want to be concerned about posterity in this city. Here, the present is all. *All*.

And so, as I said, life returns to normal for everyone… except me. I can't go back. I'd been willing to buy into this skewed reality, to accept the city for what it is and do my best to drift along unobtrusively, but no longer, not now I know that the sun can turn blue at the drop of a hat, or the moon redden any night while I'm asleep. I was lucky this time but I can't rely on the fickle hand of fate.

I've got to find out why people change into lykans, how often it happens and how it can be averted. I have to track down the answers, no matter how many blank walls I crash into along the way, otherwise how will I sleep at night or endure the days? Cheryl, Franz and the others are blessed in a way. Their position's as precarious as mine, but thanks to their fragile hold on the past, they don't realise it. I'm cursed with a fully functioning memory. I can't sit back and accept life as they do. Roll on the quest for knowledge.

The Alchemist is the man I'm after, although I'd settle for a long conversation with a sandman or a wolfer, even a bagger if that's the best I can do, but nobody I spoke with – before their memories began to evaporate – knew how to find any of those mysterious beings. They just turn up at the appropriate moment, seemingly out of nowhere.

My first port of call is a public contact box. I'm pretty sure the line of enquiry won't lead anywhere but I've nothing to lose trying.

"Operator Lewgan here, how may I help you?"

Good grief. Her again.

"Lewgie, baby," I boom. "How've you been? Are you the only one manning the lines or is Cupid trying to pitch the two of us together?"

She coughs, flustered, and I picture her blushing. "I'm sorry," she says coyly, "but who is this?"

"It's Newman Riplan. I was on to you a while back, asking about planes and outside worlds and –"

"Oh. Mr Riplan." Icy now, blushing no longer, nothing wrong with *her* memory, at least where I'm concerned. "What do you want?"

"I've a few specific queries this time, you'll be glad to hear," I chuckle. "But first, do you know anything about a red moon, a blue sun and a pack of destructive lykans who recently ran riot through the city?"

"Please, Mr Riplan, if you're going to waste my time, why

don't you –"

"No worries," I interrupt, "it was a long shot, forget it. I'd like to speak with the Alchemist if I could."

She hesitates. "I can't get you a direct line."

"How about putting me through to one of his assistants then? Somebody close to him, his right-hand man or woman."

"I'm sorry," Lewgan says, "but the Alchemist's key personnel are off-limits to the public. If you wish, I can take a message and pass it along."

"There's no other way of getting in touch with him?" I groan.

"Not through me," she says.

"OK," I sigh. "In that case, please tell him that Newman Riplan's looking for him. I assume he'll know where to find me?"

"Of course," she laughs.

"How about the sandmen?" I ask. "Can you connect me with one of them?"

"Do you mean someone who sells sand?" she asks.

"No," I tut, "I mean the guys and gals who come out when the moon turns red and dispense bags of magic sand that turn into glass cages."

She sucks on her teeth for a second. "Magic bags of sand. Cages of... grass?"

"Glass," I correct her. "With an L."

"Ah," she says.

"You don't know what I'm talking about, do you?" I smile.

"I'm afraid not."

"How about wolfers and baggers?"

"I know some garbage baggers," she says helpfully.

I press her for information for a couple more minutes but if she knows anything about the lykans and the people who combat them, she isn't telling. I ask how she accounts for the sudden population drop but she's unaware there's been one. As far as she's aware, the city's the same as ever. Long lines of jobseekers? There have never been long lines. Nourishment houses packed wall-to-wall with customers? A ludicrous notion. Doesn't happen. Never happened. Not enough people in the city.

"What about death?" I ask. "You know what death is, don't you?"

"Naturally," she says.

"What happens when somebody dies? Numbers drop then, don't they?"

"Marginally," she concedes, "but hardly enough to make a difference."

"But what happens when *everyone* dies?" I press. "All of the people alive today are going to die eventually, aren't they?"

"I assume so," she agrees.

"Who'll replace them? Where will new faces come from?"

"Hmm." She considers it a while. "It's something of a paradox, isn't it? I never thought of it like that. Still, things will work out. They always have done. The Alchemist takes good care of us."

I ask her how many undertakers there are in the city but she isn't familiar with that term. When I explain what an undertaker is, she gets it and says that they're called boxers.

"So how many boxers are there?"

"Lots," comes the vague reply. I ask her to put me in touch with one of her choice and she patches me through. The person I speak with doesn't recall dealing with a mass of dead bodies any time in the recent past.

"Business is normally pretty slow," he tells me. His firm rarely handle more than three or four bodies a day. I ask what they do with the corpses. "We strip them," he says cheerfully. "All their belongings are ours — salvage rights. Then we chop off their arms and legs and stuff them in a box."

"Why cut off the limbs?" I ask.

"Convenience," he says. "They fit into a smaller box that way."

"What happens next?" I ask, shuddering at his good-natured indifference.

"We stack them until we've got fifteen or sixteen," he says, "then cart them to the body dump. That's a big field where all the bodies of the dead wind up."

"Can anyone go there?" I ask.

"Sure," he laughs, "though why you'd want to beats me."

"Thanks for your time," I say and hang up, then let myself out and hail a public car to take me to the dump.

The body dump's little more than a huge, desolate waste area in which scores of small brown boxes have been junked. I'd like to get out and search some of them but the place is full of animals – even a couple of stray lykans who must have slipped through the net as the wolfer warned – ripping open coffins and feasting on the remains of the dead.

The driver – his name's Conor – taps his wheel uneasily and keeps a careful eye on the animals closest the car. "Never been here before," he mutters, "and I never want to come again. This place gives me the chills."

"Who stacks the boxes?" I ask.

"The dumpmen," he replies. "The boxers bring them to the edge of the dump and leave them there for the dumpmen to sort."

"Where do the dumpmen hang out?" I ask.

"Dunno," Conor says, "and I don't care. You want to look for them, fine, out you hop and off you set. Me, I'm sitting tight and getting the snuff out of here at the first sign of trouble."

I'd like to meet one of the dumpmen, to ask how many boxes they process on an average day, but I don't dare risk being stranded. Finding a public car out here would, I'd imagine, be damn near impossible. I do a rough count of the coffins — as near as I can make out, there can't be more than three hundred, which is peanuts for a city this size.

"Are there other body dumps?" I ask.

"Nah," Conor says.

"You're sure?"

"Positive. Isn't one enough? They should burn the snuffing bodies, not leave them here for scavengers. Ready to go?" Conor asks, edgy and impatient.

I stare at a tiger-like creature gnawing on the bones of an unidentifiable corpse. The snapping noises would have put the fear of God into me in the other world but I've seen worse in my time here. I'm trying to figure out what happened to the people killed by the lykans. They obviously haven't been brought here — I've no way of knowing how many perished at the hands of the lykans, but the number must have been in the thousands — so where did they end up? Maybe they were dumped outside the city boundaries. If that's the case, the dead might be able to point the way out of this city, but only if I can track them down.

"I've had enough of this," Conor snaps, losing his nerve. "I'm getting out. You with me or not?"

"OK," I sigh, sliding away from the glassless window. "Take me..." Where? Where should I start my search for the dead and those who deal with them? No point asking him to take me to the edge of town — he wouldn't know what that means. "Just take me back where we came from," I decide and spend the rest of the ride reflecting on which of the limited avenues available to me I should next set out to explore.

I continue working at Kipp's. Business isn't as good as it was but my wages have increased since he can't afford to let me go — without the small crowds my act pulls in he'd probably have to close. I'm still in a relationship with Cheryl, though I'm investing less time and effort in it these days. Who can concentrate on affairs of the heart when there are riddles the length and breadth of London's Tube system to be unravelled? Cheryl's confused and dismayed by my emotional withdrawal but she's prepared to overlook it for the time being, hoping I'll get over whatever's bugging me and find my way back to her.

I spend my days travelling, asking questions of strangers while simultaneously trying to map the city streets. I apply my own names for future reference, most of them borrowed from London, thus my maps include references to Great Russell Street, the Strand, Embankment, Oxford Street and so on. Hey, I never claimed to be original. I'm a troubleshooter, not a wordsmith.

My questions yield no answers but I don't let that deter me. I'll go through every single citizen if I have to, then go through them again in case their memories improve in the interim. At least this way I'm exercising some sort of control over my destiny. It's better than lounging around, waiting for the moon to flare and lykans to come a-knocking on my door.

I'm stopping random pedestrians in Fleet Street – about five hundred metres north of Franz's as the crow flies (not that any crows fly here — I've seen no birds in the city) – when bugle-like sounds fill the air and people drop to the floor, spreading themselves flat. I cast a panicked glance at the sun but it's its usual colour. Not wanting to appear out of place, I drop to a knee and try pinpointing the origin of the bugles.

A minute passes. Two or three. Then, sweeping round the corner that leads – if memory serves me correct – into the Old Kent Road, comes the strangest parade I've ever witnessed. Painted drones march at the fore, their skin daubed wildly with orange, pink and yellow paint. They're followed by two kangaroos which hop along in an orderly manner. After the kangaroos there's a large bus, decorated with flowers, various breeds of chattering monkeys visible through the windows. On top of the bus sits a man dressed in a flowing, multicoloured gown, liberally tossing handfuls of drone teeth over the supplicant crowds. Behind the bus trail gaggles of sandmen, wolfers and baggers, laughing and chatting among themselves. Bringing up the rear, more drones, with brushes that they clean the roads with as they pass.

I remain on my knee as the leading drones and kangaroos march (and hop) by. The man on top of the bus waves to me but I ignore him. My eyes are focused on the sandmen and co. to the rear. I get to my feet as the bus crawls past and step into the road to attract the attention of the parading humans. A wolfer spots me and frowns. "Roos," he shouts. "An agitator. Get him!"

"No," I say, hurrying towards him, smiling, "I'm not an agita–"

Something clumps the back of my head. I yell painfully and hit the pavement. Flipping around, I see the kangaroos, snarling and advancing menacingly. I always thought boxing kangaroos were fictional. Seems – in this city at least – that I underestimated the legends.

As I raise my hands to defend myself, the man on top of the bus issues a command. "Stop that," he snaps and the marsupials immediately adopt a more passive stance. "Bus — halt," the man barks and the vehicle slows to a standstill. The man walks to the edge of the roof, studies me, then jumps down and lands gracefully at my feet. Picking himself up, he brushes dust from his robes and smiles engagingly. "Are you the one who calls himself Newman Riplan?" he asks, eyes glittering. I nod numbly. "You're from an other place, aren't you? From the –" He waves a hand vaguely. "– outside world, yes?"

"Yes," I gasp, astonished.

"Thought so," he grins, then grabs my left hand and pumps it amiably. "I hear you've been looking for me," he says, then adds, though he needn't have, as I've already guessed his identity, "I'm the Alchemist. How do you do?"

The Alchemist hands his drone teeth to one of the monkeys, sends it up to take his place on top of the bus, then gives an order for the procession to continue without him. One of the wolfers – the one who first noticed me – asks if he should stay with us. "No," the Alchemist says. "I wish to exchange a few words in private with Mr Riplan. I'll catch up with you later."

The wolfer appears uneasy but accepts his commander's orders. As the last of the drones file past, the Alchemist checks the neighbourhood and spots a cosy nourishment house. "Shall we?" he asks, pointing towards it.

"Sure," I murmur light-headedly. "Whatever."

And off we trot.

"You know what the outside world is," I whisper.

We're tucking into a light meal of thinly carved drone slices. The Alchemist gulps his food down almost without chewing.

"You know what the outside world is," I say again when he fails to respond. This time he looks up and nods. "How? Nobody else does."

He shrugs and points to his mouth, which is full of food.

"Never mind that," I growl, leaning forward aggressively over the table. "What is this place? Where am I? How can I get back to the real world?"

"This..." The Alchemist swallows his last morsel of food and washes it down with a glass of sap. "This is the real world."

"Bullshit," I hiss. "The world I come from is the real one. This is a joke of a place, a cruel mockery of my own realm."

"Really?" he smiles, unoffended. "In that case, why don't you return home?"

"I can't," I moan.

"How strange," he purrs. "One would think the draw of the real world would be stronger than its fantastical counterpart. Could it be that this, as I've claimed, is real and the other was but a product of your imagination?"

I smile icily. "If that was the case, how come *you* know about it? If it only existed inside *my* head..."

"A sound argument," he admits. "Alas for you, my answer trumps it. I know about your world because I've met others who labour under the weight of similar delusions, people like you who believe there are other cities and lands, an entirely different universe, a world in which time is carefully measured and recorded, in which memories of the past stand side-by-side with those of the present, in which the moon and sun remain constant, in which glass is as commonplace as water, in which drones don't exist, in which... I could go on, but do I need to? Is this the world you believe you hail from? Have I described it accurately?"

I nod slowly. "So I'm not the first to cross between the two worlds? There have been others?"

"Many," the Alchemist says. "At the moment you're the only one but sometimes there have been five or six here at the same time. Confused, instinctless creatures, full of strange tales of aeroplanes, televisions and computers." He shakes his head. "If this world of yours does exist, it would be an interesting place to visit."

"But you couldn't visit it," I reply. "You can't get out of this city, can you?"

"No," he sighs, "I cannot. I'm not even sure what that means, though I believe my vague understanding – constructed over the course of many conversations such as this one – isn't so different to your perceived actuality. I've given a lot of thought to it over the... *years* is the term you use, is it not? A period of three hundred and sixty-five days?" He smirks when I look surprised. "I can't measure time as you do, but I can comprehend it. Weeks, months, years. In practice those terms mean nothing to me, but in theory I can absorb and reflect upon them."

"You're the only one I've met who's able to do that," I note.

"Because I'm different to other people," he says. "I'm the Alchemist."

"What does that mean exactly?" I ask. "Do you control

the city? Did you build it? Are these people your servants? Your children?"

"Please," he laughs, "not so many questions or you'll set my head spinning."

The owner of the nourishment house approaches, nervously wringing his hands. "Is everything to your satisfaction, gentlemen?" he asks, trying not to cringe as he comes face-to-face with the fabled Alchemist.

"Everything is wonderful," the Alchemist says.

"Would you care for dessert?" the owner asks, beaming proudly. "On the house, of course."

"I will have dessert," the Alchemist decides, "but I'll pay for it. No," he says, as the owner opens his mouth to argue, "I always pay my way."

"As you wish," the owner chuckles and retires to fetch a menu.

"I can't tell you the name of this city," the Alchemist murmurs, his eyes fixed intently on mine, "because it doesn't have one. I can't describe the founding of the city because my inherent understanding of time doesn't allow for such devices as starts and finishes. As I see it, the city has always been here, as have I. Other people come and go, but the Alchemist stands firm."

"Like a god?" I ask wryly.

"Ah, gods," he grins. "Several of your kind have mistaken me for one. It's embarrassing when they do. I'm not a god. I'm a *caretaker*. I watch over these people, cater to their needs, make life as pleasant for them as it can be. I arrange the distribution of drones — and no, in answer to the question I see forming, I don't know where they come from. They arrive at what you call the airport and that is all I can tell you about them."

"You control the sandmen?" I ask and he nods. "Why aren't more bags of sand made available? If you care for these people, why let so many be slaughtered?"

He shrugs. "The sun and moon change occasionally, but if there's a pattern, I can't predict it. When I sense a change coming on, I summon my sandmen. There is a room – we call it, unimaginatively I must admit, the room of sand – and when we have all gathered outside, I open the door and enter. In the room I find bags of sand. Sometimes there are many, other times few. I hand them out and the sandmen disperse. That's the way it works. I don't know where the bags come from or how they get in the room or why there are so many or so few. That's why I'm not akin to these gods of your world. Unlike them, I'm merely a cog in the machine. I know more than the people I protect, but I don't have all the answers or anywhere near."

"You don't know how the magic works?" I ask.

"Haven't a clue," he chuckles.

"You've never tried keeping a few bags aside, for use in an emergency?"

"That would not be proper," he tuts.

"Says who?" I ask.

He taps the side of his head with his fingers. "The voice in here. The voice of instinct. You don't have such a voice, do you?"

"Not as you've described it, no."

"Your kind never do," he says thoughtfully. "I've often wondered which comes first, the dream world or the loss of instinct. Perhaps this other world is your brain's way of compensating for the lack of understanding which would steer you safely through this one. Or perhaps you lost your instinct when you dallied in your world of dreams."

"Or of reality," I add sharply.

He smiles condescendingly, then cocks his head. "Tell me, if your world is real, what do you think that makes this one?"

I shift uneasily in my seat. "I'm not sure."

"But you've thought about it?" he asks.

"Of course."

"And your conclusions?"

"It could be an alternate universe."

He frowns. "That term escapes me."

"It's an idea scientists and science-fiction writers in my world have posited," I explain. "They think there might be more than one universe, that different worlds are capable of inhabiting the same space at the same time."

He thinks it over. "An interesting thought, but if such worlds existed, don't you think crossing from one to another – as you and others before you have done – would be common? Wouldn't channels have been opened between neighbouring universes, and ideas and cultures exchanged?"

"Maybe, maybe not," I sniff. "I haven't given such matters much thought."

"If this isn't an alternate universe," he says, "what then?"

"It could be a vision. A mental aberration. Something my subconscious has constructed within the confines of my brain."

"In which case," he smiles, "that would make *you* the god. If this is your mind, this is your city. You should be able to do as you please. Can you?"

I shake my head slowly, helplessly.

"What other options have you considered?" he asks.

"I could be dead," I croak.

He frowns. "You don't look dead to me."

"Dead in my world," I mumble. "I've been back there a few times — sleeping pills allow me to return. The last couple of occasions, I seemed to be dead. That would make this the afterlife."

The Alchemist's frown deepens. "What's that?"

"Where I come from, many people believe in a world beyond our own. They think people live on after their body dies, that part of them survives."

"I see," he says, though he sounds uncertain. "But if this is a place where the dead people of your world come, wouldn't the rest of us have died there too, and so share your memories of it?"

"Not necessarily," I say. "One of the afterworlds my people believe in is called Heaven, and we're told that creatures called angels live there."

"You think we're angels?" the Alchemist asks, no trace of irony in his question.

"No," I smile, "but you could be indigenous. Or you might have come from my world but lost your memories along the way."

"Hmm," the Alchemist says. "Intriguing. But if that was the case, don't you..."

The desserts arrive, cold drone innards, and we tuck in, abandoning the conversation for a time — the Alchemist isn't one to gabble and gobble. He pays the bill when we finish and we take our leave. We stroll along unnoticed in the streets, people paying no attention to us. His gown keeps snagging, meaning we have to stop frequently in order for him to adjust it.

"Where do the people of this city come from?" I ask. "You told me earlier that they come and go, but nobody I've spoken with seems to know anything about birth or ageing."

"Birth..." he reflects. "I've discussed birth with your fellow outsiders. You believe humans reproduce, that men and women mate and create babies, who grow and spawn children of their own?"

"Yes."

He smiles. "This seems logical to you?"

"Of course," I frown. "Why, what's your explanation?"

He shrugs. "I have none. People are. When they die, they are not."

"But where do they come from?" I press. "How did all these people get here? Do you know?"

He hesitates. "I think so, but I'm not sure."

"You mean it's part of your instinctual knowledge, that it only comes to the surface when prompted by specific events?"

"Ah," he winks, "you're beginning to understand our ways. That's good. Some of your kind never get to grips with us. They remain rooted in the ways of their other place, rejecting change. They generally don't survive very long. Belief isn't necessary to thrive in this city, but understanding is. I think you'll fit in nicely, Newman Riplan. You have what it takes."

"Yeah," I grin sarcastically, "I've got the right stuff."

Our talk drags on for hours. The Alchemist is an inquisitive soul and genuinely wants to aid me in my quest for answers. He doesn't come right out and say so but I think he also feels out of place. He knows – maybe only deep down – that this city doesn't make sense, that people can't just appear out of the blue, that the sun and moon should be constant, that the forces of chaos and order should be more evenly balanced.

I ask where he lives but he won't or can't tell me. Nor can he describe where the wolfers, sandmen or baggers stay, how he recruits them or what they do to kill time between attacks. "They're different to other people," he says. "Like those you met at the drone port, Jess, Phil and Bryan. They have a firmer concept of the past and more of a comprehending of the exterior forces acting upon those of us here. If this world is a successor to yours, perhaps the sandmen and the others are humans who've retained fragments of old-world memories. Maybe they wind up in their jobs because they're the best equipped to handle them."

"If that's so," I wonder aloud, "what's *my* job? If a little recollection's enough for a position with the sandmen, what does my full memory entitle me to?"

The Alchemist shrugs and smiles. "If I know, I can't currently say."

"I have a purpose though?" I push.

"I think so," he says.

"But you've no idea what it is?"

He shakes his head. "Not at the moment." The Alchemist checks the falling sun and gathers up his robes. "I must be saying farewell."

"You're leaving?" I ask dolefully.

"I've spent too much time with you already," he says. "There are things I must attend to, operations I must oversee. I don't have what you would call a schedule, but my days are full. This city doesn't run itself, even if it often seems that way."

I don't like the idea of losing contact with him. There are still a thousand questions I want to ask. "Let me come with you," I suggest. "If I see you in action, maybe I'll learn more about you, this city and my place in it."

"Sorry," he says, "but that's not permissible. I'd like to take you with me – I enjoy your company and the way you stimulate my mind – but it's not allowed."

"What if I want to get in touch with you again?" I ask. "How can I find you?"

"You can't," he says. "There's no way to directly contact me. I will know if you wish to find me – word spreads quickly – but may not be able to respond. I never know what duties I'll be required to perform day to day."

"What if I unearth the truth?" I smile. "Do you want to know about it?"

His smile matches mine. "I most certainly do."

"But how can I let you know if I don't know where to find you?" I ask.

"If the situation arises, you'll find a way," he assures me. "Of that I have no doubt."

The Alchemist shakes my hand. Ahead of us I spot a handful of wolfers waiting for him. Have they been following us or did they somehow sense where he would be and when? I think about asking the question but feel it would go unanswered.

"Good luck with your quest," the Alchemist says.

"Thanks," I sniff.

"But be careful," he warns. "This city can be cruel. You might be cut out for something wonderful in the future, but destiny – I think that's the right word – won't protect you from the perils of the present."

He joins the wolfers and they depart. As I turn and dig out my map to find the way home, I spot a giraffe loping down the road that – a quick glance at the map – leads into Piccadilly Square. I look for the Alchemist – I'd meant to ask him where the animals came from – but he's gone. Oh well, he probably wouldn't have been able to tell me anyway.

Home, I decide, to tell Cheryl about my audience with the Alchemist, and then to brainstorm, mull over and plan.

THIRTEEN

A couple of days have passed since my encounter with the Alchemist. I've spent the time pondering my next move. I haven't been very good company and can feel Cheryl growing more frustrated by the day. She's never been in a relationship that's cooled. For her it's always been hot, committed love followed by a clean, crisp break. She doesn't know how to deal with my mood swings and mixed signals. If I told her I'd lost interest and wanted to leave, she'd be fine, but she can't understand how I can want to stay but not be entirely in love with her at the same time.

Finally, having made up my mind, I arrange a special night out, the fanciest nourishment house I can find, the grandest public car to convey us there, flowers, the lot. She arrives home from the candle-making factory, unaware of my romantic intentions, and nearly drops when she spots the beautiful dress draped across the bed, the new shoes, the erotic red candles.

"What's going on?" she gasps.

"A treat," I smile. "I'm taking you out. Unless you've other plans…?"

She kisses me wildly, then slips out of her clothes and into the new gear. She almost rips the dress, she's in such a hurry to try it on. I watch with a warm smile, sad there isn't a mirror for her to admire herself in, then get into my own suit. As I'm adjusting the top button on the shirt my hands automatically slide up to rub my jowls, as they usually do when I've washed, shaved and spruced myself up, and that's when – amazingly, for the first time – I realise that, though I haven't shaved since arriving here, my face is as smooth as the proverbial baby's bottom.

Cheryl knows nothing about razor blades or shaving when I ask. "But I've seen people with beards," I grunt. "I've seen a few women with hairy legs too."

"Sure," she says. "Anyone can grow hair. I don't know about getting rid of it though. If you grow it, I think you're stuck with it."

"How do you grow it?" I ask.

"Before you go to sleep, picture it in your mind," she says, "where you want the hair to sprout and what you want it to look like."

"And it'll be there the next morning?" I ask incredulously.

"No," she giggles, "but stubble will have emerged. You keep doing the same thing, night after night, until you're satisfied with the result, then you stop."

I've never bothered with a beard before but it would be nice to try something new. I rub my face and wonder what it would look like bearded. Maybe the hair won't develop – you might need to take sleeping pills for it to work – but I think, in light of the circumstances, I'll give it a shot. After all, shouldn't every explorer have a crazy, bushy beard?

The night proceeds splendidly. We arrive at the nourishment house in style and are seated at the best table, on a hanging platform with a bird's eye view of the entire room. Waiters present us with elaborate menus, from which we choose the priciest items, no expense spared. There's no wine in this city — as I believe I've already indicated — but they have casks of specially treated sap, which lacks an alcoholic buzz but leaves something of a similar taste in the mouth.

Cheryl studies the other women and remarks on their clothes and how drab they look compared to her gorgeous costume. "I'm glad you like it," I grin. "I wasn't sure you would." (Like hell I wasn't.)

"Oh no," she assures me, "it's magnificent. But it must have cost as much as a car. How could you afford it?"

"Mugged a coach-load of drones on the way in from the airport," I smirk but the joke sails over her head.

We go for a walk after the meal, by the banks of the prettiest canal I could find. Water lilies drift across the still surface like little green messages, while frogs — a rarity in the city, where most of the animals are of the more savage variety — croak melodically in the background. Cheryl sighs happily and rests her head on my shoulder. "This is wonderful," she says softly, "the most perfect night I've known. Thank you."

"I'd spare the thanks if I were you," I chuckle edgily. "There's a stinger."

"A what?" she asks.

"I had a hidden motive. I didn't arrange this night for the noblest of reasons."

She stops and frowns. "What do you mean?"

I take a deep breath. "I'm leaving. I wanted this night to be special because it's going to be our last together for some time, maybe forever."

"I don't understand," she says. "Have you fallen out of

love with me?" I shake my head. "Tell me if you have," she snaps. "I know a bit about how your mind works. If you're saying you still love me just to spare my feelings…"

"I'm not," I promise. "I do love you. In another place, another time, I'd be delighted to –"

"Stop saying that!" she shouts. "There are no other places or times. I've had enough of those lame excuses. I've made allowances because you're different to most people, but those differences don't mean you're free to play with my feelings and treat me like a beast."

"It's not like that," I groan. "I'd stay with you if I could – God knows, it's the easiest option – but this isn't my city, not even my world. I've got to try and find a way back to my own."

"Then take me with you," she says.

"No," I say firmly. "It's too dangerous. I don't know where I'm going or what I'll run up against. Besides, if I find a way back, you might not be able to make it with me. Even if you could, I don't think you'd like my world. You'd no more fit in there than I do here. If possible, I'll try returning for you, but I can't make any promises."

"What if you fail?" she asks quietly. "What if you can't return, or wake up to the fact that there's nowhere to return *to*, that this city is all there is? What then?"

I shrug. "I'm trying not to think negatively. Things are going to be hard enough as they are without admitting defeat before I begin."

"Well," Cheryl says coolly, "if you think you can waltz back and pick up where you left off, forget it." She kicks off her shoes and starts to take off her dress.

"What are you doing?" I ask, alarmed.

"I don't want your shit," she snarls, a rare and atypical curse.

"Cheryl, don't be silly, you can't –"

"I can do what I like, you bastard," she cries. (That's a word I taught her. With no families, there can be no bastards. No sons of bitches or motherfuckers either.) "You think you're such a big man, more important than the rest of us, that we're less human. Well, I've news for you, bastard, we're not! *You're* the one who isn't human, who acts like a freak."

She's out of the dress now. Throws it in the canal. Stands before me, naked and quivering with rage.

"Leave if you want," she says, angry tears sparkling in the corners of her eyes. "Go hunt for this other world of yours. Do what you like. You always do. But don't expect me to sit here and wait for you. I'm not half the fool you take me for. I don't care that I'm in love with you. My feelings can go snuff themselves. I'm through with you, Newman Riplan. I've had it with your selfish, ignorant ways. You say you're leaving?" She sneers through her tears. "Too late, bastard, because I've already left."

And she turns her back on me and storms off, a superb dramatic exit, bare, indignant buttocks illuminated by the soft canal lights.

I've felt a lot of things since that flight out of Amsterdam took a turn for the surreal. I've been scared, confused, angry, fascinated, alienated. I've known elation when I made my first return to the real world, and despair when I returned a second time. I've felt like a king, performing in Kipp's, and like a powerless slave more times than I can recall. But right now I just feel like a rat, a complete and utter scumbag of the highest order.

I return to Franz's and pack a bag, not much, just the essentials — a change of clothes, several pairs of socks, drone teeth, my maps. I tell Franz I'm leaving but that Cheryl may or may not be staying. He takes the news in his stride. "Even if she doesn't stay," he says, "I'll keep the room vacant in case you return."

"You don't have to," I reply. "I don't know when – if ever – I'll be back."

"That's OK," he smiles, "business is bad anyway. I probably couldn't rent it out even if I wanted."

I thank him and tip him a few teeth, then let myself out and hail a public car. I give the driver the name of a shop in a street at the farthest eastern edge of my charted maps. It doesn't take long to get there — traffic is never a problem at night. I check into a local boarding house and bed down. I remember the beard just before drifting off and fall asleep visualising it.

I rise with the sun and hit the streets. I face east and take a deep breath. This is it, the start of my great escape. I haven't seriously set out to leave the confines of the city before. Now I'm going to. I'll face the rising sun every day and walk till it drops behind me, find a boarding house and tuck in for the night, then set off again in the morning. This way I'm bound to make it out eventually. What I'll find is anybody's guess – maybe it'll be worse than what's here – but one thing's for sure. Whatever lies beyond, at least it won't be merely more of the same.

Walking fills my days. Every waking hour – bar a few set aside for refreshments and asking questions of the locals – is devoted to it. My legs have forgotten what inertia feels like. Even in sleep they twitch and strain, toes curling beneath the covers of unfamiliar beds. My feet will never forgive me for what I'm putting them through. I've almost worn out the shoes I began with, and they were nearly new when I started.

I've no idea how many kilometres I've covered, but it must be several hundred. It's been at least seventeen or eighteen days since I departed – I can't be any more accurate than that, since time doesn't mean so much when you're on the road – and I must surely be covering twenty or thirty klicks a day, maybe more.

My beard has come on in leaps and bounds, the growth far quicker here than in the other world. I like playing with it as I walk. I set out to wind it into braids, but that reminded me of Cheryl, so I quit. I'm sure I look a fright – beard to the chest, dusty from the road, wide-eyed from staring at the sun to check my direction – but I haven't been turned away from any boarding houses on account of my looks. In this city, teeth talk.

Five more days of walking, maybe six — I don't think it's

been more than seven. I bought a new pair of shoes yesterday and had huge, bubbling blisters growing out of my heels when I woke this morning. I thought about resting for the day but decided against it. Popped the blisters, wrapped makeshift bandages round my ankles and walked off the pain. I'll be in agony come night but as long as infection doesn't set in you won't find me complaining.

I've been expecting the city to change but have noticed nothing new in the architecture so far. Or the people.

"Where do you think you are?"

"What does *outside* mean?"

"The end of the city? How can the city have an end?"

I've asked public car drivers if they know how to get to Kipp's or Franz's. They do. I'm not sure how to react to their familiarity with my old stomping ground. On the one hand it's nice to know I can return if things go sour, but on the other it would be encouraging to wind up in a place where nobody knew anything about that other part of the city. It would give me the sense that I was getting somewhere.

I've taken to climbing tall buildings – I've never looked on this city from a height – but to no advantage. The few which tower above the others are devoid of windows on the higher storeys and access to their roofs is restricted. I've considered trying to scale the walls from the outside but I'm no daredevil. I'd be sure to fall and plummet to my death.

What would happen to me if I died here? Would I simply blink out of existence, as I always believed I would back in the real world? (I've taken to referring to it as that again, for the duration of the quest.) Or would I move on to a world even stranger than this? Perhaps there's an endless string of these hermetic worlds and death is simply a code required to pass from one to another. Maybe the real world wasn't my first experience of life. Perhaps, because of the way life operates there, it just seemed like that. I might have been knocking about between universes for thousands – millions – of years. I may even have been in positions like this before, where the memory of one life spills over into the next.

Hell, it's even possible that death will return me to good old Mother Earth. I've pretty much given up on my body – Newman Riplan's dead and gone in the world-that-was – but perhaps I could come back as someone or something else. Maybe the reincarnationists got it right and the soul is infinite, forever moving between bodies and worlds.

I ponder coming back as a child, memory banks wiped, life to live all over again, and can't decide whether that's an attractive or terrifying prospect. Either way, I'm in no rush to put an end to my current existence. I'm not that desperate.

Not yet.

I'm all out of drone teeth. Used my last one four nights ago to secure the most flea-ridden cot it's ever been my misfortune to associate with. The fuckers are still running riot behind my ears, in my hair and through my beard. I'll be scratching from now until doomsday.

I've slept in abandoned buildings two of the three nights since. Uncomfortable but adequate. The inbetween night, I got chased by an irate landlord and, too tired to look for another abode, ended up beneath a bush on the bank of a canal. It's dangerous sleeping outside – the city belongs to its army of wild animals at night – but I got lucky. I hope my luck holds. I'm sure I'll be needing more of it.

The enemaists catch up with me every night, even when I bed down outdoors. Different crews, but they all know my name and where to find me. Most of my enemas come while I'm awake – wary of attack, my body jerks me from the murky waters of sleep at the slightest rustle of an approach – but I don't mind. It's nice to have someone to talk with, even if they're not, in general, the most stimulating of conversationalists.

Another day spent on my feet, following the sun in the morning, leaving it behind in the afternoon. I'm exhausted come evening – I woke six times last night – so I find a bench and grab forty winks. A tugging sensation on my chin interrupts my snooze. Sitting up groggily, I'm amazed to discover most of my beard gone, only a thin, bristly layer left. Then I spot a chubby man fleeing with a familiar bushy bundle in one hand. I yell and give chase and, despite my sorry condition, soon catch up with the out-of-shape thief.

"What the snuff are you up to?" I shout.

"I'm sorry, I'm sorry," he cringes. "Here –" Handing me back the severed hair. "– have it. Just don't hurt me."

"What the snuff will I do with it now?" I roar, slapping it from his hand.

"Careful," he squeals, falling to his knees. "If you don't want it, I'll keep it."

"What for?" I gawp.

"Wigs," he says.

Turns out there's a booming hair-piece trade in this part of the city. Wigs are all the rage, with eleven wiggers plying their trade in the neighbourhood, and this man is one of those.

"But if people can grow hair at will," I mutter, "why do they need wigs?"

"Oh, they're not for humans," he tells me. "They're for drones." I do a double-take but he nods earnestly. "It's true. Many people who keep drones as servants want them to look more human, so they dress them up and stick wigs on them. Some even glue a few teeth back in their mouths."

"How much is a wig worth?" I ask speculatively.

"Depends," he says. "There's the quality of the hair to take into consideration, the workmanship, the reputation of the wigger, the wealth of the customer."

"Give me a general figure," I grunt.

He chews his lip and thinks hard before answering. "For a standard wig, twelve drone teeth, maybe as much as fifteen."

"Right," I tell him, "I'll take eight for the beard."

He argues – the hair is scraggly, in poor condition, full of fleas – but I have him by the short and curlies. Not only does he stand to lose the hair by haggling too hard, but under the brutal city laws I'm within my rights to smash his skull for touching my hair without my permission. In the end we agree on a finder's fee of six teeth, in return for which he takes me back to his shop, washes my hair, cuts off most of it – I feel like a change – and shaves me bare, using a special type of sharpened stone peculiar to wiggers.

"How come there are so many wiggers in this part of the city?" I ask. It's the first time I've encountered any kind of a difference in a local community and I'm hoping it means I've wandered into a new type of zone.

"Because of Barber," Cally – the mugger-slash-wigger – answers.

"Who's Barber?" I ask.

"A man who lived here," Cally says. "He taught us how to cut hair and make wigs. Until then, those were arts we hadn't contemplated, let alone mastered."

"Did you know Barber?" I ask.

"No," Cally says. "That was before I became a wigger. But people have told me about him."

"What sort of a man was he?"

"An oddball," Cally says. "He claimed to have come from an other city, if you can believe such a thing. Constantly asking people the oddest of questions."

So this sectioned clan of barbers are the product of a man like me, a visitor who brought the barber's arts with him when he wound up here. I'm disappointed, but at least it shows change is possible. I'd thought no man could leave a mark on this place but I was wrong. Barber – that was the only name anyone knew him by – had altered the flow of everyday life and left behind a legacy, despite the ground of the past being like so much quicksand here.

I book into a nice, clean boarding house with the teeth I got for my hair, take my time over a satisfying meal, then mount the stairs to bed, where I lie, rubbing my freshly shaven chin, waiting for sleep to come.

Broke. Shelterless. Hungry. No end in sight.

I feed on stray drones. Occasionally I waylay one as it goes about its chores but usually I can find some that have been abandoned by their owners because they're no longer useful, having lost limbs or been drained of too much sap. (The drones grow lethargic when they're low on sap.) The mannequins never put up a fight. They simply stand or lie there while I rip off their fingers or bite through the tough, waxy skin of their stomach walls.

I'm growing a beard again. Not for profit – I've left the wiggers far behind – simply because I've nothing better to do.

The weather has remained constant, warm and dry most of the time. I can't remember if I asked Cheryl about seasons, if they have summers and winters here. Wouldn't surprise me if they don't. Nothing surprises me any longer.

As far as I've travelled, public car drivers still know where Franz and Cheryl live. It depresses me when I stop one of them and ask – makes me feel that I'm not making any real progress – so I only rarely do that now.

I've given up on map-making. There doesn't seem to be any point. Part of me is convinced that this city goes on forever. That part believes that no matter how far I walk,

I'll always be the same distance from the non-existent end. I should turn and head back, except I'm too stubborn to admit defeat. I'll probably die walking. Hell, maybe my body won't notice I'm dead and will continue long after my spirit's fled, unto eternity.

I was attacked by a wolf this morning. It charged me while I was changing my socks. (I wash and change them every few days out of habit.) If it had arrived a few minutes earlier or later, I'd have been a goner. As it was, I managed to stuff a shoe down its throat. While it was choking, I grabbed a noose and choked the bastard. Cut it open once I'd killed it and feasted on its hot, steaming entrails, not caring what people would think if they saw me. I cut the wolf's flesh into strips and I'm carrying them draped round my neck. They won't last long but at least I'll have something to nibble on while I walk.

The wolf gnawed my left arm pretty bad. I wash it clean in a fountain and wrap a sock around the worst section, then carry on walking, ignoring the pain and not worrying about infection, figuring it might be for the best if I catch a fever and die in my sleep.

My wounds have healed and I've made a permanent switch from drones to animals. The first thing I do every morning is go on the prowl for scavengers. Yesterday I bagged a hedgehog-like animal, much tastier than I thought it would be. I caught a monkey this morning. Didn't like the way its eyes fixed on me as I caved its head in — it looked human.

I'll be leaving my simian cousins alone in future, though I ate the one I'd killed, as it wouldn't have been right to kill but not eat it.

One of these days I'll target a lion. Just me and a noose, up against nature's most lethal killer. The thought of tackling a lion thrills me. I'm not sure why, and I don't devote much thought to it. I just keep my eyes peeled, my teeth bared and a noose close at hand.

Weeks pass, no sign of a lion. I wonder where they hang out? Perhaps I'll lay a trap for one. Capture a smaller animal and use it as bait. I could try locating them by their spoors, except street cleaners dispose of the dung on an annoyingly regular basis.

Here, kitty-kitty. Here, kitty-kitty. Here...

Still no lions. I thought I spotted one a couple of days ago but it turned out to be an overgrown cat/sheep hybrid. No good. I won't settle for anything less than the king of the jungle. Newman Riplan's never settled for second best and isn't about to start now. I'll find one eventually. All good things to those who wait.

My beard's so long, I probably look a little like a lion myself. Maybe I should start crawling about on all fours and attract one that way, like calling to like.

I remain on my steady, eastern setting. I only detour north or south if I run into a dead-end and then, as soon as I find a path around whatever happens to be obstructing me, it's east again. I'm tempted to make a camp and stick to a specific area, to scout about until I chance upon a lion – or it chances on me – but I force myself to stay focused on the trek. I've got my priorities straight, just about. Escape first, lions second, even though part of me would rather it was the other way round.

Walking. No shoes. I got rid of them ages ago. Don't need them. Feet are so tough, it'd take a hammer and nail to pierce the flesh. I walked along with a small stone imbedded in my left heel for three days before noticing it. My clothes hang on me in rags. Beard down to my navel. I haven't washed since I don't know when. People avoid me in the streets now. Some must think I'm an actual animal, a new mutation, almost human in form. The blood of many kills is stained deep into my hands, my beard, my lips. Red like the moon when the lykans run wild.

Normally I move at a fast, shuffling gait, heading rapidly east for reasons I no longer properly recall, but for the last hour or so I've been slowing down, pausing to glance around, treading carefully, sensing danger. I'm not sure why I'm acting this way. I'd as soon press ahead at full speed but I've learnt not to ignore the subtle messages of my body's defence mechanisms, so I obey my instincts and take things slow, paying more attention to my surroundings. I even stop a few worried pedestrians and ask questions of them, but by their confused responses I assume I'm not making much sense. It's been so long since I used my vocal cords, I guess

I've forgotten how.

Gradually, the further I progress, the more I understand why I'm feeling so uneasy. This place is familiar. Of course the entire city looks much the same, but this particular section...

I let my feet lead me down new but old streets, over fresh but recognisable terrain. My brain rejects the nightmarish realisation as long as it possibly can, but eventually, when I come to a halt before an unmistakable boarding house, I'm forced to acknowledge the crushing truth.

I thought I was beyond surprise but the sight I'm now presented with takes my breath away, wipes understanding away, strips me of every shred of reason I've ever struggled to cling to. I don't laugh or cry – I'm too stunned for such simple reactions – though I'm sure I will later, if I don't go completely mad first.

It's Franz's. Flying in the face of logic, despite the fact that I've been walking steadily east, I've returned to Franz's. After all these months or years of walking, I've reached the legendary end, only to find myself back at the beginning.

How's that for a kick between the legs?

FOURTEEN

Franz eyes me suspiciously as I limp from the door to the desk. He notes the filthy footprints I leave in my wake, my Gettysburg beard, the state of my clothes, my animal-like demeanour. Yet he bravely maintains his poise, and even manages a nervous little smile as I approach. "Yes, sir? May I be of some assistance?"

I open my mouth and utter an indecipherable croak.

Franz frowns. "I'm sorry, could you repeat that?"

I close my eyes and concentrate on the words. When I've got them clear in my mind, I speak. "It's... me. Newman... Riplan. I'm... back."

Franz frowns, then cautiously repeats my name. "Newman Riplan?" I watch his eyes, wondering if he's forgotten who I am. "It can't be," he mutters, leaning in closer – in spite of the stench – for a more probing examination. "Mr Riplan!" he gasps, spotting something familiar beneath the hair and dirt. "It *is* you. What has happened? How did you sink so low?"

"Long story," I sigh. "Did you keep my room as you said you would?"

Franz nods hesitantly. "But I can't let you up there like that," he says. "I have standards to maintain. My other guests would flee if they caught sight of you in such a state."

I do a little twirl, pretending to be surprised by his comments. "Why, Franz, whatever do you mean?" I wink to let him know I'm joking and he chuckles.

"Tell you what," he says, "let's go out back and see what we can do with you."

"Thanks," I smile. "You're a good friend."

He shrugs. "You're a good customer." He tuts. "Or were."

I strip naked and Franz chucks a bucket of water over me. Then another and another. After the eighth bucket he hands me a bar of rough soap and I work up a lather. He fetches more water while I'm rubbing in the soap and begins to rinse the suds out of my hair and back as I focus on my front and lower parts. When we finish, he hands me a second bar of soap and we start from the top again. By the end of the third bar I'm beginning to resemble a human being.

I use a knife to cut my hair and trim my beard. It's uncomfortable and I don't make a good job of it but it'll do for the time being. When I can afford it, I'll hire a public car and face the long drive to Barbersville. Right now I've other things to worry about.

"I can't pay for the room in advance," I tell Franz. "I haven't any drone teeth."

"I guessed as much," he laughs.

"You don't mind?"

He shakes his head. "I know you're good for the teeth. Kipp hasn't stopped talking about you since you left, whining about the drop in customers. He'll be so delighted to see you back that you'll be able to command double whatever you were earning before, which means I'll be able to hike up the rent."

It's odd that they've remembered me. I was sure they'd forget. But then, the barbers remembered their otherworld mentor as well. It seems that those of us from the outside are capable of making a lasting impression on the natives, even if they themselves are swiftly forgotten once they pass.

"Have you seen Cheryl recently?" I ask as I towel myself dry.

"Only every day," Franz replies.

"She's still here?" I'm surprised. After our last encounter, I expected her to make a clean break.

"Still here," Franz confirms. "Not in the same room – can't afford it on a single salary – but in the boarding house." He studies my naked form and purses his lips. "Would you like me to find some clothes for you before I take you to her?"

I grin. "Clothes sound like a good idea to me."

"Yes," Franz says, "me too."

Cheryl's delighted to see me. Rushes into my arms as soon as she opens her door and spots me. Drags me in and smothers me in kisses. She's been working the night shift, she tells me, which is why she's home at the moment.

"I missed you so much," she sobs. "I tried coming after you but nobody knew where to find you. No public car driver could locate you. They knew who you were but not where you'd got to. It was the first time any of them had encountered such failure. Usually they can find people, even if they're living the life of a wanderer, but not you."

"Have you forgiven me for leaving?" I ask meekly.

"Why should I have to forgive you?" she replies.

"The last time we were together, you said you never wanted to see me again," I remind her.

"No," she gasps, "I couldn't have."

"You don't recall our argument or your ultimatum?"

She shakes her head and I leave it at that. If she doesn't remember and is prepared to accept me back as if nothing untoward has happened, so much the better. I don't think I could handle a complicated reconciliation scene. Right now the simple life is the most attractive one. With no other worries, I can concentrate on trying to make sense of how I got back here and where I went wrong.

An evening of love-making, soft words and dim candles. Cheryl doesn't ask if I've been faithful — when you're in love in this city, you never cheat. She'd like to take the night off work but they're busy and she's been recently promoted.

"I'll be back before dawn," she promises. "We'll have more fun then."

"Can't wait," I grin and pat her bum as she scoots off. Once she's gone, I return to my own, old room – it looks the same as ever – make myself comfortable and fall to pondering.

Try as I might, I can't figure it out. I stuck to the same direction through the entire journey. I got pretty confused during the latter days – wanting to fight a lion with my bare hands and a noose! – but even in that wild state I stayed true to my course. Even when I'd forgotten why I was walking, I knew I had to walk east. One way, so there could be no mistakes. I'm not much of a navigator, but I know how to tell east from west. If I'd been working by compass or maps, I could put it down to faulty, misleading equipment, but the sun doesn't make mistakes or send you the wrong way. It can't. At least... in my world it can't. Here? Who knows. Maybe in this place it's a wandering, deceptive star.

I'm depressed by the failure of my quest but comforted by Cheryl's embraces, the warm bed that I can relax in every night, the regular meals, the softening of my calluses, the slowing to normality of my mind. If I'd known life on the road would be so hellish, I might never have set forth. Once committed, I had to see it through – I couldn't have settled for a mid-trek retreat, as I'd have been forever haunted by dreams of what might have been – but now that I understand that the city boundaries, if they exist at all, lie somewhere beyond my reach, I'm able to accept it. I feel no need to set off on another quest – west, north or south – as I'm sure I'd fare no differently.

I'm trapped. There's no way out, no way home, nothing other than this city, this time, these people. If I run into the Alchemist tomorrow and he asks me about life in the outside world, I'll say, "*Outside?* What's that, old boy? What's that?"

I pick up where I left off and it's as if I'd never been absent. I take to the stage at Kipp's and regale my audiences with tales of mad scientists, werewolves, crooked businessmen, gangsters and – of course – drones. I restock my wardrobe. Make what should be the long trip to Barbersville to have the remains of my beard removed, only to find that it takes less than an hour in a public car. (I don't reflect on the impossibility of that, as I'd only drive myself insane.) Cheryl goes back on day shifts so we can spend our nights together. I fatten myself up with plenty of meals. I even continue asking occasional questions of random passersby – Where am I? Where does the city end? How can I get out? – going through the motions, though I no longer anticipate or hope for answers. Everything back the way it was in what I failed to realise were the good old days.

Except it's not *exactly* the same. I've changed. I act as I did before and nobody – not even Cheryl – notices any differences, but the old Newman Riplan is no more. As relief at having come to the end of the quest recedes, bitterness and anger seep in. I'm stuck here, no say in my destiny, at the mercy of elemental changes, waiting for the lykans to reappear.

The days drag. Before, I was genuinely interested in this city and how it functioned. No longer. I don't care how things work. I've stopped popping into factories – as I used to do before the quest – to ask questions of the foremen, to see drones being melted down, to see cars being manufactured. I no longer wonder how they get by without glass and electricity and computers, how everything falls into place, how people know instinctively how to act and react.

I now spend my time brooding in Kipp's, or sitting by fountains and staring moodily into the water, or going for long, directionless drives in public cars. I spotted the Alchemist parading down a road yesterday but didn't even stroll over to say hello. Couldn't be bothered. I chewed on a crispy drone finger instead and kicked a stone into the canal that I was resting by.

It's not just the city I feel bitter towards. It's the people. I'm being nice to Cheryl, taking her wherever she wants to go, smiling, kissing, playing the part of the lover, but inside I'm starting to despise her. I tried telling her about my quest but I might as well have been talking to a drone. "I walked for days and days and days, in one direction, and ended up back here."

"So?" she asked, smiling prettily.

"You don't think that's strange?"

"No."

"I went straight, Cheryl. Straight ahead. Yet I ended up back here."

She shrugged — couldn't see the problem.

It's not that she's stupid – she's not – it's just the way these people are. I've nothing against her personally, but as the person I'm closest to, she bears the brunt of my disgust and frustration for her unquestioning, gormless clan. I'm trying hard not to hate her but I'm fighting a losing battle. One of these days I fear I'll snap and evict her from my life. I don't want to, but my wants no longer serve me as they once did. That's what happens when you take a man's control over his life out of his hands.

I've just got through making love with Cheryl. She's sensed my antipathy. She was straining too hard to please me during sex. She lies on the bed, naked, and tickles my testicles with her toes. I force a smile but it's thin and unconvincing.

"Do you want to talk?" Cheryl asks and I shake my head wordlessly. "You were wonderful at Kipp's tonight."

"Thanks," I grunt.

"Wonderful in bed too," she giggles, poking me playfully with the toes.

Again, a weak smile and a muttered, "Thanks."

"Did you sprinkle the sperm?" she asks, abandoning the small talk.

"Yes," I sniff. I always sprinkle the sperm. Sex wouldn't be permitted if I skipped that routine.

"Good." She stares around the room – she's moved back in with me – and searches for something further to say. Finds nothing. "Well, it's sleep for me then," she sighs and pops a pill. "See you in the morning."

"Yeah," I reply and remove her toes from between my thighs as she falls into a deep, instant sleep.

I spend a few sour hours reflecting on life and the blows it's dealt me. I wonder if I did anything to deserve such a fate, if this is a godly punishment that's been meted out. I can't think of any awful, dark deeds. I've screwed over some business colleagues but nobody ever suffered unduly as a result of my efforts to get ahead. Could it be the whoring? I haven't treated women with much respect – if I'd met Cheryl back in the old world, I'd probably have dumped her by this stage without thinking twice – and if God, as the feminists claim, is a woman...

The more I think about it, the more it seems like something only a spiteful god could dream up. "He loves computers and technology — right, out they go. He likes to know how things work, so we won't tell him. We'll even strip the city of names and history, so he feels doubly confused. And to top it all, we'll ruin his sex life by interfering with the natural rhythms of intercourse."

Am I being childish? Certainly. But this city would retard the most magnificent of minds, so there was never much hope for poor old Newman Riplan, who was a smart operator but hardly a genius. I think it's to my credit that I've come this far with only one minor breakdown – my lion-hunting phase – along the way.

I study Cheryl's slumbering form and feel jealous contempt. How dare she sleep so soundly while I'm writhing in the flames of a waking hell? Life's so simple for her. If things go wrong, all she has to do is wait a few days for her subconscious to smooth over the cracks. She wouldn't last pissing time in my world. Give her a fortnight and she'd be a gibbering, howling wreck. It's not fair that I'm suffering while she blithely carries on, nothing to rock her boat by even a fraction.

My eyes narrow as I think of a way to ruin her day, so that she can understand what it feels like when the universe doesn't work the way you want it to. She breathes deeply when she's asleep. I know from experience that nothing short of wild yelling and shaking can wake her. I murmur her name — no response. I say it louder this time but her face remains the same, composed, oblivious. I dig her in the ribs. She emits a groan, her face puckers, but otherwise there are no changes.

I roll on top of her, bitterness directing my actions. Part of me screams with outrage and orders me to stop but I ignore it. I've had enough of bowing to this city's bowdlerized ways. It's time I flexed my muscles. I'm not ruled by the same laws as the others and I'll be damned if I go on pretending that I am. Newman Riplan is through being dictated to. From now on *I* make the rules.

I slide inside Cheryl as I have done so many times since we hooked up, but this time with a cruel end result in mind. I'm hard before contact and begin pumping away as gently as possible, ready to withdraw at the first sign of consciousness.

It doesn't take long to climax. At the last moment I almost pull out — afraid that something terrible will happen — but I stick to my guns as I explode silently inside her. I lie tensely locked in for several minutes, waiting for the predicted big bad to happen, but nothing does, apart from the natural limpening of a certain appendage.

I eventually slip out and recline on my own side of the bed, both disappointed and relieved. She was so sure I'd do damage if I came inside her that I'd started to believe it, even though I knew it must be nonsense. All that fuss — for what? A few minutes later I clean up the mess, check to make sure Cheryl's still asleep, then lie back and wait for Morpheus to claim me too.

FIFTEEN

I've never felt grimier. Two days have passed since I took advantage of Cheryl while she was sleeping and I've spent them calling myself every foul name under the sun. How could I have done such a thing? I'm sure she would have agreed to have sex with me if I'd woken her and asked – she's never refused – but I didn't. I stole in like a thief while she was sleeping, no better than a rapist, and did the one thing she's always vehemently resisted. It doesn't matter that my sperm didn't do any harm. She believes it's a dangerous substance and I promised never to shoot it into her, yet in the heat of the moment I reneged on that promise and became a vile, spiteful, predatory bully.

I've been extra nice to Cheryl, buying her all sorts of gifts in a futile attempt to ease my guilty conscience. She doesn't know about the nocturnal transgression – I watched her cautiously as she woke and she was completely unaware of what had taken place – but that makes me feel worse. She's so happy that I'm being nice to her again. To see trust and love in her eyes and know I'm undeserving of them...

God damn this city for what it's made of me. I can't shift responsibility for the blame – I'm guilty, hands-down, no arguments – but if not for this wretched, rat's shit of a purgatory I'd never have resorted to so cheap a shot. If I ever get out, I'll return with a couple of nukes and level the joint.

I'm beginning to lose my audience at Kipp's. I can't work up the enthusiasm any longer. I sleepwalk through the stories, adapting *Frankenstein* and *Psycho*, but I've lost the knack for rousing a crowd's interest. They no longer hang on my every word or sit glued to their seats in anticipation of my story's next terrifying twist. I try different approaches – I give Westerns and war movies a shot – to no great effect. Kipp keeps me on – I'm still a good opening act for better yarn spinners – but cuts my pay.

"I don't like doing this," he says miserably, "but with business so poor, I can't afford to pay you more."

The money's not a problem – with what Cheryl earns, we've plenty to survive on – but my stage failure does nothing to lift my spirits. I feel like someone who's wandered in from a lousy Ingmar Bergman movie, having to suffer through endless replays of ten reels of Swedish depression and angst.

I've been having a hard time sleeping since that night with Cheryl. I'd take a pill if I dared, but I've experienced nothing worse than that time I returned to what should have been the real world, only to find myself immersed in timeless, conscious blackness. I'm tossing and turning, trying to drop off, when the door opens and a pair of enemaists enter.

"Sorry," one says, realising I'm awake. "Want us to come back later?"

"No, that's OK, come in," I reply. As the enemaists set to work on Cheryl I recognise one of them. "It's Isaac, isn't it?"

The enemaist looks up and smiles politely. "You got it. Know me, do you?"

"We spoke a long time ago. My name's Newman Riplan."

Isaac frowns. "That sounds familiar. When did...?" He

clicks his fingers. "You were the snuffer who said he was going to piss in the sink."

I laugh. "Right. That was me."

"Here, Fen," Isaac says, nudging his partner. "Remember me telling you about this guy?"

"Yeah," Fen says, rubbing his nose. "Didn't think it was funny though. Pissing in a sink — a revolting idea."

I ask Isaac where his old partner – Andy – is, but he doesn't know who I'm talking about, so I write Andy off. We chat about what Isaac has been up to – that lasts all of a minute – and I tell him the names of some of the enemaists I met in the course of my quest. He knows a few of them and is amazed I got about that much. "I'm stunned you've any feet left," he laughs. "All that walking, I'd have bet on you wearing them down."

He recalls attending one of my shows at Kipp's and asks how things are going. "Not so good," I sigh. "My tongue's turned traitor. I can still think up stories but I can't deliver them ably."

"That's a shame," he says earnestly. "You were good. I would have gone to see you again if I hadn't been working so hard. Are you planning to give up?"

"I don't know," I shrug. "What else am I fit for?"

"You could always join us," Isaac chuckles. "Plenty of openings in the enemaists." He laughs and so does Fen.

"That's a joke," Fen explains. "Plenty of *openings*. Get it?"

"I get it," I grin. "Thanks for the offer. If I ever get desperate, I'll bear..."

I stop as a half-remembered thought flickers through my brain.

"What do you do with the waste when you finish your rounds?" I ask.

Isaac squints. "It goes down the Swanee."

"The Swanee?" I echo.

"A load of pipes in our factory. They lead beneath the city."

"Pipes?" I blink. "Beneath the city?"

"Yeah. Hey, are you OK?" Isaac steps towards me, concerned, as I sink back on the bed. "You look white around the gills all of a sudden."

"I'm fine," I gasp, waving him away.

Pipes beneath the city. I can't leave by conventional methods – walking, driving, flight – but I've never tried burrowing out. Perhaps I've been looking in the wrong places for the exit signs. Maybe this city comes equipped with an underworld, through the tunnels of which freedom lies.

"Are there really vacancies?" I ask.

"Sure," Isaac says.

"Do you think I could apply?"

"You're serious?" he asks.

"Yeah."

"Well, I won't say anything to deter you," a surprised Isaac mutters. "We're severely undermanned, so we'll take any recruits we can get. And it won't so much be an application as a signing on — they're not turning down anyone."

"Could Cheryl join too?" I ask on a whim.

"Who's that?" Isaac asks and I give her a slight shake. "Oh, your woman. Sure. There aren't many female enemaists but that's not because we don't want them, we just can't normally convince any women to join."

"So it won't be a problem if we turn up looking to start work tomorrow?" I ask.

"You're eager," Isaac laughs. "You ain't got nothing devious on your mind, do you? Because, listen – and this is the voice of experience speaking – if you're looking to join so you can fiddle with people's privates while they're sleeping…"

"No," I say, grinning sickly, "that's not why I want to join."

"Well, great," Isaac says. "Tell you what, drop by my place in the afternoon and I'll take you down to the recruiting office, put in a good word for you and get things fast-tracked."

"That would be wonderful," I smile. "You don't mind?"

"Course not," he says. "We get a bonus for bringing in newbies. See you later."

"Later," I agree, shaking his hand and escorting him – once Fen has emptied my bowels – to the door.

I do a little dance as soon as I'm alone – pipes beneath the city! This is it, freedom, I can sense it – then pace anxiously round the room, forming plans, some wild, some reasonable, some that might actually work, waiting for Cheryl to wake so I can tell her the news about her revised employment prospects.

*

Cheryl, understandably, is less than thrilled. "Give up my well-paying, enjoyable job to go sticking pipes up people's bums? I. Think. Not."

I try explaining that the job has nothing to do with my decision. "This is a chance for us to escape," I tell her, "to get out of this crazy hell hole. Things mightn't work out as planned – given what happened to me on walkabout, I'm pretty sure they won't – but we have to try. At least *I* have to. This city is your home. If you don't want to leave, I'll understand."

She studies my face, tears in her eyes, wanting to say yes to me but afraid.

"This world of yours," she mumbles. "If it exists and can be reached... is there a place in it for me?"

"I don't know," I answer honestly. "I love you, Cheryl, and want you to come with me, but it would be a huge change. You might not be able to cope. Still, I'd like you to try. If things don't work out, you can come back."

I'm not sure why I'm so eager to take her, given that I was happy (*determined*) to leave by myself before. Maybe I think I'll be rewarding her by taking her into my world, and wish to make things right with her that way.

"This means a lot to you, doesn't it?" she asks quietly.

"It means everything," I croak, thinking about what I did to her when she was asleep. "I'm rotting here, turning into something I despise. If I don't get out, it's going to prove the end of me."

Cheryl smiles bravely. "Alright. I'll hand in my notice and accompany you."

"Seriously?" I gasp.

"Seriously," she says.

"You're an angel," I hoot, kissing her.

"I'm a fool," she sighs. "I wish I wasn't in love with you, Newman. Life would be much simpler if I could walk away and forget about you."

"Simpler," I agree, "but would it be as much fun?"

"This isn't fun," she says solemnly. "This terrifies me. But I'll do it because I love you and I'm hoping that love will win out over terror in the end."

If I wasn't so desperate to escape, that would stop me, and out of love for her I'd drop the crazy plan. But this city really will grind me down if I stay, so I selfishly allow her to live with her terror and send her off to hand in her notice ahead of the move into our new jobs.

We fill several canisters with water and stuff them in a bag. I've no idea when the chance to explore the pipes will arrive – it may be weeks or months before access is permitted – but it's best to go prepared. Maybe Isaac or one of his colleagues will offer to show us round the plant and a situation will arise where we can slip away on the quiet. There's no telling how long we'll be down there. The exit – if one exists – could be minutes away or it could involve another long and arduous trek. That's why we're bringing the water.

"What about extra clothes?" Cheryl asks and I laugh.

"We're going down sewerage pipes," I remind her. "Clean clothes aren't going to be an issue."

"Food?" she says. "Shall I pack some drone slices?"

"That's a good idea," I reply, "but only bring enough for a few meals — we don't want to weigh ourselves down too heavily. We can always catch a couple of rats if we get hungry."

"Eat an animal?" she moans.

"We might have to," I sigh, as if that repulses me as much as it does her.

When we're ready, we quench the candles and let ourselves out. I've told Franz about our new jobs. He was worried we wouldn't be able to afford the room on our new salaries but I said that wouldn't be a problem, though I suppose – if we don't get down the pipes sometime soon – it might be. I've no idea what enemaists earn but I'm guessing it isn't a lot or they wouldn't be understaffed. Anyway, I paid him in advance for the next several nights, so that's not something we have to worry about for the time being.

We hail a public car and discuss the future on our way to Isaac's. I'm full of optimism. Cheryl isn't but pretends she is. I'm not sure it's a good idea to involve her in this. She'd almost certainly be better off here. What does my world have to offer someone like her? Oh well, as I promised, if we do escape and she decides she prefers it here, I won't stand in her way if she wants to come back. And who knows, after such a long time away, maybe *I* won't fit in either. It might be that I won't be able to adapt to my old way of life, that I'll return with her or, more ironically still, that she'll fall in love with my world and stay, while I'll find I can't stand it and make the trek back to the city on my own.

"Tell me more about the other world," she urges. "They've no drones?"

"Not a one."

"What about drone teeth?"

"We use paper and metal. Not ordinary paper and metal," I add, spotting the sceptical lift of her eyebrows. "They're specially designed."

"And glass is plentiful?" she asks.

"Yes. It's everywhere."

"There are no lykans?"

I smile. "Well, we tell fairy-tales about werewolves, which are similar, but... Hold it," I interrupt myself, disturbed by her questions.

"Yes?" she smiles.

"You mentioned glass and lykans."

"So?"

"You know what they are?" I whisper, mouth suddenly dry.

"Of course," she smirks. "Why wouldn't I?"

Ignoring her question, I lean forward and tap the driver on the shoulder.

"Sir?" he responds politely.

"Do you know what lykans are?" I ask, a cold claw of dread tugging at my entrails. "Glass? Sandmen? Wolfers?"

"Certainly, sir," he chuckles.

Fuck! I stick my head out of the window and stare at the sun. At first it looks normal but after a couple of seconds I spot blue tendrils dancing round the edges, beginning to spread towards the centre.

"Stop the car," I yell and the driver screeches to a halt.

"What's wrong?" he yelps. "Why did you... Hey!" he shouts as I scramble out, dragging Cheryl with me. "You haven't paid your fare. Come back." He slams open his door and gets to his feet, preparing to give chase. Then he notices the panicking crowds beginning to emerge from nearby buildings. He glances up at the sky, spots the changing sun and groans. "Oh, snuff!" Forgetting the fare, he jumps back in the car and takes off. He mows down a couple of people – a kid among them – further up the road, but doesn't even pause to wipe the blood from his face when it flies across the bonnet and spatters him.

In the distance, the first of this season's flock of lykans begins to howl.

Cheryl's drawn towards the natural flow of the crowds but I drag her away to the quieter back streets. "We mustn't get caught in a stampede," I tell her, assuming control even though she's been through more of these things than me.

"But we have to find a sandman," she gasps.

"Yes," I pant, "but we stand a better chance this way. The lykans will be attracted to the noise and smells of the crowds and won't be concentrating on these alleys until later, when the pickings are scarce."

We each grab a noose and begin jogging, eyes peeled. A lykan darts past us at one stage, close enough to rip both our throats open, but it's focused on the scent of the hysterical masses and pays us no attention.

We spend longer on the streets than we did before, three or four hours by my estimate. The red moon replaces the blue sun in the firmament. The killing goes on. I pass a woman changing into a beast and put a quick end to her misery.

"I thought people changed as soon as the sun or moon turned," I remark.

Cheryl shakes her head. "Sometimes transformations don't occur until a day or two into the cycle."

"Any idea why?" I ask.

"No. That's just the way it is."

Finally we spot a sandman hiding in the arch of a doorway, his guards either having abandoned him or lurking out of sight.

"You don't know how pleased I am to see some customers at last," he says as we draw up. "How goes the slaughter?"

"Don't know," I grunt. "We didn't stick around to find out. Have you sand?"

"You're in luck," he says. "This is my last bag. I only had two to begin with. I would have sold this one long ago, except my guards were jumped by lykans and I decided it would be safer to linger in the shadows."

"Lykans got your guards?" Cheryl asks with surprise. When the sandman nods, she says, "I thought that couldn't happen. Sandmen and their protectors are sacred, aren't they?"

"Supposed to be," he agrees mournfully. "It seems things have changed. These lykans aren't acting the way they normally do. They're smarter, more vicious, less predictable." He sighs and looks up at the moon. "I hope things return to normal soon. I fear the worst if they don't."

"How much for the sand?" I ask, emptying my pockets in search of some teeth but finding none — I gave Franz those that I'd been saving for a rainy day. Cheryl gave him hers too.

I'm starting to panic when the sandman shakes his head and hands over the bag of sand. "Forget it," he says. "I'm glad to have discharged my duties. The sooner I get out of here, the better. So long and the best of luck."

"Same to you," I mutter and lead the way to the middle of the road. "Ready?" I ask Cheryl. She nods, we shut our eyes, and I sprinkle the sand over our heads.

Magic. Nakedness. Glass. Safety. Calm.

We huddle together for warmth, not saying much. I try instigating conversation but Cheryl isn't in the mood. She seems troubled, but it can't have anything to do with the lykans, because we're safe from them in here.

"How long do you think it's going to be this time?" I ask, trying again to get her talking.

"Don't know," she mutters.

"It's handy it happened while we were carrying water," I note. "We won't have to rely on drone sap so much."

"Mmm," she replies.

"And we have those drone slices too, in case the drones take a while to come this way."

"We'll survive," she sighs and there's a long silence after that.

"I hope Isaac makes it," I chirp eventually. "We might

not get the jobs without his support."

"I don't think that will be much of a problem," she murmurs. "There will be plenty of jobs on offer when this is over."

I get up and test the glass bars of the cage. I'd love to know how these things form. Next time – assuming my escape plans fail to reach fruition – if I've money and run into a sandman with extra bags of sand, I'll try to buy two and keep my eyes open while pouring the first over my head. That way, if it doesn't work, I'll have a bag to fall back on.

A lykan comes ambling along, so I step away from the bars and turn to tell Cheryl my plan, only to discover her staring at me, eyes wide, breathing hoarsely. "Cheryl?" I say with alarm. "What's wrong? Are you –"

"Don't!" she gasps as I start towards her. "Stay back. Don't come any closer."

I stop. "Cheryl, what is it? What's happening?"

Her hands are shaking. The muscles running the length of her legs and arms are undulating as if an electric current is coursing through her veins. Her bare breasts shudder and her lips peel back from her teeth.

"You did it," she snarls. "You... *ejaculated*... inside me."

"No," I lie immediately. "You know I always pulled out before –"

"You did it!" she screams. "I warned you not to – said it would lead to disaster – but you did it anyway, you stupid, stupid man." She lowers her head. Saliva drips from her lips in white, foaming pearls. I spy tiny bushes of hair sprouting along the breadth of her shoulders. Her breasts are narrowing, growing smaller. The hair round her groin has spread to cover the majority of her abdominal area.

"Oh God," I moan, understanding now – when it's far too late – why women are the first to turn into lykans, women who've been tricked and betrayed by men like me who didn't heed their warnings and pleas. "Oh Christ, no."

Cheryl's head comes up. Her jaw is stretching, her eyes no longer recognisably human, her ears beginning to point. A few more seconds and she'll be...

She opens her mouth and screams. No, not a scream — a *howl*.

Stunned out of inactivity, I scour the floor for something to use against the creature that is forming and which will shortly attack. I dropped my noose while buying the bag of sand but Cheryl held onto hers. It lies near her convulsing, altering body. I take a deep breath and dive across. The fingers of my left hand close around the handle as I come to my feet. I force the O of the noose over Cheryl's/the lykan's head. My right hand grasps the spindle and turns sharply. The noose tightens and Cheryl/the lykan is choked into silence.

I hold the spindle firmly in place. The struggle at the end of the noose ceases. I could let go now – it's over – but instead I turn the spindle another notch. I can't ease up. The noose seems glued to my hands. Soon I begin to cry, to sob, to howl in pitiful mimicry of Cheryl's final utterance. But even as I fall to the floor, moaning, howling and weeping, I continue to exert pressure, cutting deeper into my dead lover's throat, unable to stop until I've sliced through all the flesh and cartilage, severing the head, so that the wire loop closes into a compact, final, all-damning knot.

SIXTEEN

It's been five days. I'm hungry, bored, guilt-ridden, borderline suicidal. Cheryl's body lies stuffed by one of the cage walls, a constant reminder of my neglectful crime. I killed her. I'm not talking about finishing her off with the noose – that was self-protection – but before that, the night I assaulted her while she was asleep. That's when the dirty deed was done, when I condemned her with my seed, sentencing her to turn when the moon or sun next issued its transformative call. I was pissed-off, bitter, cruel, and because of that Cheryl is dead.

I take a sip from one of the water bottles. I've been rationing them, so there's still plenty left, but there's nothing I can do about the food situation. My stomach is rumbling and I'll most likely starve to death if this siege doesn't lift soon. The sandman was right when he said the lykans were acting unusually. Drones started milling by a couple of hours into the cycle, but unlike last time, when the lykans gave them a wide berth, now the savage beasts are interfering with the natural order of things. Several have established a vigil round my cage and are violently preventing the drones from coming to my aid.

With no enemaists on hand, I've had to start pissing in a spot near Cheryl's feet that I've designated as a toilet. It feels strange after all this time. *Dirty*. The smell is acrid and foul and lingers in the air. I'm dreading my first dump, though without anything to eat, that's not an issue just yet.

I head to the defecatory spot after my sip of water to empty my bladder. One of the lykans rushes up to the bars of the cage as I'm pissing and slams its head against the glass, then staggers away to howls of applause from its colleagues. It's become a regular performance, repeated a couple of times an hour, a different lykan each time. I've stopped paying attention to them and no longer shriek or shudder when they strike, though it's impossible to sleep through the racket.

They take no notice of Cheryl, even though she's jammed against the bars and would be an easy target. I was half hoping they'd feed on her, rip her to pieces and cart her body away, but they don't spare her a second glance. Perhaps they sense my anguish and want me to suffer. Maybe this is psychological warfare, designed to induce me to smash my head against the bars until my brain pulps and my body drops.

They'll have a long wait if that's the case. Not because I'm super-resilient. I just fear physical pain more than mental torment.

A couple more days trickle by. It's night. The red moon hangs above me like a bloated strawberry. The lykans cavort outside the cage, though their numbers have dwindled as stragglers slip away to feast on less well-protected subjects.

I've seen nobody aside from the lykans and drones. I'd kill for company right now. Uh-oh – a quick glance at Cheryl – bad choice of words.

Starving. I've never been this hungry. I've tried calling to drones, praying that one will slip through the ranks of lykans, but although they come in their obedient droves, the lykans make short work of them. The entire area beyond the cage is a wide, ragged circle of severed waxy limbs and sap. Lykans slip and slide on the mess, sometimes howling indignantly, other times making a noise that might just pass for laughter in a house of the insane.

Some of the limbs lie within reach. I drool as I stare at them, imagining the taste of the flesh, the refreshing nectar of the sap, forgetting the many times that I've complained about having to eat drones in the past. I'm tempted to make a grab for an arm or leg, but the lykans are watching out for that. They're not obvious about it – sometimes they deliberately look away and act as if they're unaware of my presence – but I know they're waiting to pounce. They're faster than humans, especially one as famished and weak as me.

I worry that hunger will warp my senses, that I'll start to think I'm swifter than the lykans, that I'll succumb to temptation and try to help myself to one of the limbs lying just outside the bars of the cage. If I make that mistake, the lykans will pounce, rip me up and pull me through the gaps between the bars in pieces. I understand that now and can restrain myself. But give it time. Give it time.

One especially smart lykan – apart from occasional forays to fill himself up, he's been hanging round from the start – was privy to a stroke of genius yesterday. Rather than throw himself at the cage, he paused, picked up a drone's severed head and jammed it up to one of the gaps between the bars. He shook the head and made gurgling, quasi-literate sounds, then stuck his fingers up through the neck and began working the lips and eyes from the inside, so it looked as if the dead drone was trying to talk.

I fell back from the manipulated drone face, nauseated beyond all due measure, and dry-retched. The lykan – for no particular reason, I'd decided a few days earlier to refer to him as Theo – cackled gruesomely and barked at his demonic cousins. Soon there were drone faces pressed between various bars, some arms, legs and entrails too, lykans behind them, howling and shaking the flesh from side to side, extracting much pleasure from my obvious distress.

It's hard to describe how terrifying those faces were. I'd come to look upon drones as dispassionately as everybody else in the city, mindless dummies, there for my convenience. Now, with so many of them converging on the cage, staring at me with dead, fish-like eyes, I felt as if I was in a supernatural dock and they were my ghostly accusers. I knew they were mindless mannequins being puppeteered by lykans, but lack of sleep and hunger played tricks on my mind and I was unable to rid myself of the nightmarish belief. I lost control and started bellowing and sobbing, begging the drone spirits to leave me alone.

After a while, as I was beginning to emerge from my screaming fit, Theo had another bright idea. He ripped a drone head in two, discarded the rear section and jammed the mask-like face over his own, making it appear even more animated than the others. That set me off again, and soon the rest of the lykans were copying Theo's lead and I was reduced to a weeping, wailing wreck of a ball.

*

The faces don't bother me any longer. Not even the human faces that the lykans have been appropriating since morning. I'm too hungry to care. Hunger has invaded every cell of my body. Fear and all other emotions have been forced out. Emptiness has taken over. I'd probably eat my own faeces if I could produce any, and I don't say that lightly. I've never known starvation before, not on anything approaching this scale, and I'm unable to deal with it. I must have something to eat. A few days ago I assumed I'd simply waste away. I'd no problem with that. I thought I'd drift off to death in my sleep, miserable but painless. But it's not like that. This is worse – or so I imagine – than being crucified. My insides feel as if they're on fire. If I move, hunger pangs haunt my every gesture. If I remain motionless, they grow slowly, in waves, until I'm forced to beat the walls of my stomach with my fists in a futile attempt to drive out the pain.

In one of my quieter moments I study a handful of lykans on the other side of the glass, tossing a man's body into the air, pulling it to bits between them, ripping the flesh from his bones with their teeth, gorging themselves on his blood. No word of a lie — if I could get out there right now, I'd join them. It wouldn't matter to me that he was once a living, breathing, thinking human being. If I could escape this cage, and human flesh was all that was on offer, I'd dive in with my fork and knife – fingers if I had to – before you could say...

The thought dies between synapses. A new one takes its place, propelled by an inhuman craving. I don't have to go outside the cage to find human flesh — I turn and study the familiar body tucked away by the glass wall — I've got my own ready-made supply inside.

I won't eat Cheryl. I won't eat Cheryl. I won't eat...

Hours have passed. Hours of sitting, staring, contemplating, drooling. Hardcore vegetarians claim that meat is murder. Well, it works the other way too — murder can be meat. Dead cow, dead sheep, dead human... is there any real difference? I may have had it before for all I know. The many restaurants I've dined in around the world, in less developed countries... who's to say one of them didn't run short of beef, rip a human arm from a corpse and stick it through the grinder? Even if that hasn't happened (and the rational part of my brain knows it's unlikely), aren't we all cannibals by proxy? People die, are buried, get eaten by worms and insects, which feed birds and animals, which get eaten in turn by...

No. That's bullshit. A student could get away with it in a debating class, but in the real world — even this sham of a one — it's bullshit. I won't kid myself. I'll go into this — *if* I go into it — with my eyes open. Eating Cheryl would be the act of a barbaric, tortured, pitiful man. I won't try to ease my conscience with soothing rationalisations. The choice is clear — violate millions of years of conditioning and become the basest of creatures, or cling to my humanity and starve to death. For the time being, I'm lucid and moral enough to plump for the nobler of options.

I won't eat Cheryl. I won't eat Cheryl. I won't eat...

*

I won't eat Cheryl. I won't. I won't. Not even a nibble. Not even one of her little fingers, though there couldn't be much harm in snapping off a finger and popping it into my mouth. That would hardly count. I mean, what's a finger between friends? Cheryl wouldn't mind. A little finger, a cut of thigh, a slice of breast, a...

I won't! I won't! I won't!

There's a voice in my head and it's talking to me as if I'm another person, not letting me tune out, demanding I listen.

Don't be a fool, Newman. You're going to give in to temptation eventually. If you were in poorer condition, perhaps you could hold out for death, but you're a fine, physical specimen of a man. Look at yourself, still able to stand without feeling dizzy, able to walk, to reason. There's days left in you, at least four or five if I'm any judge. You can't hold out that long. If you think things are bad now, imagine what they'll be like after another two or three days.

What are you afraid of? Nobody will see. Nobody will know. The lykans? You don't think they're likely to stand in judgement, do you? Go ahead. They're waiting for you to die, so they can laugh and piss on your bones. Don't grant them the satisfaction. Picture their faces when they realise you've beaten them, that they failed to break you down. One little bite. The first will be the hardest. After a couple of mouthfuls you'll never know what took you so long to get started. Do it, Newman. Do it. Do it. Do it. Do it. Do...

The sun and moon can't stay like this forever. They have to change back. I must ignore the voice of damnation and stand firm against it. How will I feel if I start munching on her, only for normality to set in a couple of minutes later?

That won't happen, Newman. The sun doesn't give a fine flying fuck about you. It's not doing this to tease you. You have to –

"Shut up!" I scream, startling the nearby lykans. "I won't eat her. It's Cheryl we're talking about. The woman I've had sex with. The woman I love."

Now who's talking bullshit? the voice jeers. *You never loved her. You used her. She was your easiest way of getting to grips with this place, of figuring out how things worked, learning the rules. It could have been anyone. You needed her to survive and that's why you stuck by her, not because you were in love.*

Well, wakey-wakey, Newman, you still need her. You've got good mileage out of the lovestruck old girl but it isn't time to trade her in yet. She'd want you to get your money's worth. She loved you. If she's in heaven now, she'll be urging you on. You don't want to disappoint her, do you? You don't want Cheryl to cry and –

"Shut up! Shut up! Shut up!" I roar, and the lykans howl gleefully.

You're weakening, Newman. I feel it. Only a matter of time, then…

"Shut up," I croak, but weakly.

She's in good condition. I examine her thoroughly – just curious, I'm not going to eat her, I'm *not* – and apart from some toughening of the skin she's almost as fresh as she would have been alive. Hairier, granted, but not stiff or decomposing. Which would be good news if I was going to eat her.

Not that I am, of course.

But if I was...

I make no big production of it when I finally cave in. I don't throw my arms wide and beg forgiveness, or burst into tears, or offer the devil my soul. I simply pick up her left arm, tear through the tough, outer skin, and gnaw.

It tastes like raw meat and that's all it is, really. Think of it that way and it doesn't seem so bad. Rare steak, no worse than raw drone.

The lykans don't approve of recent developments. They rattle the bars of the cage and scream abuse at me. Theo seems particularly irate. He slams his head so hard against the glass that he busts open his nose. The lykans nearest him lose their minds when they catch the scent of blood. They fall upon Theo and he disappears beneath their claws and teeth. He puts up a brave fight but is powerless in the face of so many foes. When the melee dies down and the dust clears, there's no more Theo. I pause to mark his loss, then gnash on up past Cheryl's elbow to the meatier sections of her arm.

I have bad moments, when I snap to my senses, thrust away from the corpse I'm devouring and run screaming around the cage, but not as many as I was expecting. If Cheryl had been from my world, perhaps I'd feel differently, but I doubt it. The shameful truth of the matter is it's a dog eat dog world and I'm the King fucking Kong of canines.

I eat twice a day, not long after waking and at dusk. A

few mouthfuls of water with each meal and a couple over the course of the day. I'm running low on water, have to be careful, don't want to die of thirst, especially after the grisly lengths I've gone to in order to live.

I spend the rest of the time drawing in the dust, hunched over shitting (my movements are a torment, because of dehydration, and it takes me ages to pass even the smallest and most shrivelled of stools) or trying to count the stars at night. The lykans have abandoned me, but not before moving all the drone limbs out of reach, the bastards. A few pop by every now and then to check I'm still here and bang their heads against the bars for old times' sake, but they've realised I won't crack and they can't frighten me any more.

I wonder what people are doing in other cages. Are there die-hards like me chowing down on their partners? I can't see anyone except us cannibals making it through intact, not if the lykans have been preventing the drones from reaching the survivors. Maybe this is the start of a new phase for the city. Perhaps the next person who arrives from my world will have to face hordes of flesh-hungry cannibals, me among them, cooking pots in tow.

Oh, Mother, if you could see me now.

Finally it ends, one dark and lonely night. The moon changes fluidly, red draining away like coloured bleach from a toilet bowl. The city looks strange in the white light. I'd grown accustomed to the crimson sheen. Strangely, I'll miss it.

The wolfers sweep through the streets, eliminating the lykans. They're excited when they spot me. "Look!" their leader yelps in a most unleaderly-like fashion. "Somebody's alive in there."

They crowd round the cage, faces crinkling as they spot Cheryl's corpse — not much left on the gleaming bones — and work out what I've been living on.

"Need anything?" the leader asks, nervously handling his sword, as if afraid I'll attack.

I cock my head and grin. "If I had some carrots, onions and a pot, I could try my hand at a stew."

"Pardon?" he frowns.

I laugh flatly. "Forget it. I'm fine. Best I've ever been."

"He's acting strangely," one of the wolfers mutters to the leader.

"Can't have been easy for him," the leader sighs. "Everybody else we've seen chose to starve or kill themselves. To hang on in there all this time, with nothing to eat except…" He points at Cheryl.

"Do you think he killed her or waited for her to die?" another wolfer asks.

"Like it snuffing matters," the leader snorts, then orders his troops back into shape and sets off to continue the killing.

"Good luck," I shout after them. "Give the Alchemist a kiss from me. But no tongues!" And I laugh hysterically, like that's the funniest thing I've ever heard.

I play difficult with the sandman when he arrives, refuse to stand in the middle of the cage and shut my eyes. He doesn't try to force me, a model of understanding and sympathy.

"Whenever you feel up to it," he smiles. "No rush. I'll wait. You've been through an ordeal. You're not responsible for your actions."

"Know what I'll do when I get out?" I growl. "I'll slit your throat and eat you raw. That's what I do. That's who I am."

"You're angry, Mr Riplan," he says, "but that's alright, you're entitled to be angry. It's good that you don't keep it bottled up inside. You must –"

"Oh, shut the fuck up," I snap.

After a few hours of stubborn, pointless resistance, I capitulate. The walls come down and the sandman goes about his business. I don't attack him. For all my threats, I'm not a violent man. Besides, he's a big, healthy-looking son of a bitch. Probably beat the living shit out of me if I squared up to him.

I spend the rest of the night searching for fellow survivors but find none. The streets are deserted. I shout as I go and bang on the doors of houses but nobody answers. It's starting to worry me. I surely can't be the only survivor, not in a city this size, but there probably aren't a lot of us. It might take days, weeks before I find anybody. I don't want to spend all that time alone, not after the solitude of the cage.

I spy a troop of wolfers tracking a herd of lykans and hurry after them. "Hi, I'm Newman Riplan," I introduce myself when I catch up. "You guys don't mind if I tag along, do you? Only I can't find anyone else and I –"

"Sorry, sir," their leader says, "but we can't be responsible for civilians."

"But you're the only people I can find," I whine.

"Sorry," he says again, "but we don't have time. We're normally wrapping things up by this stage of the hunt, but because there were so many lykans, we aren't even halfway through. You'd slow us down and we can't have that."

"Let me trail along behind," I say. "If you get into trouble, I can back you up."

"No," he says politely but firmly.

"Listen, shitface," I growl, "I know the Alchemist. We're buddies. He won't take kindly to the news if I tell him I asked for help and you turned me down. He'll hand you your head on a plate if I say the word, so if you don't –"

The leader turns swiftly and, with the butt of his sword, slams the side of my head. It's either a perfectly landed blow or a lucky one, but it works a treat and I'm two-thirds down the road to unconsciousness by the time I hit the ground.

SEVENTEEN

The streets are deserted when I come to. No lykans, no wolfers, no people. There aren't even drones, though I find some round the bend as I set out to explore, standing in a motionless little group, looking more than ever like showroom mannequins.

I wander the streets for hours, calling for help, seeking others who survived the prolonged massacre, but no one answers. I knock on doors, check inside factories, pop into nourishment houses, but all are devoid of life.

The bodies of the dead have been removed from the streets, except those inside glass cages, which the sandmen have left intact. I don't want to get too close to these reminders of my cannibalism, but have to check to make sure the people in the cages are dead.

They are.

Most let themselves starve, though a few slit their own throats or choked on their nooses, each of them nobler and braver than me, more human in the end than I was, despite all the time I've spent here claiming to be the advanced one.

There aren't many glass cages. I come across only five during my hours of searching. An ill omen, though I try not to dwell on it.

Two days and not a sign of life anywhere. Even the animals have disappeared. I haven't bothered dressing or eating, though I have stopped to lower my face into a canal every so often, to stave off thirst.

The enemaists seem to have gone down with everybody else aboard ship, so I piss against walls or into canals. But I can't bring myself to shit out in the open. Even after all I've done, that just feels wrong. So when I have to pass a stool — and that's much easier now that I'm drinking properly — I enter a building, find a dark room, and do my business in a corner, using old scraps of clothes that I pick up while walking to wipe myself clean.

I refuse to believe that I'm the only survivor, though that's what I feel in my gut. A whole city can't have been wiped out, not even one as bizarre as this. I've no idea how big it is, but from my failed escape attempt I know it's huge, home to hundreds of thousands, if not millions. All those inhabitants can't have perished. It's ludicrous to think that I alone had enough savvy to pull through the ordeal. There must be others. Finding them is surely just a matter of time.

And yet these people are (*were?*) different. Maybe their will to survive is (*was?*) less than that of people from my world. They may have simply rolled over and died, the lot of them, like lemmings.

There's also the enigma of Barbersville. I was well into my trek before I reached that part of the city on foot, yet in a public car it was a short trip. Geography doesn't work here the way it does on Earth. Maybe the city somehow wraps on itself and isn't actually that big a place, home to mere thousands rather than millions. In that case annihilation wouldn't be such an improbability.

But even if my fears prove to be accurate and the general populace has been wiped out, what about the sandmen, wolfers and baggers? *They* were still around when the flood of lykans broke. They must be alive, waiting for the next cycle, holed up somewhere safe. But how to find them? How?

I light huge bonfires that are visible from kilometres around. It's not as easy as I thought it would be, but after a few failed attempts I work out how to encourage them into wild, flaming life. I stack drones inside a building and set fire to a couple of them. The fire spreads through the waxy dummies, then to the walls of the building and its neighbours – the safety measures here are appalling – and soon there's a blaze burning that would give the bravest of firemen nightmares.

I was nearly trapped by the fast-moving flames a couple of times, but now, after much experimenting, I have the process down to a tee. I know exactly how quickly a fire will spread, how to stack the drones and which direction to take when making my dash for safety.

But fierce and bright as the fires are, nobody comes to investigate. No survivors straggle in, weeping for joy, falling into my arms to share their tales of woe. No sandmen or wolfers roll by to berate me for my destructive behaviour. The Alchemist doesn't track me down and say how pleased he is to see me. I might as well be flicking lit matches into an ocean for all the good my pyres are doing.

I continue lighting fires, but only sporadically, and nothing too elaborate. I don't want to waste time arranging drones and dodging flames when I could be out searching for humans.

*

After an especially nasty dream – in which I was chased by hundreds of drones with Cheryl's features – I awake one morning and suddenly remember where I was heading when the sun changed. The enemaist factory and the pipes underground. I should forget about survivors — even if some exist, so what? My whole plan had been to get away from this city and its people. That's what I should focus on. If I can find the factory and discover a way out...

It's easier said than done. This city's full of factories, one pretty much the same as the other, most unlabelled. A public car driver would have had me there in a matter of minutes but they perished along with everyone else. Their cars remain, dotting the roads like the evacuated shells of giant, metal snails, but what good are the chariots without the charioteers?

I search high and low for the fabled factory but no luck so far. If I ever find it, I'll take drones down the pipes with me, eat them for nourishment, set them on fire for light, send them ahead if the way looks dangerous. I've been thinking a lot about drones, wondering how to get the best out of them. I've been writing notes, pinning them to various mannequins and ordering them to roam the city at will. The notes probably won't lead to anything – even if one is discovered by a human, I doubt if he or she would be able to find me – but it's better than leaving the blank-faced dummies hanging about on the streets like inert zombies waiting for a scent of blood in the air.

*

Cheryl. Franz. Kipp. Isaac. They're all dead. It only hits me occasionally, usually at night. The rest of the time I don't think about it. I concentrate on the search, on marshalling drones, leaving clues and pointers so that others might find me. Then, out of nowhere, the knowledge of all that has been lost will hit and I'll sink to my knees, sobbing. Often it'll be hours before I can rise again.

The nights are so dark, nobody to light the street candles. I hate when thoughts of the dead immobilise me after sunset. There's nothing worse than crouching in the dark, crying, imagining ghosts brushing by on all sides. I've tried teaching the drones to light candles but they're too clumsy. More often than not they set fire to themselves and end up as waxy, bubbling puddles of waste.

I've started talking to the mannequins. They can't answer, but the noise of my voice is preferable to silence. I outline my plans, my ideas, my hopes, my fears. I explain various theories to them and bounce questions off their unchanging faces, imagining responses, pretending their foreheads are crinkling thoughtfully, their lips lifting into a smile. I even give names to a few of them, though none learns to respond to the calls and I soon forget the names myself.

It can't be healthy, associating with the drones this way. The more I indulge in the madness, the greater the strain on my sanity. I can see how it will end, me surrounded by drones, treating them as real people, no longer able to tell the difference. Maybe I'll fall in love with a female, adopt a few kiddies and come to think of them as my own. Invent brothers and sisters, maybe even a mother, old friends and neighbours, an entire community. And if real people turn up out of the blue one day, perhaps I'll see them as a threat and kill them.

Can a few meaningless exchanges with a pack of wax dummies lead to such potentially devastating consequences? Probably not in a normal person, but I'm not normal. I've been through every kind of wringer imaginable. I've been ripped from the fabric of my own world, cast into madness, seen people die, eaten the flesh of the woman I professed to love. I'm not walking on the knife-edge of insanity — I'm dancing naked through its fiery fields. Anything less than utter resistance on my part and lunacy won't have to claim me for its own, as I'll have already booked into the hotel. I mustn't talk to the drones. I mustn't.

And yet, when my defences are low, I can't help myself. As they used to say back in that other world, it's good to talk.

I still haven't dressed. I enjoy gambolling naked through the streets. It's not like I'm an exhibitionist — hell, there's nobody to exhibit to, just the drones, and they don't care one way or the other.

I've tried reaching Operator Lewgan many times, but the lines in the public contact boxes are dead. Either nobody home or nobody answering.

I've been all over the city, driving when I don't feel like walking – the cars are easy to manage, simpler than their Earth counterparts – and I still haven't run into anyone.

Where are the damn sandmen and their associates? I've scoured basements and the roofs of buildings — I finally worked up the courage to scale a few of the taller edifices — all to no avail. There's a small army of wolfers. They should be simple to track down. There should be traces that even Inspector Clouseau could find, but there aren't, unless I'm denser than I think and lack the brains to make sense of what I'm looking at.

More fires. (Wishing I had marshmallows to toast.) More walking. (The soles of my feet are leather.) More driving. (I prefer walking.) Chatting to the drones. (When I shouldn't be.) Picking at my pubes. (Old habits die hard.) Drinking. (Sap — the choice of kings.) Eating. (I have to keep up my strength.) Excreting. (Not an issue any longer. I even shit in the middle of the streets, in front of the drones, without blinking.) The usual.

Maybe I dreamt them all. If I died back in my world, and this city is a product of my decaying brain, the people were never real. Perhaps part of me simply tired of the pretence, changed the sun and moon and wiped out the insubstantial locals. If so, I should be able to bring them back to life again.

I close my eyes and concentrate, willing the humans back into existence.

It doesn't work.

I try again, this time focusing on bringing only one human into the world. Still no joy, but I don't give up. It's a new routine that I add to my days. In between the walking, driving, setting fires and not talking to drones, I relax every now and then and tinker with the mental dust of creation. I haven't succeeded so far but I'll keep trying.

So lonely. Desperate for company. I never realised how well-off I was before. I try filling my days with quests and experiments and grand plans, but the hollowness of my endeavours is growing ever harder to ignore. Is this life of mine worth sticking with? Maybe I should try my luck on another world. Climb to the top of one of the tall buildings, jump and see where my crushing landing leads me.

But what if it leads nowhere? If death is the timeless void that I experienced on my last return to the normal universe, and this world is a midway zone, and death here results in an irreversible return to the nothingness... what then? Time's dragging at the moment but it isn't suspended. My days are long but not indefinite. I might be the only person left but there are buildings, canals, cars, drones. There are hours and minutes and periods of sleep. There's a chance that I'll find someone or discover a way out.

This life is nothing to envy, but it's too soon to give up. I'm miserable and self-pitying at the moment but suicide should never be considered. If life is truly unbearable, ending it will be the only viable option and you won't hesitate. Where there's doubt, life should always be granted preference. I'm not going to kill myself just because I'm feeling pissed-off. That would be stupid.

Got that, Newman?

Yes, sir, Mr Riplan, sir.

Good boy. Essay on my desk, summarising the main points of the lecture, nine o'clock tomorrow morning. Detention if you screw it up.

I've had a horrible thought. It would have been funny any other time, but fills me with self-loathing here and now. I'll push it from my mind if I can, though I'm sure I won't be able, that I'll act on it before this ordeal comes to an end. I feel it in my boner. My naked, lonely, desperate boner. My...

Did I say *boner*? I meant to say bones. Dr Freud, where are you now?

Don't think about it. Don't think about it. Don't...

Oh, sod it. I've put it off for nine days – ten? more? – but no longer. I've come up with all sorts of excuses why I shouldn't, but the truth is I'm just a chickenshit, afraid someone – God? – is going to tap me on the shoulder halfway through to jeer at me.

I check around – I don't know what part of the city I'm in, or if I've been here before, and I no longer keep tabs on such things – and spot a cluster of drones. I saunter across and give them a once-over. Nah, nothing here to interest the libido. I move on, eyes peeled, and dismiss six more groups before locating the type of model I've been looking for.

She's five-six or -seven, a cute, round face, full lips, may have been black in the real world – black or white originally, all drones share the same skin pigments here – carefully moulded pubic hair. "You," I croak, and she follows obediently, padding softly along behind me.

I unearth a clothes store and deck her out in the finest costumes I can find. Sift through several dresses – long, short, revealing, demure – before settling on a pink, frilly number, which best accentuates her curves. I wish I could purchase a wig for her but I've no idea how far I am from Barbersville. Never mind, I'll just pretend she's a fashionable skinhead.

As we're leaving the store I notice the mechanical rhythm of her walk, the same as every other drone's. "No," I sigh, stopping. "We can't have you parading about like a robot. Ruins the effect. Watch — like this." I perform an atrocious mimic of a model's catwalk stride, swaying my hips from side to side like a ship caught in a storm, arms writhing like horny snakes, lips puckering up, eyelids fluttering. The drone – I'll come up with a name for her but can't think of anything suitable at the moment – watches expressionlessly, then has a go.

Oh dear. She looks worse than I did. I guess drones weren't built to strut sexily. Her limbs refuse to contort gracefully. We spend an hour working on it, by the end of which she's improved – or else I've grown accustomed to her clumsiness – but not considerably. Not that I'm overly bothered. It's not how she looks walking that I'm interested in. It's how she looks lying down. Woof-woof!

I think of a name for her while searching for a nice boarding house. *Savova*. I like it. Sounds Russian. That's why she's cold and stiff, because she's a Russian model, fresh from Siberia. All she needs is a bit of warming-up. Given my hot and feverish state, by the time I'm finished with her she'll look like something out of *Baywatch*.

I finally locate the ideal *chateau de bonk* and lead the way up to its finest room, one with a boudoir and its own tiny pantry. I tell Savova to make herself at home and she lowers herself into a chair and reclines – after a lot of unsubtle hinting on my part – in a vague approximation of sultriness.

"Beautiful," I grin, having told her to raise her right leg a little to display more thigh. "Perfect. Hold it there, my dove, and I'll be with you shortly."

I flutter through the bedroom, making sure everything's right, clean linen, carefully made bed, drapes closed – just in case God's watching – candles lit. It takes a few minutes to get everything the way I want it but Savova's in no rush.

I pause, satisfied with the room, and glance down at my penis. It's standing to attention, as it has been since I first set eyes on my Russian princess, waving from left to right with the general sway of my body. I'd feared it might be rusty after such a long period of inactivity – no wet-dreams in this city – but I needn't have worried. I should have found some clothes for myself, to add to the illusion, but I was so busy concentrating on Savova's body that I never paused to consider my own. I think about nipping out to dress up but discard the idea before it's fully formed. I've waited long enough. I'm ready for action. I'll dress up another time. There'll be plenty of opportunities as long as this one passes smoothly.

I call Savova and she emerges – obeying my voice, not

the sound of her name – from behind the thin curtain that separates the boudoir from the bedroom.

"Hello, beautiful lady," I grin, wiping sweat from my flushed cheeks. "Doing anything tonight?" Savova stares at me blankly but I pretend her eyebrows rise tellingly in answer to my question. "Thought not," I chuckle, striding like a disco love god towards her. "Well," I murmur, taking her in my arms, "fear not, your evening has purpose and direction now."

I kiss her – "Yuck." – and pull back. Waxy. Her lips didn't move. Not in the least bit sensual. Oh well, who needs kissing? I've more interesting avenues of pursuit in mind. Humming a Beatles song, I lead Savova into an impromptu waltz round the room. She's awkward on her feet but I was never a great dancer myself, so we're evenly matched. After a couple of minutes of horseplay – in which I reel out a string of corny and coarse chat-up lines that I never would have used in a real situation, such as, "Do you come here often?" "My, that's a nice dress you're almost wearing." "Did you pee your pants or are you just pleased to see me?" – we stage-fall onto the bed and I laugh throatily, pretending to be surprised by where we've ended up.

"Well," I growl, smiling wolfishly, "I wonder what's going to happen now?" She says nothing. Stares up at me – or the ceiling – unperturbed by the sequence of events. I cup her covered left breast with a hand and watch her face for signs of passion. None. I nibble her ear — no reaction. Sighing, I shut my eyes and imagine her smiling wickedly, breasts heaving, lips parting to breathe that one intoxicating word, "*Yes...*"

Operating in self-imposed darkness, I massage the folds of the material clear of her breast and lightly run my tongue over it. Again, the distasteful waxy residue. I guess oral sex is out of the question.

Leaving the breast, I slide my hand down to her smooth, perfectly cast calves. My fingers knead the flesh, then creep up. This is more like it. Her legs could almost pass for a real woman's, long and shapely. I whisper in her ear, "Part your thighs, honey, I'm coming through."

She practically does the banana splitz, destroying the moment.

"Not so far apart," I mutter, opening my eyes a slit so I can coax her into the right position. When I'm happy with the spacing arrangements, I close my eyes again, take a few seconds to recapture the exotic visions that I'd been entertaining myself with, and proceed.

I meant to make a big deal of the foreplay – fingers slowly inching towards her panties, tenderly working them down, lots of huffing and puffing – but when push comes to shove it doesn't seem worthwhile. Grabbing the lining of the knickers, I yank them off and fall on her. My penis shoots forward like a guided missile, only to be slickly repelled. I chuckle hoarsely – "Feisty little wench!" – and make a second lunge. Again my manoeuvres result in rebuttal.

Frowning, I shuffle back and drop down for a closer examination. Savova's vagina looks as if it was carved out of wax, but apart from that it seems no different to any normal woman's, so why have my attempts at penetration proved futile?

Parting the opening folds of her plastic-like labia, I discover it's a facade. There's no depth. A narrow, shallow slit in an otherwise sexless crescent of solid, penis-resistant flesh. Dismayed, I check her rear and it's the same. It looks like there's an opening but in reality there isn't.

I toy with the idea that she could be a dud, that the rest of the drone population might be different, but I don't get far with that line of thought. They're asexual, the lot of them, I'm sure they are. Carnally incompatible.

I roll off Savova, groaning. For the first time in weeks I was actually excited about something. I'd been looking forward to this more than my first real female as a spotty-faced teenager. Back then I'd known it was only a matter of time before I got lucky. If it hadn't been with Kia at her seventeenth birthday party, it would have been with one of her friends, maybe not that night, but before long, as we were all young, frisky and eager to experiment. I'd taken sex for granted. It held no secrets from me, not even when I was a virgin, since I'd seen so much of it online. But here, with a drone, after all this time on my own, it was something new and unknown.

As disappointed as I am, there's no point tormenting myself. Sex is a washout — so what? I wasn't even thinking about it until a couple of weeks ago. Celibacy's hardly the pits. I've survived far worse blows than that.

I slide off the bed and cast my eyes over the drone – Savova is no more, I see only a mannequin now – which has held its position, legs apart, awaiting my instructions. I could always carve a hole...

My face wrinkles. Bollocks to that. If I was a sex-starved pervert, maybe, but I'm not. I'll settle for a hand-job, thanks very much.

So I fall back on the devices and vices of my youth. It's been years since I pumped myself manually. I feel embarrassed. I thought those days were behind me forever, that I'd never run out of women. Just goes to show you never can tell. It doesn't take long to climax. Less than a minute and I'm spraying the floor with my sperm, a gift to the great god Onan.

Sighing with a mixture of happiness and self-contempt, I sit on the edge of the bed and stare moodily at the sperm. I've got the post-ejaculation blues and the minutes tick slowly by. The thought of sprinkling the liquid – as Cheryl always had me do – crosses my mind, but what's the point? With nobody to act as a receptacle for its evil, altering ways, it can't do any harm. I'll just leave it where it is and...

The pool of sperm begins to pulsate.

"Oh Christ," I moan, more disgusted than alarmed. "What now?"

I lean forward and watch as the thick, white liquid wheezes up into a milk-cloud bubble. It's multiplying in size at a ferocious rate, double, treble, now ten times its original mass. I laugh at the surreality of it all, hop off the bed and step over the rising semi-sphere to view it from the other side. I drop to my knees and press up close to the expanding sperm bubble, careful not to touch it.

Judging by the darkness at the heart of the sperm, I think there's something inside, but I can't tell what it is. I consider popping the encasing bubble with a sharp object but I've a feeling I don't need to. Whatever's in there will be forcing its way out pretty soon.

I return to the bed and hum tunelessly while the bubble levels out at about the half-metre high mark, a diameter of a metre or more. I'm enjoying this. I could be moments away from death — there could be a lykan in there — but the thought fails to stir me. I don't even think about leaving. In fact my biggest worry is that the bubble will burst and I'll end up splattered in my own spunk.

To think I used to be normal once.

The drone still hasn't moved. I lie back against one of its knees and make myself comfortable. This is better than the cinema. A front-row seat at the theatre of the absurd. There are people in my world who'd pay a fortune for an encounter like this, and here's grinning old me, catching the show for free.

A few minutes of inactivity follow. I detect tiny grunting sounds, emanating from within the bubble. What on earth could it be? I'm tingling with anticipation. I hope it doesn't turn out to be something mundane, some weird type of trapped air bubble. I'm in the mood for dramatical surprises. I want...

Ah. Whatever's inside is beginning to move. I can see a head — I assume it's a head — twisting this way and that. Now its body, a slow rippling of indefinable muscles. A loud grunt. The thing backs up, then charges at the wall across from the bed, still encased in the bubble of sperm. It bounces off the wall and collapses, takes a few seconds to gather itself, rises, thrusts forward again. A tiny rip appears in the fabric of the bubble. Air rushes in and a happy sigh drifts out. Another charge. One more. The hole's about the size of two fists stuck together by this stage. I could probably peer inside if I wanted but I'm content to wait. I don't want to spoil the thing's big entrance.

A short, stubby horn appears and begins to carefully work at the edges of the hole, widening and lengthening the tear. This is too marvellous to be true. A *horn*. Maybe it's Rudolf the Red-Nosed Reindeer, or a medieval knight sporting an especially intricate codpiece, or a unicorn, or...

Hold it. No need for further guessing. The moment of birth is upon us. The creature bites its way through, gnawing at the wall of the bubble, which begins to drop from its flesh. The head's out. Shoulders. A leg. Here comes the rest. All bets are off. The result's in. It's a... a...

A rhinoceros.

Big pause. And I mean BIG.

I do a double-take but there's no change. It's still a rhinoceros. Smaller than usual, somewhat timid looking, but unmistakably a rhino.

The rhinoceros looks at me. I look back. Hard to tell which of us is the more confused. I hope it doesn't think I'm its mother. I've no intention of trying to breast-feed a rhino.

Seconds pass and the rhinoceros loses interest in me. It starts sniffing round the room, grunts when it finds the door and butts it lightly with its head. The rhino doesn't look back over its shoulder at me, but that's what it would do if it was a smarter animal. I decide to let it out, so I rise and open the door. It snorts its approval and trots out into the corridor, discovers the staircase and heads down, taking its time, not fazed in the slightest.

I stroll across to the window – stepping over the vacated pool of sperm – and draw back the curtains. The street below is deserted, but not for long. About a minute into my vigil the rhinoceros emerges and makes its way to the middle of the road. It sniffs the air, decides on a direction and moseys along.

I follow the rhino's progress until it passes from sight, then let myself out of the room – forgetting about the drone, who remains on the bed, positioned for an act of coitus which is doomed never to be consummated – and methodically plod down the rhino-trod stairs.

"Well," I mutter as I depart the building and take to the streets, "I guess now I know where the animals come from."

EIGHTEEN

And so I find a new calling in life. I've been Newman Riplan, the King Kong of troubleshooters. Newman Riplan, explorer of a brave new world. Newman Riplan, (failed) escape artiste. Newman Riplan, (fine young) cannibal. Now I'm Newman Riplan, *wanker*, and proud of it.

I wander the streets, no longer thinking of enemaist factories, ways out and other survivors, too busy being the giver of life. I masturbate four or five times daily. My testicles feel as if they're being squeezed dry but otherwise I'm fine. No signs of blindness setting in or hair sprouting along the lines of my palms. True, there isn't much left in me by the fifth ejaculation, but enough to do the business.

Stimulation proves the biggest difficulty. It's not easy stirring my penis into life with only my imagination — never my best asset — to work with. If I was fifteen or sixteen, no problem, I was more up than down in those days, but a man in his late twenties (it might even be early thirties by now, depending on how many months have passed since that night on the plane) has long lost that teenage, lustful drive. The first couple of wanks are easily accomplished — fresh after a good night's sleep, raring to go — but by the fourth I'm delving deep into my carnal memory banks, stringing together the most outlandish scenarios to excite the wilting beast to life.

I utilise the drones when all else fails, dress them up in sexy gear and have them pose erotically. I tried getting one of them to give me a handjob — my right arm's feeling the strain and my left is no good for that kind of operation – but she nearly squeezed the life out of my frightened little man. I only just managed to yell at her to let go before it was too late. Another few seconds and I would have been maimed for life.

I've given birth to every kind of animal under the sun. Tigers, dogs, monkeys, elephants, mice, cockroaches, cows, giraffes. Hybrids as well, creatures unheard of in the annals of zoological history. I've created more mutations these past few months than a nuclear power plant manages in thirty years or more. The creatures never attack me. They seem to instinctively understand how vital I am and afford me a wide berth, even the great predators like the lions and panthers.

My sperm doesn't just produce single animals. More often than not, one load will give rise to three or four of a species, or scores when it's something like insects. The siblings aren't always of the same family either. In one memorable load I spawned a horse, a cat, a llama, a wolf and an armadillo. They don't attack each other while emerging from the embryonic sac, though I suppose it's possible they prey on one another during later encounters. It takes about a week for the larger animals to grow to their full size, but bugs and the like are fully formed upon arrival.

Realising one day that all of my creations had been land animals, I fell to wondering about fish and birds. I trotted along to a nearby canal and shot my load into it. Sure enough, when the sperm cleared, a school of salmon could be seen swimming about. I've populated many bodies of water since. So far all my aquatic children have been on the dull side — salmon, trout, frogs, carp, eels. No whales, sharks or dolphins. Perhaps, since they can't flourish in these conditions, I'm incapable of creating them, but I'll go on trying. Wouldn't it be great to make a whale? Given its groin of genesis, there won't be any prizes for guessing what I'd call it!

I've let my beard grow again. I figure I look more biblical this way, which is appropriate, given my godly stature. Oh, don't get me wrong, I know I'm no god, certainly not *God*, but I can't help feeling I'm not too far removed from those heavenly beings of yore. Who but a godlike figure could bestow life as I'm doing? Isn't that one of the prerequisites for godhood, the ability to create life on one's own? I'm sure plenty of tribes on Earth would hail me as a hero of the celestial spheres if word of my exploits trickled back to them.

It's fun imagining the reaction I'd get back home. People would think it was a hoax. TV crews would place me under constant surveillance. Scientists would want to dissect me. Pornographers would offer vast sums for my services. I could make a fortune keeping zoos supplied, maybe even resurrect the dodo or the dinosaurs. If I wanted to take a despotic road to riches, I could demand protection money from towns and cities — pay me X amount in gold bullion or I'll unleash a horde of locusts on your sorry asses!

Following my success with the fish, I tried creating birds, but without any luck. I climbed to the top of a tall building and aimed over the edge. I hoped birds would emerge during the sperm's short-lived flight and automatically take to the skies, but instead it shattered into oblivion on the road below, putting a premature end to whatever was growing within. Maybe birds aren't permitted here. If they existed, they might be able to soar beyond the confines of the city and set people – if there were any – thinking about boundaries.

I miss birds. I used to enjoy watching them swoop and soar and do all that birdy business. This city is a lesser place without them, and although it's not something I can directly control, I feel that I've failed, and keep thinking about ways that I might bring them into being. What if I knocked together a hang-glider and shot my load into my left hand mid-air?

I haven't given birth to any humans. In the early days of my masturbational frenzy I felt sure it wouldn't be long before the walls of a sperm bubble parted to reveal a cowering, naked and confused Homo sapien. Hasn't happened though, and after so much spunk under the bridge, I don't think it will.

It'd be interesting if I *could* make humans. If a woman emerged and fell in love with me and we made the beast with two backs, would it be incest? Technically speaking, I guess it might be classed as such, though I doubt if any court in the land would convict me. But what would our actual relationship be? Father-child, brother-sister, kissing cousins? That's the kind of conundrum that would leave a genealogist whimpering over his maps of family trees.

*

Hi-ho, hi-ho, a-wanking I will go,
With my penis out,
Shooting sperm about,
Hi-ho, hi-ho, hi-ho.

My poor foreskin's been rubbed raw. A pity I'm not circumcised. I should give the little fellow a day or two of rest, dip it in a cool glass of drone sap and leave it to soak, but I can't tear myself away from the animal production line. I've never been this fascinated by anything, wondering what sort of creatures will hatch, watching them emerge, tracking them as they set off to establish their territory. I'm like a kid in a toy factory, dashing about from one…

No, that's a crappy comparison. A kid in a toy factory — *tchah*! I haven't much of an imagination but surely I'm not that drab up top. I feel like… like… Ah! Like God in the primordial ooze, selecting pockets of matter from a sea of bubbling chaos, bringing life and order into existence, lord and master of time, space and creation. I can no more tear myself away from masturbation than God could have turned his back on the world just three days into his planned series of universal renovations.

"Never mind, penis," I cluck. "You neither, testicles, milked dry as you are by this point. I'll make it up to you one day. How does a month in Tahiti sound, lying naked on a beach, soaking up the sun and frightening the ladies? Another few months of wanking and I'll quit. Honest. You can trust…"

I trail off into silence. Hmm. Talking to my reproductive

organs. Is that more or less disturbing than talking to the drones?

I'm strolling down an avenue, tugging at myself, working up a head of steam for my next piece of procreative art, when a familiar-looking building gives me reason to pause. It's a fairly ordinary establishment, not visibly different to the thousands of others I encounter during the course of an average day, so why am I standing here, staring up at it like Charlton Heston encountering the Statue of Liberty at the end of that film about the ape planet?

After a few minutes of troubled deliberation, I abandon the mystery and move on. I reach the end of the street and turn before a memory sparks and inspires me to dart back in a flurry of excitement. I barge into the building, scout about and find a door which, once opened, reveals the start of the dark and lengthy tunnel to the drone port — what I used to refer to as an airport in my previous life.

The drone port. Sweet mother of Rico, I haven't thought about that place in so long. Why the hell didn't I head there when civilisation fell and I alone survived? The lykans killed a lot of drones but the city has been filling up with them since, which means they must still be arriving, which means there must still be people at the drone port, offloading them from the planes.

People!

I set off down the tunnel, then recall my wild, naked state and backtrack. If I turn up in Jess's office looking like this, she'll probably sic her wolves on me. I jump into a nearby canal and wash off the worst of the accumulated filth. Hop up and down on the bank until dry, then find a clothes shop and kit myself out in the finest garb on offer. I can't do anything about the beard, though I pick out as many stains as I spot. When I've made myself as presentable as possible, I return to the building, gain access to the tunnel, calm my jitters as best I can, and start walking.

The journey doesn't seem so long this time, probably because I know where I'm going and what to expect, and also because my leg muscles have come a long way since that historical day and I walk much quicker than I did then, longer strides, breathing easily.

I emerge via a concealed hole in a wall, a little way down from the personnel buildings, which is confusing — there were no junctions in the tunnel, meaning I should have arrived at Jess's office. Oh well, just another small mystery to add to the city's myriad cache.

The drone port's as I remember it, surrounded by towering walls, encased in pure darkness. I can't spot any planes on the landing strip, though there's a bus waiting, so they must be expecting one. It's quiet out here, much quieter than the city, which has livened up since the return of the animals. I feel peaceful, like I've come home after a long trip away.

I check the bus first, hoping to run into Mannie, but it's deserted. From there I head for Jess's office, knock on the door and, when there's no answer, let myself in. The room's as neat as it was during my previous visit, but dusty and damp, as though nobody's been here in quite some time. I check behind Jess's desk. Her chair is lying on its side and doesn't seem to have been used recently. I bend and look into the cages beneath the desk, where I spy two desiccated skeletons. The panels at the back of the cages have been distressingly clawed and gnawed, so the wolves clearly didn't die a happy death, but what about Jess? Is she dead too or simply on a leave of absence?

I check the other building, where the off-loaders — Phil, Bryan and Mannie — hung out. It's in better nick. There are beds in the corner, neatly made. A cupboard stocked with drone slices and sap. Spare shoes, caps and gloves.

"Hello?" I call. "Anybody home?"

No reply. I don't hang about. I recall how curt Phil and Bryan were, and don't think they'd appreciate discovering me here, invading their privacy.

As I emerge I spot a set of rolling steps being trundled into position next to a plane which must have pulled up while I was inside. I'd love to know how those fuckers set down so quietly. It's a pity I missed the landing — it might have provided a clue as to how I arrived here. Hurrying across, I wait until all the drones from the plane have filed past — not many, no more than thirty — then scuttle up the steps. I pass through the cockpit and find myself back in the archaic setting of an airplane cabin. Two off-loaders are halfway down the aisle, cleaning up.

"Yoo-hoo!" I shout, and beam as they turn suspiciously. To my surprise — and, oddly, delight — they're the same two I originally encountered, the blue-suited Phil and Bryan.

"Who the snuff are you?" Bryan snaps.

"Where'd you come from?" Phil growls. He's not as green-looking as he used to be, seems to have settled into his job.

"It's me," I say, stepping forward. "Newman Riplan."

"Who?" Bryan asks, eyeballing me warily.

"Newman Riplan," I repeat. "We met a long time ago. I came in on a plane — I mean, a drone hold like this. Remember? You kicked me off. I met Mannie outside, then went to see Jess, then –"

"Hold it," Bryan interrupts. "You're making my head spin. Mannie? Jess? Who the snuff are they? I don't know any Mannie or Jess."

"I don't either," Phil says, "but I feel like I know this guy. There's something about him..." Phil clicks his fingers. "Got it. He's the drone hold man. Remember when you told me about drone hold men and how we should be careful what we said around them, or we'd have the Alchemist riding our backs?"

Bryan frowns and thinks for a few seconds, then relaxes into a smile. "Sure," he chuckles. "Newman Riplan. You didn't have a beard last time. How you been doing?"

Ha! If I tried answering that one, I'd be here all night, so I just say, "Fine, fine, how about you?" They've been getting along nicely, they reply. I ask again about Jess and Mannie but they've forgotten them, so I assume the pair are dead. Phil and Bryan haven't been to the city for ages. They barely even remember the world of buildings, moons, suns and lykans.

"Oh yeah," Phil finally recalls, "the lykans. They're why we've been staying here. The last few times we went back, the place was full of the bloody things. We decided we'd be safer where we are."

I tell them the lykans are long gone and it's safe to return but they shake their heads.

"Won't be safe till the Alchemist says so," Bryan insists. "This happened once before, a long time ago. The sun and moon stayed changed for ages and just about everyone died. We were warned not to go back until the city was repopulated."

"How did that happen?" I ask. "Where did the people come from?"

Bryan shrugs. "What am I, a know it all?"

Phil looks out the window. "The drones have left," he says. "We'd better get a move on. Could be a new drone hold arriving any time now."

"Yeah," Bryan sighs. "No rest for the wicked."

They return to their cleaning duties. I stare out the window. There's no sign of the bus.

"Who drove them out of here?" I ask.

"Don't know," Bryan grunts. "That's not our area of expertise. We off-load them, that's all."

"But surely —" I start to protest.

"There," Bryan says curtly, reaching the rear of the plane and turning. "Done and dusted. Time to leave."

The two men head back up the aisle. I step out of their way to let them pass but they stop when they reach me.

"Come on," Phil smiles. "You can't stay there. Out you come."

"Please," I gasp, "leave me here, OK? I want to escape. I've been going mad. I can't take it anymore."

"Sorry," Bryan says, "but nobody stays on the drone holds. Company policy."

"I'll pay you," I screech. "I can get drone teeth, more than you can imagine, a mountain of them. I'll make rich men of the both of you. You'll be able to retire and live in the lap of luxury."

Bryan laughs. "Hear that, Phil? He's going to make us rich."

"I like the sound of that," Phil cackles. "I could always see myself living a life of leisure."

Bryan takes a firm hold of my right arm and tugs me out into the aisle.

"I'm not lying," I shout. "I can get the teeth, I swear. All you have to do –"

"– is disobey orders," Bryan grunts, shaking his head. "There aren't enough teeth in the entire city to sway us from our duties. The Alchemist trusts us. That's more important than wealth."

"Besides," Phil adds, "we get all the teeth we need, whenever we need them — just pick them from the drones as they're going past. The Alchemist doesn't mind. It's messy, so we hardly ever bother, but on the odd occasion, if we're planning to live it up a little…"

I try thinking of something else to bribe them with. When I come up blank, I resort to brute force, take a swing at Bryan and lash out at Phil with my feet, but they've been expecting this and subdue me with an embarrassing lack of fuss. Bryan swipes aside my clumsy punch, Phil kicks my legs out from under me, then the two of them are on my back, pinning me to the floor.

"Try that again," Bryan says pleasantly, "and we'll carry you out in pieces."

"Bastards," I sob, grimacing into the rough cabin carpet. "I'll pay you back for this. I'll unleash an army of animals on you. See how tough you are when you're staring down a lion's maw."

"He's crazy," Phil mutters.

"Of course he is," Bryan agrees. "He wouldn't have come all the way out here if he wasn't. Ordinary folk don't bother with this place. No reason why they should. All drone hold men are loopy." Bryan manhandles me to my feet, twisting my left arm up behind my back. "You going to give us any more trouble?"

I shake my head tearfully.

"We don't like doing this," Phil says comfortingly, playing the good cop this time round, "but it's our job. If we helped you, it'd mean the chopping block if the Alchemist found out. And he would."

"It's OK," I moan. "I understand."

"You don't hold it against us?"

"No," I whimper.

"Good man," Phil says and tells Bryan to release me.

They walk me off the plane, closing the doors as they leave. We descend the steps and the two off-loaders start rolling them away.

"Can I watch the drone hold taking off?" I ask.

"Taking what off?" Phil frowns.

"Can I watch when it flies away?" I clarify.

The men laugh uncertainly.

"*Flies?*" Bryan snickers. "How could a thing that size fly?"

"Well, how does it leave, then?" I ask.

He shrugs. "Beats me. We turn our backs and sooner or later it's gone."

"You mean you've never seen...?" I stare at the plane. "Can I hang about until it goes? I won't try to get on. I just want to stay and watch."

Phil and Bryan exchange questioning looks, then shrug. "Sure," Phil says. "No harm in that. But if you spot the Alchemist, scarper, and if he catches you, you never saw us and we never saw you, alright?"

"It's a deal," I agree and settle back to watch the motionless metal bird.

After hours of determined scrutiny, in which the plane shows no signs of activity, my eyelids begin to droop. I yawn, sit up and slap my cheeks. I wish I had someone to talk with. Mannie would have sat by me and told tall tales to while away the hours. He was a nice bloke, even though I didn't get to know him well. He wouldn't have booted me off the plane, not like sour old Cain and Abel, the officious pair of...

My eyelids droop again and this time close. I come close to falling asleep but at the last possible second snap awake. I take several deep breaths and blink rapidly. I won't let sleep spoil things for me. I'm not going to miss this. I'll stand here as long as it takes and won't budge until...

The plane's gone. I stare at the space where it should be, then check the rest of the airport, in case I'm just disoriented, but it's nowhere to be seen. I don't bother with the sky — I know I won't find it up there amidst the blackness. My shoulders slump and I turn towards the buildings. It isn't meant to be. It's no coincidence that the plane disappeared while I was momentarily napping. Whoever controls the flights in and out of here doesn't want to share the secret with me. By now I've learnt to accept such disappointments as par for the course.

Departing via the departed Jess's office, I head back to the city, walking slowly this time, in no rush, enjoying the dark monotony of the uncomplicated tunnel.

NINETEEN

I don't feel like masturbating these days but continue all the same, since I have no better way to kill the time. I trudge the familiar, anonymous, unexciting streets, study the forms I've given life to, feed and drink from drones when my body demands. Deep thoughts are rare and unsought. I prefer the silence of mindless acceptance. Thinking only brings suffering. How sweet the world would be if we could all tune out and leave our brains on standby. Ambition and inquisition are the whip-cracking, back-riding scourges of humanity. To the devil with them!

Time has passed but I've no idea how much. That's a question for the inquisitive. Who in their right mind cares about time? Who wants to know that he's a minute more removed from the womb, one day closer to the grave? Only the interested. Only the aware.

Awareness is my foe. I shun it, recoil from recognition, sink down within myself, where images have no names and thoughts mill around like sheep on a desert island. I aim to be like the drones. They've got the world sussed. No cares, no worries, no future, no past. I must sink down as deep as they have before I can truly know peace. Down, down, down...

Sunk. Nestled snugly on the ocean bed of consciousness. Stray shoals of eel-like slivers of insight disturb my rest every once in a while – as they do now, when I pause to reflect on my lack of reflection – but most of the timeless time I'm lost in the still, calm, murky waters of tranquil nothingness. Bliss.

I've retreated so far within myself that for days on end I fail to take notice of the growing rivers of humans passing by as I wend my dazed way through the streets. Perhaps if one had stopped or spoken to me, I might have reacted sooner, but they've been slipping past like drones, silent, expressionless, naked. I might have initially overlooked them even if I'd been fully conscious.

No specific encounter disturbs my waking slumber. Rather it's the cumulative counts registered by distant parts of my brain — there are just too many tiny, mental *pings* to ignore, even in my zombie-like state. *Those are people*, my brain notes repeatedly. *Those are people. Those are...* And so on, until the information becomes an irritant, forcing me to rise on the bubbles of cognition in order to investigate the situation and quell the flow of unwanted stimuli.

I'm reluctant to rise. Part of me fears that if I surface, I might never return to the depths of the lost. Sinking this deep within myself hasn't been easy. The curse of humanity – dreaded intelligence – may combine with my self-protective drive to counter further attempts at immersion. Though I don't want to, I'm sure I'll learn from this experience, maybe making it impossible to replicate. Still, rise I must. As little as I care about the city and its denizens, something inside me still needs to *know*.

The city appears more vivid after my virtual leave of absence. Drab walls now glitter with promise. The monotonous sky arcs over everything like a wondrous gateway to eternity. The weak afternoon sunlight feels as if it's bronzing my bones. The rough stone pavement could be a dance floor and my feet could belong to Fred Astaire. The people look...

Ah! The people. They're why I've returned. I almost forgot about them on the way up. I abandoned the peaceful depths of oblivion to check on the humans. I can't quite remember why I should be so interested in them, but I'm sure it will come back to me.

I watch them filing past, men and women, moving stiffly, eyes thin slits in their faces, breathing lightly, in no hurry but proceeding with purpose. They operate singly, though in certain places – outside factories and boarding houses – they converge and stand in silent crowds, waiting stoically like trees in anticipation of rain.

What's interesting about these humans? Why should their faces and forms have disturbed my slumber and dredged me up from the placating depths? In their somnambulistic appearance, they're not that different to the hordes of drones. What is it about them that...?

Of course. They were extinct. I begin to remember the changing of the sun and moon, the coming of the lykans, Cheryl, death on a Holocaustal scale, my aimless wandering, the absence of humans, how much I longed to find one to talk with and share my woes with and dance with and have sex with and...

I hurry towards the nearest human and stop, breathless,

smiling nervously, trying to think of something to say. "I... I'm Newman Riplan," I finally wheeze. The man stares straight ahead and doesn't acknowledge me. I step back, deflated. Have I offended him? I approach a different member of the species — a beautiful woman with a kind face, long legs and delightful breasts — and try engaging her in conversation, but she blanks me as well.

I try several more, none of whom spares me as much as a glance. I'm starting to panic — is something wrong with me? Am I so hideous that nobody will talk to me? — when I realise they're not just ignoring *me*, they're ignoring everything, the drones, the animals — a few of which have already attacked and made their first kills — and each other. These people are like I was, adrift within their forms, living but unconscious.

Happier now that I know there's nothing personal in their aloofness, my mind settles into the fleshy conduits of its old stomping ground and I ponder the scenario. I check a few of the humans in closer detail, thinking that perhaps they're elaborate drones, but they seem to be real. Flesh, bones, eyes, tongues, teeth, sexual organs. But where have they come from? Why so mechanical? And what are they waiting for?

The humans seem to be emanating from the same place, somewhere to the west of my current position. I decide to track down the source and set off, heading into the flow. (See? Back no more than a couple of minutes and already off on another bloody quest. Intelligence should be outlawed.) I stop humans occasionally and ask questions — I'd even welcome an old, "Where do you think you are?" – but none displays any sign of awareness. Silent, stony-faced, detached.

The trail leads to a huge square. There are four openings into it, each guarded by a phalanx of wolfers. Those on my route of approach study me cautiously as I draw near. Their leader barks at me to stop when I'm about ten metres away, and stop I do. "Who the hell are you?" he shouts.

"Newman Riplan," I answer meekly.

"Where did you come from?"

That makes me smile. "Where do you think I came from?" I taunt him.

He glares at me. "What do you want?"

I shrug, figuring if the wolfers are part of this, their boss is probably mixed up in it too. "Is the Alchemist nearby?" I ask and he nods. "Then I want to meet him."

"What if he doesn't want to meet you?" the wolfer growls.

"In that case I'll trot along and leave you be."

The leader mutters something to his troops, then disappears into the square. I spend the time while he's gone examining my nails and beard, surprised by their length, realising I must have been out of it far longer than I imagined.

The wolfers part sharply and a naked man strides through their midst. They close ranks again and the man passes me by, paying me no attention, instinctively knowing his path.

The leader's smiling when he returns. "It's OK," he tells his troops. "The Alchemist knows this guy, says we're to let him in."

The wolfers slide aside. If this is a trap, I'll have a hard time getting back through them to escape, but I've no choice but to press on. I didn't struggle all the way out of my coma-like state just to study my nails and chew split ends.

As they close behind me, I spot the Alchemist. He's in the middle of the square, clad in a simply awful pink outfit. "Stay there a minute," he shouts cheerfully and I stop. Through one of the other openings into the square, a handful of wolfers are dragging a panther. They have it noosed and roped and are trying desperately to avoid its thrashing limbs and claws. They manoeuvre it to the centre of the square, where the Alchemist waits patiently, smiling like a dentist.

The beast stops struggling when it's brought before the Alchemist and stares at him suspiciously but harmlessly. The wolfers remove the noose and ropes, pause for breath, then retreat and head off in search of their next animal.

The Alchemist smiles down upon the majestic panther and spreads his arms. The pink billows of his costume flap in a light breeze. The Alchemist brings his arms together again and places his hands over the ears of the panther. He bends down as the creature opens its mouth. Showing no fear, the Alchemist presses his teeth to the animal's lower lip and gently bites it. Then he raises his head, a pearl of blood on his extended tongue, and spits the panther's blood down its throat. Stepping back, he removes his hands, reaches into a huge sack of sand lying by his side, and sprinkles a measured pinch of grains over the beast's head.

The panther stands transfixed, then shakes its head and howls. A second later, as its scream is dying in the air, it convulses and falls to the ground, mouth working itself open and shut, foam making a rabid mask of its lower face. The Alchemist stands calmly over the writhing animal, not even blinking.

A cloud of dust begins to envelop the panther, and then I realise it isn't dust, but sand. A tiny, swirling sandstorm blows around the animal, obscuring it from sight. It builds up to a funnel about two metres in height, then all of a sudden stops and drops in a hail of individual grains. At the centre of the scattered sand, the beast stands erect.

Only it's no longer an animal.

It's a human.

I watch as the woman – short and frumpy, lacking all of the agile grace of a panther – raises her palms to the Alchemist, who kisses them both. She smiles once, then assumes the blank expression common to all I've seen on my way here. She turns and walks towards the northern exit. The wolfers part, let her through, close ranks once she's gone. By the eastern exit another group of hunters are dragging in one of my masturbation-spawned animals – a large pig – and awaiting the Alchemist's nod.

"Would you mind hanging on a while?" the Alchemist asks me. "I'm rather busy at the moment."

"Take your time," I tell him, squatting against a wall. I lean my head back and close my eyes. "I'll grab forty winks. Give me a shout when you're ready." And with that, as if what I've witnessed was no more spectacular than the unwrapping of a box of chocolates, I slip instantly asleep.

*

It's dark when he wakes me. The square's deserted, save for several wolfers acting as bodyguards to the Alchemist.

"Work over for the day?" I ask, getting to my feet.

"Yes," he says. "It's too dangerous to hunt at night. I know the animals don't attack you but the rest of us are not so fortunate. Come."

He leads the way to a boarding house which the wolfers are using as a base. The downstairs floor has been converted into a nourishment house and a makeshift waiter takes our order as we wend our way to the Alchemist's table. It's been a long time since I dined indoors. I hope I don't make a fool of myself.

"You've changed since our last meeting," the Alchemist comments as we wait for the meal to arrive. "You were unhappy. Confused. You seem to have adapted to our way of life in the interim."

"Hadn't much choice," I tell him. "One must change when faced with change. It was either embrace the madness or be swamped by it. There was a third option – total retreat – which I tried and was enjoying, but I knew it couldn't last. I'm too inquisitive, that's my problem."

The waiter brings our meal and departs. We tuck in. It's nothing grand – they obviously don't have professional cooks on the books – but far better than anything else I've been treated to recently.

"How went your quest?" the Alchemist enquires as we eat.

"Which one?" I snort. "There have been so many, I've lost track. Do you mean the quest to find out where the people of this city come from?"

"No," he smiles, "I know that now. I'll forget it again, but for the moment it's not a secret to me. I meant the quest to find a way out, to discover where the city lies in relation to your *other* world. Any luck?"

"Nope," I say brightly. "Hit a blank wall."

"Oh," he says, "I'm sorry."

"Don't be," I laugh. "I'm not."

I ask if this is how the city has always populated itself, if the people present when I arrived were products of some other outsider's masturbational frenzy.

"Yes," the Alchemist replies, "this has always been the way. Men arrive from an other place every so often. Some don't learn the ways of creation and pass from the city along with its natural inhabitants. Others figure it out but choose not to act upon their knowledge, and they too pass unmarked. Then there are a rare few, such as yourself, who serve to regenerate the city after it's been purged."

"What happens to the men like me?" I ask. "Do we pass as well?"

The Alchemist sighs. "There's a saying among your people — *all things must pass*. So it is here. Nothing lasts forever, not even the Alchemist. My time is finite, the same as yours. Eventually I'll be replaced by a younger man who'll assume my identity and role. Like all the others of this city, I'll be forgotten.

"But *you'll* be remembered," he says, patting my arm comfortingly. "That's the glory of creation. These new citizens will treasure the memory of Newman Riplan, because you sired them. They'll recall the yarns you spun, even though none was present to hear them. They'll remember the strange man who asked odd questions and tilted at imaginary windmills. Public car drivers will, at certain times, say to their passengers, 'Newman Riplan once travelled in this car,' and their passengers will nod sombrely and study the vehicle with interest, even reverence."

"Sounds wonderful," I remark drily. "Well worth all the misery and effort."

"I don't know about *wonderful*," the Alchemist says, "but you should take some measure of pride from it. As you've noted, the present is all to the people here. They have no real concept of pasts or futures. In this realm, legacies are unheard of. The greatest and wealthiest leave no more to mark their passing than the smallest and poorest. Nobody will remember me or those who fill this boarding house tonight. In the marathon of time we're also-rans, each and every one of us, but *you* will be glorified by remembrance as long as the city stands."

"Whatever," I shrug, returning to the meal.

"My words fail to impress you," the Alchemist notes.

"Being remembered never mattered to me," I tell him. "You say it's an honour, and I believe you, but I won't turn cartwheels. The way I see it, it's how you're thought of while you're alive that matters, not what happens when you're dead. You think, if Van Gogh's spirit is knocking about somewhere, he takes comfort from the success that art dealers have enjoyed at his expense? You think he wouldn't have swapped those decades of posthumous fame for a couple of months of recognition and cash while he was alive?"

"I'm sorry," the Alchemist frowns, "but who's Van Gogh?"

"Precisely," I grin. "Who's Van Gogh? Who's Newman Riplan? A dead man and a lost one. Does it matter if we're remembered? I don't think so. Death is death, and memories – legacies, whatever you want to call them – are bullshit. If I've learnt only one thing in this city, it's that. Your people are right — live for today and sod the rest of eternity."

"Time has embittered you," the Alchemist says sadly.

"No," I contradict him, "it's opened my eyes. I thought I was superior to the people here when I first arrived. I realise now that I wasn't. Knowledge is a drag. Acceptance and resignation are the keys to a happy, fruitful life. If I had it all to do over again, you know what I'd change?" He shakes his head slowly. "I'd have a lobotomy." I lift my glass, tap it against his and wink. "Cheers."

We retire upstairs when we're done with dinner, where we recline in twin chairs and stare out an oversized window at the ever-darkening city beyond.

"No candles being lit in the streets yet," I note.

"No," the Alchemist says, "they won't be ignited until the city has a full, working complement of humans."

"When will that be?" I ask.

He shakes his head. "My concept of time is nowhere near as developed as yours. I can't recall exactly how long this operation takes. I spend two or three days in a location, my wolfers haul in as many animals as they can find, I transform them into humans, then we move on to another sector and begin again. It is, I believe, a long and arduous task."

"Do you transform every animal in the city?" I ask, unable to put a halt to the questioning spheres of my brain.

"Of course not," he says. "I transform a lot of them, but it would take forever to track down each and every product of your emissions. Besides, it's good to have animals. We can feed on them if we run out of drones."

"Can that happen?" I ask.

"Oh yes," he says. "We've never completely exhausted our supply, but once we were down to a couple of hundred, with no sign of any new loads, so those of us with the stomach for it tucked into the animals, although even they were running out by the end. Eventually the drone holds began to arrive again, but many citizens died of starvation before the larders could be restocked."

"What if I hadn't survived?" I ask. "If I'd died and there was no outsider left to create the animals?"

"Another would have arrived from your place sooner or later," the Alchemist says. "He'd have found an empty city and wandered the streets, bewildered, alone. At some point he — or another, if he'd failed to grasp his potential — would have discovered his powers and things would have started over. That's how life sustains itself — the elements cut us down, men from your world build us up. No matter how low our numbers sink, or how high they soar, we always return to a happy medium."

That sets me thinking. Is the world I came from really so different to this one? They reproduce by a mixture of masturbation and alchemy, we reproduce by sexual contact, but the result's the same — regeneration. Their numbers are controlled by changing suns and moons and the unleashing of lykans, ours by wars, diseases, storms and earthquakes — again, the same result, the trimming back of numbers, the freeing of space for new life to take hold and blossom.

"Have your numbers ever fallen as low as this?" I ask.

"Not in my time," he says. "There have always been survivors, sometimes only a few dozen, but never less than that. This time, apart from my assistants – wolfers, sandmen, baggers, drone off-loaders and some others who exist in sections of the city inaccessible to lykans and the general populace – you were the only one to pull through."

"Any idea why that should be?" I ask.

He frowns. "It may have been simple bad luck, or…"

"Yes?" I prompt when he doesn't continue.

"When you arrived," he says quietly, "this city was bursting with people, more than I ever remember seeing previously. It had been a long time since the sun and moon last changed and several men from your world had been operating throughout the city, adding to the ranks. Jobs were becoming scarce. Buildings were getting crowded. That parade you saw me in when we first met? I often go on such outings, to track down animals and transform them, but I'd ceased that part of my work by the time I ran into you. I just paraded through the streets, waving my arms at the people, unwilling to add to the chaos. It was the first time – the only time – I've acted contrary to instinct."

I muse on that awhile. The city became overcrowded, things got out of control, balance was lost. As a result, there followed a purge of humanity that puts the worst of my people's war crimes to shame. An entire cleanout, down to the roots. I think of my world and its ever-increasing billions, people living longer and longer, babies being born in their multitudes, major wars on the decrease, technology and medicine continually figuring out new ways to save and prolong lives.

Then I think of the alleged meteorite that wiped out the dinosaurs, and how one could strike from the heavens any time. I consider the nuclear weapons we've stockpiled, the diseases we've cultivated, the way the world has been moving so quickly since the early days of the twentieth century, the leaps we've made, the incredible bounds we've taken. I used to assume that it was down to us, that we were smart monkeys in control of our destinies. But maybe we aren't so smart. Maybe our brains are doing the job that the lykans did here. Perhaps our world is also due for a cleansing. Maybe...

I turn away from the thoughts. Even if I'm correct, what good will brooding do? I can't get back to warn the people of my world about the possible impending apocalypse. Even if I could, I couldn't change anything, as no one would believe me. The people I left behind will have to grapple with their own affairs and deal with their future as best they can. I can't reach them from here.

We continue to chat, of this and that. I ask about the humans I've seen and why they've appeared so mechanical.

"They're always that way right after creation," the Alchemist informs me. "In time they'll become more animated — it's remarkable how swiftly they click into the swing of things once they get going."

"What about names?" I ask.

"They'll have those too," he says.

"How?" I ask, to which he only shrugs.

"That's not information I currently possess," he says, "though I think it has something to do with the sandmen."

"And jobs?" I continue. "Do they walk straight into employment?"

"Yes," he says. "There are positions which must be filled immediately, teeth extractors, public car drivers, cooks, enemaists and so on. People are assigned those roles arbitrarily. When things have settled down, they'll be free to chase their own careers, though most will choose to stay where they are — with no real sense of the future, few feel the need to improve upon their present."

"What about your people?" I ask. "The sandmen, wolfers and the rest. Are they created the same as everybody else?"

He nods. "As I said, we're protected from the lykans, but some of us invariably wind up caught outside our shelters when the sun or moon changes, while others meet sticky ends in the course of our hunts — it's not easy tackling lions and the like. I replenish the ranks occasionally, when they fall below acceptable numbers."

"You're going to need a couple of people at the drone port," I advise him. "Mannie and Jess are no more."

He frowns. "The names aren't familiar, but I was aware of the vacancies." He raises an eyebrow. "Are *you* interested in filling one of the positions?"

I think about spending my days in the company of Phil and Bryan. "No thanks," I grunt.

"So what will you do now?" he asks.

I scratch my beard thoughtfully. "Dunno," I mutter. "Go on creating animals for you to fiddle with, I guess."

"A noble pursuit," he smiles, "but hardly fitting for one of your ambition and drive. Have you no other plans? A new quest, perhaps?"

I shrug. The truth is, I haven't a clue. The future stretches out ahead of me like a desert and I don't know what I want of it. Retreat back inside my mind and try losing myself again? Not with people around — you need solitude of an exacting quality in order to sink that deep within yourself. Go back to a nourishment house and spin stories for a living? Can't picture it. Fall in love with one of my surrogate daughters and settle into domestic bliss? After all I've been through, it's hard to imagine myself in such a cosy situation. Climb a tall building and step off the…?

Best not to think about it. Time will provide the answer. And if it doesn't, who gives a snuff? Stop worrying, Newman old boy. Tension doesn't suit you.

We talk our way through to dawn. I'm bright-eyed following my afternoon nap, while the Alchemist never seems to feel any strain. We'd go on talking, except one of his wolfers interrupts and reminds him of his duties in the square.

"I must take my leave," he sighs. "Time waits for no man, not even here. Do you wish to accompany me?"

I shake my head. "No, I'd only be in the way. Let's meet

for another chinwag when your work is done and you have time to spare."

"I'll look forward to it," he says, though by the melancholic shade of his eyes I can tell he doesn't think we'll enjoy a night like this again.

We shake hands and he departs. The rest of his team are leaving as well. This is their last day in this location and they wish to establish their new base before nightfall. I wait until they're gone, then explore the boarding house, examining the refuse they left behind.

People begin to arrive later in the day. They stand outside the building, waiting patiently to be activated. I never asked the Alchemist how the people select their homes, but I guess it's something they just instinctively know. I do a head count — eleven. Even if two or three times the number arrive later, there'll be plenty of rooms available. I look round, decide this is as good a spot as any to situate myself, and head upstairs.

I choose the best room in the house – first dibs! – slip off my clothes and leave them outside the door, marking my territory. Then I lie back on the bed and wait to see how things develop.

TWENTY

It's weeks before the humans are released from their (e)motionless shells. I pass the time pottering about the boarding house, cleaning the rooms, fixing broken pieces of furniture, making the beds. I don't leave the premises, and keep a careful watch on the inert crowd outside, afraid I'll miss their revival if I turn my back for more than a couple of minutes. I dine on drones, plenty of which pass by each day. Animals came sniffing round during the first few days but I chased them off, even the more vicious creatures like bears and cobras, and now sightings are rare.

I'm upstairs cleaning the sinks when things start to happen. I hear footsteps on the stairs, then doors opening and bed springs creaking. Abandoning my duties, I rush down to the next landing and begin slamming open the doors to the rooms. About halfway along I barge in on a naked, fat man sitting on a bed. His head jolts up and he shouts, "Hey! What the snuff are you doing in my –"

I'm gone before he can finish, down the stairs, through the lobby and out the front door. A sandman and four wolfers are outside with the statue-like humans. The Alchemist's men jump with alarm when I burst into the open and the wolfers raise their heavy swords and advance threateningly.

"Wait," the sandman stops them and steps forward, eyes narrowing. "Are you Newman Riplan?" he asks and I nod warily. "I thought so. The Alchemist told us to expect you. It's alright," he says to the wolfers. "He's an ally." They retreat and the sandman approaches. "You could do with some clothes," he says critically.

I glance down at my naked body. "What's wrong with the natural look?" I ask.

"Nothing," the sandman says, "except you're going to have to start interacting with people again. They won't take kindly to your nudity."

"Snuff 'em," I sniff.

The sandman shrugs. "Have it your own way. Just thought I'd mention it. You won't get far in job interviews undressed like that."

"Snuff jobs too," I grin.

The sandman sighs and shakes his head. "The Alchemist said you'd want to watch me breathing being into the humans."

"Can I?" I ask excitedly.

"Of course," he says. "It's no secret. Just don't get in my way."

Returning to the line of people, he beckons a woman forward. She steps up and kneels at a signal. The sandman licks his thumbs and nods at the wolfers, one of whom brings him a pouch of sand. He rubs both thumbs in the sand, then gently rolls them across the woman's open eyes. Her body shudders but she doesn't pull away. Rubbing his thumbs in the sand again, he murmurs something I can't hear. The woman's mouth opens and he places the thumbs on her tongue and leaves them there a couple of seconds before casually removing them.

The woman coughs, blinks, looks around, gets to her feet. She appears both aware and confident, not in the least awed by her sudden ascension to the ranks of the conscious living. The sandman hands her a bag of drone teeth. She thanks him, turns and enters the boarding house, simple as you please.

"She'll buy clothes later," the sandman tells me. "Stores will be opening soon. The teeth are to get her started, to spend on clothes, food, rent. These people won't be fully cognisant for another couple of days — they'll dress, eat and work, seemingly of their own volition, but actually in accordance with the Alchemist's will — but they're capable of speech if you wish to engage them. They'll even overlook your disregard for clothing conventions, but only for the time being."

"Is that all you have to do to bring them to consciousness?" I ask, feeling let down by the procedure. "Just rub some sand over their eyes and tongues?"

"Of course," he says.

"It's a tad simplistic," I gripe.

He laughs. "If you think it's easy, try it yourself — you'll be in for a surprise."

"What about names?" I ask. "Do they know their names now?"

"Yes," he says and shows me the balls of his thumbs. The flesh of both is raised into boil-like letters. $D\ E\ L\ N\ A$.

"Delna — that's her name?" I ask.

"Apparently," he says, studying the letters as if wondering how they got there.

"What about the next human?"

"The letters change every time I pass my thumbs across a

pair of eyes," he explains. "I draw the name from the eyes and, by pressing down on the tongue, make the host aware of his or her identity."

"Cool," I whistle.

I watch as the sandman animates the rest of the humans. He doesn't seem to take much pride in his work, just brings them to life, sets them on their way, then yawns as though he's screwing nuts onto bolts on an assembly line. The joys of creation are wasted on this guy.

The sandman brushes the last crumbs of sand from his hands when he finishes and smiles tightly at me. "You may accompany us on our rounds if you wish," he says, though I can tell it's politeness and not desire for my company prompting him to make the offer.

"You won't be doing anything different further along the line, will you?" I ask.

"It's always the same," he says.

"Then that's alright," I reply. "I'm happy where I am."

"Please yourself," he says, not bothering to disguise his mild relief.

"When will the city be back to normal?" I ask as he gathers the wolfers around him and prepares to depart.

"Soon," he promises.

"You're not the only sandman doing the rounds?"

"Snuff no," he snorts. "There's a whole fleet of us out on the streets, covering the entire city. I'm almost finished in my sections, and the others will be wrapping up too. A day or two more and everything will be back to normal."

"*Normal*," I smile, only half-remembering the time when

that would have made my upper lip curl.

"Well, goodbye," the sandman says. "Mustn't linger. I don't want to fall behind schedule."

"Goodbye," I say curtly.

We don't bother shaking hands.

I head inside and up the stairs as the sandman and wolfers move on. I'm still smiling, taking the steps slowly, dwelling at some length on that word – *normal* – and looking forward to finding out what the new normal plays like.

Within a week it's as if life in the city had never been interrupted. Nourishment houses open their doors for business. The hum of production lines can be heard inside factories. Cars return to the roads. Candles are lit every night to illuminate the streets. People meet and chat and fall in love, and it's like they've always been here — they don't realise how new to this world they are or where they came from. Had this happened months (years?) ago, I might have tried telling them about my adventures and the debt they owe me, but I'm a different man to the one I once was. I no longer wish to rock the boat or disturb its passengers. They have no answers, so why bother them with questions?

My new landlord, Rick, is nowhere near as pleasant as Franz. He gets greedy and unreasonable as his senses return, demands payment up front, won't cut me any slack. "Show me your teeth or a clean pair of heels," he growls, giving me two days to come up with the exorbitant rent.

I could bash out some sperm, give birth to a ferocious

beast and sic it on him, but I'm in a mellow mood, so I shrug, pack my few belongings and leave. There are plenty more boarding houses. I'll sleep just as sweetly elsewhere.

To my surprise, I find the other landlords equally cold and unhelpful. They ask for teeth in advance and slam the door in my face when I fail to produce any.

"There are loads of jobs going," one snarls. "Nobody has an excuse to be broke unless they're lazy, good for nothing layabouts."

I ask if my beard and shabby clothes — I've taken to dressing again, but my duds are the worse for wear — have anything to do with his hostile attitude.

"No," he says, "just your ugly face."

And *slam!* goes the door.

Charming.

It's not just the landlords. I try a couple of nourishment houses for jobs, only to meet with rejection at every turn. Some owners won't even give me an audition — they say they've too many acts as it is — and those who do rarely listen for more than a couple of minutes.

"I can't believe you're telling *Frankenstein* and *Dracula* stories," one of them snorts. "Everyone knows those old chestnuts. Try something new, why don't you?"

The Alchemist was right — I *have* made a lasting impression on the locals, only not the sort I would have wished. My pilfered stories have passed into common parlance. Everybody — and I mean *everybody* — is familiar with them. I've rendered myself old-fashioned.

I could probably think up new stuff if I wanted – there are lots of TV shows and films I never got round to regurgitating – but I'm so bemused by the whole thing, I just don't bother. I'll get work in a factory when I feel the need. At the moment I'm happy enough pounding the streets and sleeping rough. I don't have to worry about animals attacking. My beastly children are kind to their poppa. Work can wait. Life can wait too. Consider this my paternity leave.

One evening, by chance, I stumble across an enemaist factory. I clock it by the workers filing out. Though I've long since abandoned thoughts of escaping the city, I pop in to see what it's like.

The girl in reception is nicer to me than most of the newcomers have been and politely listens to my request to explore inside the plant. I tell her I'm thinking of joining but want to check it out first.

"There's no problem with having a look around," she says, "but getting a job here might not be so easy — our books are pretty full at the moment."

So, I'm not even wanted by the enemaists. The pity, Iago, the pity!

As I suspected, the factory turns out to be a dead end. My guide – the girl from reception, happy to double-up on her jobs – leads me down past a series of pipes to a seemingly bottomless pit of liquid waste.

"That's where it goes," she tells me, smiling proudly. I ask where it comes out but the question's lost on her. "Out?

It goes in, not out."

I stare down into the yellow-brown waters of the pit. If I had scuba diving gear, I might be able to investigate further. As things stand, forget it.

I thank the girl for her time and leave. I'm not upset to come away knowing that I'm well and truly trapped, as I wasn't expecting anything else. In a way I'm glad. Now that I've been in one of the factories and scoped it out, I can push the last, lingering hope of escape from my thoughts completely. Hope is nothing but a hindrance in this hermetic hodgepodge of a city. I'm better off without it.

The days and nights blur into one another again. I don't lose myself on the seabed of my mind this time – as I predicted, the proximity of people proves too much of a distraction – but I fall into an agreeable state of listlessness which enables me to function without exerting too many brain cells. I shuffle through the streets like a tramp, preying on drones when I'm hungry, dipping into canals or ponds when I need to wash, sleeping rough beneath the always temperate sky.

I have little to do with the locals – bar encounters with the ever reliable enemaists – though I keep a fascinated eye on them as they go about their daily business. Like a father who's forsaken his children in a fit of rage, I can't entirely divorce myself from my interest in them.

It's an interest which isn't returned. They treat me worse than a drone, making no attempt to hide the disgust they feel at seeing me pollute their pearly streets. The citizens of yore would have had some modicum of sympathy for my plight. This lot — perhaps reflecting their cold paternal creator — are a harsher breed. I suppose, with a cannibal for a father, it's only natural that they're more hardened.

I've used my name on a few occasions, to see what sort of an impact it carries. "I'm Newman Riplan," I've muttered, and each time there's been recognition.

"The guy who used to tell those super stories? Sure, we know you. Snuff, man, what happened? You look like something a rat threw up."

I've spun a number of hard luck stories in reply to their enquiries, sometimes resulting in a welcome handout, but I haven't made any friends. Intrigued as they might be in the legend, nobody wants to associate with a deadbeat. This is a city of class, of go-getters, of — God forgive me for spawning them — yuppies. It's surely only a matter of time before Filofaxes come into fashion.

I wander into Barbersville one day, chat with some of the new clan of barbers, have my beard cut and hair trimmed. I make a lot of drone teeth from the sale of my hair — "So long," the barber murmurs appreciatively, "and such high quality." I use the teeth to buy new shoes, even though the soles of my feet are so tough that I don't really need them.

It's nice to see the barbers flourishing. I wish I'd done more than tell stories before I helped create the recent crop of citizens. It would have been nice to gift the people something revolutionary, like glass, electricity or clocks. If I'd applied myself to making timepieces before the purge, would that have provided my offspring with a better understanding of time? Maybe I could have changed the nature of these people in a truly meaningful way.

But it's too late now. Unless there's another purge in my lifetime — and that's something I don't wish for, even in my darkest moments — I'll never get a chance to shape the population of this city again. The stories, good, bad or indifferent, will have to be enough.

I've plenty of drone teeth left after buying the shoes. I let them slide from hand to hand, smiling blankly at them, trying to make a count but constantly losing track. Eventually I stack them in a neat little pile on the pavement and leave them for somebody else to find. I've no real need of them. Apart from the shoes, this city has nothing to offer that I truly desire.

One more day in the endless legion of uncharted days. I'm moseying along, taking my time, thinking about nothing in particular, when I spot a man who doesn't seem to fit in. Unlike the usual citizens, who know what they're up to, where they're going and what they want, this man is milling about, stopping people, asking questions and looking distressed. Most curious.

Avoid him, part of me whispers. *Turn and walk away and don't look back.*

"Why should I be afraid?" I ask.

The voice in my head sniffs and says, *If you don't listen, you'll be sorry.*

I decide that's not a satisfactory explanation and choose to ignore my own advice, so I proceed as before.

The man – dark-skinned, casually dressed, sweating, frightened – spots me studying him and powers his way towards me, perhaps hoping to get more from a tramp than the respectable people. I slow to a standstill and wait for him. That annoying part of my brain is shrieking at me now – *Don't engage! Don't engage!* – but I silence it with a mental bellow. "Who's the boss?" I roar. "Me or you?"

You, it whimpers, *but you'll soon wish you weren't.*

Then it retreats into a sulky silence.

"Sir!" the black man shouts and stops before me, panting as if he'd been racing. "You've got to tell me where I am, man. I was at a party on a plane. One of my friends, he has his own jet, it was his brother's twenty-first, we went up to party among the clouds. I'd popped a few pills – you know what it's like at parties – and downed a shitload of shots, then all of a sudden I started to cough. I doubled over, fell to my knees, thought the end had come, but then my throat cleared. I was able to breathe again. I sat up, laughing, expecting everybody to be crowding round to see if I was OK, only to find the lot of them in their seats. I was pissed at them – uncaring bastards – and started to complain, but then I realised they... they..."

He starts to cry. I stare at him wordlessly.

"They weren't human anymore," he moans. "They'd turned into white fucking mannequins. Like –" He points at a nearby drone. "– that fucking thing. Then the plane sets down, the mannequins leave and a couple of goons come in. I tried getting sense out of them but they herded me off the plane and into some guy's office. He gave me a bag of teeth

– fucking *teeth*! – and threatened to set a pair of wolves – fucking *wolves*! – on me when I got heavy."

The black man pauses to gulp down sobs. I wonder about Jess's replacement while the stranger struggles to regain his breath. Sounds like the new guy is as fond of wolves as she was. Maybe they come with the job.

"Then I walked through the longest fucking tunnel in history," the black man resumes, "and emerged into this nightmare of a city. I've been trying to find out where I am but people treat me like I'm mad and talking gibberish. Please, man, you've got to tell me what's happened."

He shakes me desperately. His fingers hurt my arms where he grips them but I don't react. I can understand why he's upset. I don't blame him for the roughness.

"You've got to tell me," the black man weeps. "Where the fuck am I?"

A human. A *real* human. From *my* world. I never thought I'd meet one again. I was sure I'd die alone among these strangers and that would be that. But fate has smiled on me. I can link up with this man. I know what he's going through. I can explain things, regale him with my story, prepare him for what's to come. He won't believe me to begin with – he might even resent me for being the bearer of ill tidings – but as he settles in and realises I've told the truth, we'll grow closer. Perhaps together we can figure a way out of here. I'll be able to tell him about the sleeping pills. He might be able to return to the real world with a message and ask for help, not waste his trip back like I did. Even if escape proves beyond us, we'll have each other. I don't have to be a lone outsider any longer.

The black man is still shaking me, crying, asking questions. I raise a hand and pat his back, hoping to calm him down. "There, there," I try to whisper but my lips won't form the words. It's been so long since I spoke, even longer since I had to use words which meant anything.

"You've got to help me," he sobs. "What is this place? Where the fuck *am* I?"

An old question. I step back from him, breaking free of his grasp, smile and open my mouth to initiate conversation. As the words come out and I realise what they are – the only words I'm capable of forming – my smile disintegrates and I start to retreat.

"Where do you think you are?" I croak, horrified by what I'm saying but unable to produce any other answer.

"Where do you think you are?" I gasp, turning to run, ignoring his pleas, leaving him behind.

"Where do you think you are?" I scream hysterically, as much to myself as to the man I've deserted, and I disappear into the city, stumbling blindly down the capillaries of my black-hearted abomination of a prison, of my... *home*.

I still can't believe what I said to the black man. It haunts me day and night, whether asleep or awake. My one chance to make contact with a member of my own world and I blew it. What hurts the worst is knowing it wasn't forced upon me. I didn't answer his question the way I did because some unseen power was acting to control my tongue. I did it because I was afraid, terrified of announcing myself to a fellow Earthling and exposing my pitiful shortcomings, having to describe my fall and how low I'd sunk. The people of this city don't matter to me. I could tell them about eating Cheryl and masturbating naked in the streets and they wouldn't blink. But to parade the truth before a man of my own world...

I'm one of them now. At long, lonely last, I'm a true citizen. I've been angry, sad, crazy, paranoid, hopeless. I've blown through every emotion in the book, including some which weren't included in any book I ever read, but this is the end of the line. I can't go on as I have been. I don't know who I am. A member of the city, yes, but what does that mean? What does it make me? The rest of them were brought into this world with assigned roles. Each knows their place in it. I'm one of them now, yet I'm not like them. What role can *I* fill? What slot can *I* slip into? I'm no one. I'm nothing.

I feel a crushing sense of desolation. I haven't just lost hope or my sanity this time. I've lost *me*. I'm no longer the man I was. No longer any sort of man at all. I live, breathe, eat, think. But I'm not Newman Riplan. I'm something else... anonymous... out of time and place... completely and utterly adrift. I have no meaning, and no hope of ever having a meaning. Lacking that single, most simple of driving attributes, what is there in all this world of a city that could possibly inspire me to carry on?

I'm thin. Haggard. Haven't eaten for three or four days. Didn't eat for nine or ten before that. Thirsty. Naked. I've abandoned my rags, even my shoes. Back the way Mother Nature intended. I stagger from street to street, as if part of a crucifixion parade, bowed beneath the weight of that most terrible of questions — "Where do you think you are?" I can't get it out of my mind. It torments me.

I belong nowhere, not in this world, not in my own. I'm a miserable specimen of a creature, a badly timed joke, bereft of purpose, meaning, dignity, passion. How did I end up like this? The situation was extreme, but others would have coped, dealt with the change and fashioned new, exciting lives. They'd have taken the shapeless clay of this city and imposed themselves on it, used their superior mental faculties to bend things their way. They wouldn't have retreated into their shells or feasted on the dead or wasted their time on useless quests. It would be easy for me to blame the city for my failure but in truth it's my own. A challenge was set and I failed to rise to it. Simple as that.

The future... Christ, I don't want to think about that. Don't even want to acknowledge it. All I really want is to...

The moon turns red and distracts me. A pity — I'd have liked to know what I really wanted. No time now. I have to flee. I can hear howling already. I start to run, though in my weakened condition I can't work up much speed. People pour out of buildings, screaming and panicking. Nice to see some things don't change. I'd feel sorry for them if I was capable of empathy.

Loping along, I turn a corner and spot a sandman. He smiles and beckons me on. I don't have any drone teeth – foolish, foolish Newman – but I start towards him regardless, thinking I can maybe spin him a tale in lieu of the teeth.

Less than halfway there, I pause, then stop and sink to my haunches.

Why continue? Is there one good reason – even a lousy reason – why I should go on living? If there is, I can't isolate it. I'm not brave enough to take my own life but I might manage to hold still long enough to let another to do the business for me. A couple of minutes, that's all it will take. A brief flurry of bloody activity, then peace and silence.

I sigh happily – I've assumed responsibility for my life again, even if it's only to end it – and smile up at the sky. What I see brings a frown to my face. Though I should be looking at the moon, somehow I'm also aware of the sun. It hangs in the firmament, fiery blue, horizontal to the moon. Lykans round the corner behind me – I can tell by their snarls and the click of their claws on the pavement – but I pay them no heed. I'm focused on the sun and moon, gazing up, awed, childlike.

I realise now that the heavenly bodies are eyes in a huge black face. Twinkling, mischievous eyes. And the stars are teeth. The giant's dark lips part, lifting into a sneering smile, no longer bothering to hide, aware that it's been rumbled. The lykans close in on me, a circle of them, but slowly, perturbed by my peculiar behaviour, taking their time, fearing a trap.

The glittering, celestial teeth extend towards me – or I rise towards them, I'm not sure which – and I feel the powerful breath of the sky creature, hot as an inferno on my face, knocking me back with the stench of death. The lykans growl and prepare to leap. The eyes continue twinkling in the heavens. A dark cavern of a mouth surrounds me.

The teeth snap shut. One swift motion, faster than an exploding star. A sound of galaxies grinding together. Lykans leap, claws and fangs bared. I hardly hear their howls over the clashing of the universal teeth. I sense...

Lykans. Stars. Fangs. Eyes. The drone of plane engines. A hooker asking what I do. King Kong. A second of madness. Pain. Light. Red. Red everywhere. Darkness. The stench of animals. The taste of human flesh in my mouth. Then a voice in my ear, a familiar voice, the voice of the Alchemist. *Where do you think you are?*

...and then I'm swallowed whole.

TWENTY-ONE

In nothingness, all is revealed. In destruction, new life is conceived. In loss, new paths are found. Everything has a reason and happens for a reason. I see that now. I always saw it. I just wasn't aware of my awareness.

I walk the familiar, beloved streets, and marvel at the fact that I ever thought of them as alien. I know I once did. The memories hover, murky and scattershot, but inescapable. I was afraid of this city once. It didn't feel like home. There was... an other place.

I pause in the middle of a street. People are smiling at me, bowing to me. I wave distractedly to them but my thoughts are elsewhere.

An other place.

I'm not sure what that phrase means. There's nowhere but here, no city other than this one, yet I have dreams and occasional visions of places that are not to be found in this metropolis, buildings with glass in the windows, cars with wings that soar high in the sky, a world of cities with gaps between, open stretches of land, enormous bodies of water.

I stand in the street, frowning, wondering where the visions hail from, where *I* hail from. A shudder runs through me as I recall times of hardship and suffering. A strange taste fills my mouth, something foul that I ate. I look at my hands and know that once they were red with blood.

The troubling sensation fades and my smile returns. I don't know how long I've been here – I'm not even entirely sure what that means – but I'm settling into my role. The visions are nothing to be afraid of. Everything happens for a reason. To become who I am, I had to explore a path unknown to my fellow citizens. To care for them, I couldn't be one of them. To rise, I had to fall. To embrace, I had to abandon. Thus it has always been.

The city makes great demands of those it entrusts with its secrets and powers. To build its key players, it must strip their trappings from them. Very few are suited to the position that I hold. The city tests many and the majority are found wanting. But every so often one emerges to be the man that the city requires. (It's always a man, never a woman. Part of me knows why that must be the case, but I can't put my finger on it right now. There are many things I can't put my finger on, but that's fine, just the way it is and always has been.)

It's evening and the first stars are starting to show. I look up, half-remembering a time when I saw a face in the sky, the face of the city, with eyes only for me, choosing me from among the masses.

I remember howls too, claws raking my flesh, fangs ripping me apart, at the same time as they tore apart my predecessor. It was incredibly painful but the pain was shortlived and the body was meaningless. We're never as dependent on our bodies as we believe, never as tied to them as we feel. It took me a long time to realise that – indeed, I had to lose my body to understand how little I needed it – but I understand now. Bodies are merely the bridges through which the will of the city flows.

I have a sense that those were interesting times, when I was linked to that body. I feel like I lived an interesting life. There was a woman, a partner. I told stories. I sought to get away from the city, to escape to that other place that I sometimes dream about. Ludicrous notions, but they motivated me for a long time, drove me in a way that I needed to be driven. The city required one who knew it intimately but who wasn't in awe of it, who could cherish its secrets but not be crushed by them, a man who'd scaled heights and been destroyed, who'd fought and chosen surrender, who had accepted the city as his lover, his tormentor, his enigma, his annihilator, his all.

The city is constant but the rest of us are transitory. As my predecessor so aptly noted, all things will pass. All people too, no matter how mighty, no matter how small. I will be replaced, as the one who wore these robes before me was replaced, and I've no idea what will happen after that, if the city will have further use for me in a different guise, or if darkness will claim me for its own. Perhaps the city will abandon me, as I once would have abandoned it if I'd been able to.

But that's a worry for another day, and in truth it won't be much of a worry then either, because I'm at peace with the city. I accept its decisions, its whims, its cruelties and mysteries. Everything happens for a reason. We come, experience, fade. It's not our place to know any more than that, merely to serve if asked, in whatever way we can.

I lower my gaze and chuckle guiltily. People are staring at me. They're not accustomed to seeing me hesitate. I mustn't do this again. Their faith in me needs to be rewarded. No visible slips or cracks. They look to me for so much and I must provide it, for that is the deal I struck with the city when my bones were crushed and my new body was forged.

(How? When? Why? Those are questions I let the lykans strip away with my flesh. I don't ask them these days. I rarely even think about them now, and I sense that soon I won't think of them at all. I'm still in the act of becoming.)

I spread my arms and move among my people, offering comfort and support, along with the assurance that all is well. Bad times will come — they always must — and everything will pass, but I'm the living proof that nothing truly changes, that all that seeps out will ebb back in again. I am their anchor and their hope, their guide and their monitor, their protector and their comforter. I am a *new man* (that makes me smile morosely, though I'm not sure why) but an old, established figure.

I am the Alchemist.

These are my people and this is my city.

Everything else is but a dream.

AN OTHER PLACE

was written between 6th february 1998 and 19th october 2016

Printed in Great Britain
by Amazon